Listening in the Dusk

By Celia Fremlin

Novels

LISTENING IN THE DUSK
THE PARASITE PERSON
WITH NO CRYING
THE SPIDER-ORCHID
THE LONG SHADOW
APPOINTMENT WITH YESTERDAY
POSSESSION
PRISONER'S BASE
THE JEALOUS ONE
THE TROUBLE MAKERS
SEVEN LEAN YEARS
UNCLE PAUL
THE HOURS BEFORE DAWN

Short Story Collections

A LOVELY DAY TO DIE
BY HORROR HAUNTED
DON'T GO TO SLEEP IN THE DARK

Listening in the Dusk

CELIA FREMLIN

A CRIME CLUB BOOK

DOUBLEDAY

New York   London   Toronto   Sydney   Auckland

A CRIME CLUB BOOK
PUBLISHED BY DOUBLEDAY
a division of Bantam Doubleday Dell Publishing Group, Inc.
666 Fifth Avenue, New York, New York 10103

DOUBLEDAY and the portrayal of a man
with a gun are trademarks of Doubleday,
a division of Bantam Doubleday Dell
Publishing Group, Inc.

Library of Congress Cataloging-in-Publication Data
Fremlin, Celia.
Listening in the dusk / Celia Fremlin.—1st ed. in the U.S.
p. cm.
"A Crime Club Book."
I. Title.
PR6053.R45L5 1990
823'.914—dc20   90–34996
                                                CIP
ISBN 0-385-41502-8
Copyright © 1990 by Celia Fremlin
All Rights Reserved
Printed in the United States of America
December 1990
First Edition in the United States of America

Listening in the Dusk

CHAPTER 1

Dusk was the best time for Mary; especially the winter dusk, and especially in London. Leaning out from her third-floor window, breathing gratefully the sharp, anonymous air, she felt, for a few minutes, perfectly normal; just an ordinary young girl who has left her home town and come up to the big city in search of a new life, a new job, new friends—new everything.

And she had, indeed, already done a number of the things this ordinary girl would do. She had looked for the cheapest room she could find; with a landlady willing to take her on trust despite her lack of references and her vagueness about her previous address. She had even—though so far unsuccessfully—tried to find a job. Nothing unusual in that, of course, unemployment being the way it was. Though what *was* unusual, in her case, was that she could not make use of any of her qualifications. Dared not even mention them, not to anybody, let alone to a potential employer. Still, no one knew of this problem. No one *could* know, so long as she didn't tell them. From the point of view of her landlady, and of her fellow-lodgers, she was just one more young woman unlucky in her search for work. And it had only been five weeks after all; nothing at all remarkable about it so far.

Still, this was one more reason why she welcomed the coming of twilight, the beginning of darkness. Soon the world's workers would be on their way home, and she would no longer be the only one with nothing to do. There they would all be, slacking off after their day's work, indulging in a bit of leisure, maybe leaning idly out of their windows, just as she was doing, watching the lights coming on here and there in the houses opposite, while beyond the still faintly-gleaming slate roofs the massed clouds, grey on grey, gathered themselves to-wards the coming of the dark.

Twilight. Bat-light. Though of course there were no bats now, not in December, not in the middle of London: and even if there had been, she could not have borne to watch them; not after what had happened.

With every advance of darkness, Mary felt a little bit safer. If anyone looked up now, all they would see would be the pale blur of a face that might be any face. Besides, no one *would* look up; why should they? They would be hurrying along, head down, eyes on the pavement, minds focussed on getting to wherever they were going, out of the cold and damp. But even as this vaguely reassuring thought crossed her mind, someone *did* look up. A woman, of indeterminate age, hair and face almost invisible under a plastic rain-hat, was pausing outside this very house, looking it up and down with an air both uncertain and purposeful.

Mary withdrew her head so precipitately that she banged it quite sharply on the raised sash. With violently beating heart she retreated into the recesses of her room, already scolding herself for so ridiculous an over-reaction.

A strange woman happening to glance up at a house—why on earth should it be anything to do with her, Mary? This was a city of six or seven million people—which was precisely why she had come here in the first place—and the chances of any random one of them being one of those she had reason to fear was so remote that . . .

And at that point, she heard the knock on the front door, really loud—and once again Mary's heart was beating wildly, irrationally. She tiptoed to her door, full of dread, and opened it softly, just a crack, to try and make out what was going on.

Her landlady answering the door, of course. Voices. The landlady's voice buoyantly welcoming—as it always was, to absolutely anyone, in absolutely any situation—and then the other voice, the strange one. Yes, strange. A total stranger.

So *that* was all right. It was nothing to do with her. All the same, when she heard the double set of footsteps beginning to mount the stairs, she found herself holding her breath again. Softly, she closed her door—it would never do to be caught peeping—and through the crack listened tensely to the approaching sounds. How far up were they coming? There were two sets of tenants on the floors below her—doubtless this was a visitor to one of them. But no . . . on came the laboured footsteps . . . past the first floor . . . past the second . . . on and on, with agonising slowness.

Outside her door, they paused, and Mary's heart missed a beat. It was for *her*, then, a visitor for *her!* An unwelcome visitor—for all visitors were unwelcome, and there could be no news for her but bad news.

Mary cowered, tensing herself for the knock on her door . . .

But it was all right! With a rush of utterly disproportionate thankfulness, she heard the footsteps start up again . . . on past her door . . . across the landing, and then on up the narrow uncarpeted stairs that led to the topmost part of the tall house—the lumber-room, and the big gurgling water-tank that murmured all night long, the pipes clucking and whispering up and down the old walls. She had found it frightening at first, these unfamiliar intermittent sounds when she was trying to sleep, but she had grown used to them after a while, and they didn't frighten her anymore.

It was everything else that frightened her now.

CHAPTER 2

On the third landing, Alice paused to remove her rain-hat and shake loose her damp hair. Ahead of her, the fourth and last flight of stairs was uncarpeted, and already awash with darkness. Through a small, grimy skylight the fading remnants of daylight filtered down to show up the worst of the cobwebs and the peeling wallpaper; and for a moment Alice felt a wild impulse to turn and run, her heels clattering first on these bare wooden treads, and then slithering, stumbling over worn stair-carpet, round and round, down and down, to the narrow entrance-hall with its clutter of bicycles, free newspapers and unclaimed letters, and then out through the front door, back into the rainy December street.

She didn't, of course. Too many things were against it, some of them harshly practical, others verging on the idiotic; and, as commonly happens at such moments, it was one of the idiotic ones that forced the decision on her.

Simply, she didn't want to hurt the feelings of this vague and amiable person in orange slacks (if they were orange; it was hard to tell in this light) who was labouring up the stairs ahead of her.

Unlike most landladies, Mrs. Harman ("Call me Hetty," she'd urged, almost before Alice was through the front door) was making not the smallest attempt to minimise the deficiencies of the accommodation she had on offer. On the contrary, she seemed bent on making the worst of it, even, at the beginning, declaring it unfit for human habitation.

"No, I'm awfully sorry, I've nothing left at all," she'd said at first, shaking her mop of rust-coloured hair and blinking sleepily, as if just roused from a belated afternoon nap; and then, perhaps taking pity on Alice's look of weary disappointment, she amended: "Well . . . that is . . . But it's an awful room, you know, it really is. Right up at the top of the house, no cooking facilities, not even a gas-ring, and the bathroom three flights down. I don't really have the nerve to let it at all, the rain coming in under the slates like it does in winter-time—well, it *is* winter-time, isn't it, right now? It'll be at its worst. And it's not furnished, either, just an old chair or two, and a grotty old divan bed that's got shoved up there because of no one wanting to sleep on it. It's probably damp right through by now.

"And then there's the *junk*, you wouldn't believe it, everyone shoves their junk up there, I can't stop them, you know how it is. I keep meaning to have a good clear-out one day, tell them, once and for all, anything that's not gone by Sunday, it'll go straight to Oxfam! 'OK, Hetty,' they'll say, 'We'll get onto it right away, no problem!' And of course there *is* no problem, not for them, because they don't do anything. And Oxfam would never look at it anyway, a pile of rubbish like that, and half of it too heavy to shift . . . Believe it or not, my dear, there's half a motor-bike up there . . . more than half, actually"—here she glanced a little anxiously at Alice, to see how she was taking it—"two wheels, anyway, as well as no end of bars and bits and bobs of metal. And I can't tell you how many clapped-out TVs there are up there, I've given up counting. And then all the labour-saving stuff, mixers that don't mix, full of fluff and dried-up bits of food; slicers that don't slice . . . Things with their handles missing, or their insides, or something. It's enough to make you weep!"

Actually, Alice had felt much more like weeping *before* hearing this tale of woe. A list of disamenities on this scale had a sort of bizarre splendour of its own, and was oddly cheering.

"Well, let me see it, anyway," she said. "I'm not looking for luxury, you know, and I might be able to stack things up somehow . . . make a nice little area to live in . . ."

"Oh, do you think you might?" Hetty's face lit up. "That'd be a grand thing for me. I'd feel really good if that room could be a room again and not a rubbish-tip. Living under a rubbish-tip, it makes you quite depressed sometimes, when you think about it. Well, here goes; you're the first person I've even dared show it to!"

She made it sound like a singular honour, and Alice felt quite absurdly elated, as if she had at last come top in something. After all the months of coming bottom, in nearly every test that life can set up, it was really quite exhilarating.

Afterwards, looking back, Alice realised that this was the moment when her decision was made; the moment when she suddenly became irrevocably committed to this room, whatever it turned out to be like. At the time she imagined that she was still undecided, still waiting to make a rational choice after having inspected the room.

"I'll fix a light-bulb, of course," Hetty was saying as they reached the shadowy top landing. "I've got one somewhere; isn't it funny how the bulbs you've got are always either fifteens or hundred-and-fifties, nothing in between. I keep buying sixties and hundreds, but can I ever find one when I want it? I can not! Do you think it's like that for everyone?" Without waiting for Alice to answer this possibly profound philosophical question, Hetty continued, "Well, here we are now: just take a look!" Here she flung open a door—or, rather, tried to fling it open, for after the first six inches it stuck groaningly on a bulge of lino swollen up with the damp. She had to go down on her knees, reach through the crack and hammer with her clenched fist at the offending bulge, until at last the door could be edged open.

"You see?" she exclaimed, puffing to her feet and brushing ineffectually at the knees of her orange trousers, "That's just typical! Nothing works up here! *Nothing!*" She spoke with gloomy triumph, in the tones of one who has at last won a long and closely-reasoned argument.

"Damn, there isn't a light here either!" she exclaimed, flipping ineffectually at the switch just inside the door. "What a nuisance! Now you can't see properly how frightful it is!"

Alice peered into the shadowed spaces ahead. Such light as filtered in from the fast-fading afternoon came through a small dormer window set high in the sloping attic ceiling, and her first impression was of a monstrous army standing to attention, shield-to-shield in silent battle-order. Huge shapes loomed; as her eyes became accustomed to the darkness she could see the floor at her feet awash with old newspapers and cardboard boxes.

Discouraging. But so what? Discouragement is hardly relevant to one whose courage is already just about drained away.

"How much?" Alice found herself asking, and Hetty gave quite a little start of surprise, as if taken unawares.

"How much what?" she began; and then gave an apologetic little laugh. "How much rent, do you mean? Well . . . it's a problem, isn't it? I don't know how I've the nerve to charge *anything* for such a hell-hole, but on the other hand . . . Look, what do *you* think, Alice? What would *you* charge, if it was yours?"

It was heart-warming to be called "Alice" after such short acquaintance; and the more so after all the weeks of formal letters from lawyers starting "Dear Mrs. Saunders"—a name which anyway seemed to belong to her less and less as the day of the divorce approached.

By now, she felt that her prospective landlady was almost an old friend, and she tried to answer the question in the simple, unembarrassed way that it had been asked.

"I do see what you mean about the—well—all that," she said, gesturing vaguely into the darkness. "But, on the other hand, to have *any* sort of room in London these days—*any* sort of a roof over one's head . . . Well, it's quite something, isn't it, to get *anything* . . . ?

"What I'd charge? Well, I think I'd see what the person could afford —the kind of person, I mean, who'd be wanting a room like this. I'd try to find out how desperate they were," she continued, and then wished she hadn't. It not only sounded rather rude, but it drew quite unnecessary attention to the question of her own desperation, and the reasons for it.

However, Hetty seemed unperturbed, and certainly not offended. A somewhat un-typical landlady-tenant argument ensued, with the landlady citing all the manifold disadvantages of the place, and Alice countering these as best she could by extolling the quiet and privacy afforded by an attic and enthusing about the superb view. (Well, this high up you surely could see *something?*)

"Oh well," said Hetty finally, "I'll tell you what. Let's leave it vague for the moment, shall we, and any time I'm short I'll ask you for something towards the rates, or something. Or if the electricity bill is too frightful . . . that sort of thing. How about that?"

For a moment, Alice had an alarming vision of what Rodney would have said to a business arrangement of this nature. But this was followed almost immediately by the realisation that it didn't matter what Rodney would have said. Not anymore. She could say "Yes" to anything she liked now.

So, "Yes," she said, and it was like a signpost pointing to the unknown. It was wild, and terrible, and exhilarating, like being cast adrift in an open boat.

"Yes, that will be just fine," she said.

CHAPTER 3

When she came back about two hours later, with her suitcase and her set of Jane Austens, Alice found that her landlady had added what she could in the way of homely touches by fixing a 150-watt bulb in the light socket, and throwing a dirty lace bed-cover over the dismembered motor-bike. In the relentless glare from the low, sloping ceiling the room looked derelict beyond description. Each broken-down discarded object now obtruded not only itself but also a bizarre and jagged shadow cast by the low-slung naked bulb; the whole presenting a sinister tangle of interlacing darkness, black on black, far into the narrowing recesses of the room where the ceiling sloped almost to the floor. It could have been a film set for one of those sci-fi movies about the collapse of technological civilization: enlarged to monster size on the big screen, it would look like the whole world crumbling to ruin. And there in the middle of it was Alice, the last humanoid left alive after whatever-it-was, inter-planetary war or something. Only of course in the film she wouldn't have been a deserted wife, pushing forty, hunched into a winter coat and boots, mouth ugly with anxiety and cold. She would have been a dazzling blonde in a bikini, her lithe body tanned to perfection and impervious to danger, cold and discomfort as it preened and cavorted its way to pre-ordained happiness.

Pre-ordained happiness. Not so long ago, Alice had thought—indeed had taken for granted—that happiness was pre-ordained for her, too; that she had a right to it, somehow, as a consequence of all the pleasant, uneventful years during which disasters had only happened to other people. She had got into the university of her choice; had graduated from it with a first-class degree, found a satisfying job in a school where they actually wanted a teacher of Classics. She had married the man she loved, and found herself totally happy with him. After such a run of good luck, it was hard not to feel like a fully paid-up member of some mysterious elite to whom Providence had granted special immunity—and to feel correspondingly outraged when Providence suddenly reneges on the bargain.

It's not *fair!* Alice found herself silently protesting as she stared at her new home under the cruel light. It's not *fair!* This is something that can't happen to *me!*

For several seconds, she felt like flinging herself onto the narrow sagging divan that flanked one wall, covering her eyes with both hands against the glare, and screaming aloud until somebody came and did something. But of course no one would. Or, rather, they *would* come, they *would* do something, but inevitably it would be something intolerable to her pride.

Pride was the only thing she had left now (apart from the Jane Austens), and having hung on to it so grimly through all the bitter weeks since Rodney's ultimatum, it would be absurd to squander it now.

Or had it, rather, been absurd to hang on to it in the first place? Why had she not done what the other forty-ish wives of her acquaintance had done, and fought (through solicitors, of course) for every penny she could screw out of her errant husband, for every stick of furniture, and above all for the right to stay in her comfortable, well-equipped home with its fitted carpets, its constant hot water, its books, its pictures, its plump cushions and softly-shaded lighting . . . ?

She could have demanded all these things, quite easily. Rodney would have been reasonable; her own solicitors would have been pleased, and so, she suspected, would Rodney's, committed though they were to fighting such claims. They would have known where they were then: they could have set in motion the familiar machinery for bargaining with bitter, rapacious wives—the sort of wives they best understood—and after the long, formal wrangling, everyone would have got their rights. Or what they wanted. Or what they ought to want. Or something . . .

But she hadn't given them the satisfaction—none of them, neither the friends nor the foes.

"I'm not taking *anything!*" she had cried. "Not a penny of your money, not a stick of furniture! Nothing!"

And out she had walked. With nothing. Well, nothing that she couldn't carry to the bus-stop in her own two hands, anyway.

To what purpose? In the interests of whose happiness? Certainly not Rodney's, who would have vastly preferred a fair—even a generous—settlement. And as to her own happiness . . . ? Well, look at her now, spread-eagled on a damp, lumpy mattress in a derelict junk-room, icy cold, trying not to scream.

You're crazy! You want your head examined! her friends had said when they heard of her plans—or, rather, her lack of plans. How do you think you're going to manage? they'd said. Where can you go, anyway? How do you think you're going to get another job at your age? And it's not fair on Rodney, they'd pointed out, when all other arguments had failed. It's making him feel awful—this last from her sister-in-law.

Well, OK, so it *wasn't* fair on Rodney. Why should it be? And *of course* it made him feel awful. Was this, perhaps, the whole object of the exercise? She had chosen to think of her motive as pride, but was it, rather, revenge? The subtle, sophisticated revenge that a woman like her, an intellectual sort of a woman, was turning out to be rather good at? The woman she had become, that is. The woman she had been only a few months ago was immeasurably nicer in every way, and would never have dreamed of hurting anyone deliberately, let alone her own husband.

It had been a good marriage, despite being childless. Or maybe *because* of being childless, each of them having no one but the other to please. Over the years, they'd had lots of fun together as well as love; indeed, it was the memory of the fun, and the betrayal of it, that hurt even more than the betrayal of love. She felt that she could perhaps have forgiven Rodney's loving another woman: it was the drying-up of intimate, long-standing jokes that hurt most: the blank, uncomprehending stare with which he began to greet her amusing little anecdotes that would once have sent them into fits of shared laughter. This was the real betrayal. This was the pain which had lodged in her heart like a fish-bone and would not go away.

The most recent of their shared jokes was the one that hurt most to look back on.

"Watch out!" she remembered calling across the bedroom to Rodney one summer Saturday morning, her voice full of laughter, "Watch out! *She's* there again!"

"Oh God—no! Where?" he'd answered, laughing likewise; and together they'd peered from behind the bedroom curtains, giggling like schoolchildren, as they watched the lumpy figure in its too-youthful summer dress sauntering by with would-be nonchalance, looking everywhere except up at the windows of the Saunders' home.

Ivy Budd. A silly enough name in its own right, and conducive to a certain amount of idle mockery, even if it hadn't been compounded by a degree of actual silliness almost beyond belief. Since parting from a rather shadowy Mr. Budd some two or three years ago—whether by divorce or by some other form of natural wastage was unclear—Ivy had developed a forlorn and hopeless crush on Rodney Saunders, trailing him along the corridors of the polytechnic where they both worked; hanging about in the car-park at the end of the day in hopes of seeing him come out and get into his car; even—who knows?—cherishing the even fainter hope that he might notice her, and offer her a lift to the station.

Which, in the early days, he had quite often done, as befitted a friendly colleague as yet unaware of his passenger's girlish and unrequited passion.

It was Alice who had noted the symptoms first. She'd been walking up the road with the weekend shopping one Saturday morning when she'd encountered—slightly to her surprise, for the quiet residential road with its bright front gardens and flowering cherry-trees didn't really lead to anywhere—this colleague of Rodney's whom she knew at the time only very slightly.

"Hullo," she'd said, with the small polite smile one gives to near strangers; and was about to pass on without further exchange, when the woman came to an awkward and jerky halt right in front of her, gulped uncomfortably and burst into rapid speech.

"I . . . I'm just on my way to post a letter," she gabbled, displaying the envelope with a flourish as if it was a key exhibit for the defence. "I only meant . . . that is, I thought if I could maybe catch the midday post . . ."

Vaguely puzzled by the gratuitous volley of information, Alice was at a loss for a reply. Why on earth should the woman find it necessary to explain to a near stranger her reason for walking peaceably along a public highway?

Oh, well. No business of mine, Alice had reflected, and passed on with a vague smile. She had thought no more about it until the following Saturday, when looking out of the bedroom window she noticed once again this same woman, strolling this time at a leisurely pace, as if waiting for someone to catch her up. But no one did, and not many minutes later, back she came again. Her pace was that of someone out for a stroll in the spring sunshine, and yet there was something intent and purposeful about her, an air of expectancy. The day was warm, and she was wearing a short cotton dress from which her muscular thighs projected like roof-supports, while her arms, scarlet with sunburn, hung from the sleeveless garment heavily, and somehow helplessly, as if they didn't know what they were supposed to be doing. No handbag. No load of weekend shopping. Just two thick, freckled arms with hands on the end of them.

"That woman from the Fine Arts Department," she remarked to Rodney at lunch-time, "Ivy somebody—the one you sometimes give lifts to—has she come to live in our road, or something?"

"Ivy Budd? The one with the legs? No, I don't think so. Not that I know of. Why?"

"Well, I keep seeing her around, that's all. It seems funny, if she still lives over in Fulham. I saw her last Saturday, she said she'd come to post a letter. Can you credit it—travelling all the way from Fulham to post a letter in our pillar-box instead of in her own!"

Rodney shrugged. He didn't seem very interested, and merely murmured that there were no zoning regulations about pillar-boxes, were there? Anyone could post anything anywhere they liked, and anyway it takes all sorts, especially in the Fine Arts Department . . .

But the next Saturday, there she was again—hanging about on the other side of the road watching Rodney cut the front hedge, and finally crossing the road to ask him, blushing furiously, for a spray of the cut privet to take home with her—and even Rodney was a bit taken aback.

"A spray of *privet*," he speculated over lunch. "What on earth can she want it for? I started asking her, does she keep stick-insects? But she seemed terrified. She just gave a great gulp, and ran off down the road. *Ran!* Did I say something wrong, do you suppose? Is "stick-insect" the latest rude word, or something?"

Alice laughed. "She's potty about you, darling, that's all it is," she explained. "She's going to press that privet spray between sheets of blotting-paper, and keep it for ever! She's got a crush on you, like a lovesick teenager."

"*Teenager!* She's fifty if she's a day," protested Rodney—though actually she wasn't, she was only forty-four, as Alice was to discover later. "Are you seriously suggesting that a grown woman . . . ?"

"Yes, I am," Alice insisted. "It's not as extraordinary as you seem to think. A crush isn't peculiar to teenagers, you know. It's a kind of loving that people go in for when the object of their love is unattainable. It can happen at any age, in fact it's quite common, to judge by what one hears. Middle-aged women and their doctors. Vicars and devoted female members of their congregations . . ."

"Well, I'm not a bloody vicar," Rodney grumbled. "Vicars are paid to be pestered, the topping-up of half-empty souls is their job. But it's not mine, and I'm damned if I'm going to be press-ganged into it! I'll take out an injunction against her if she's not careful!"

But very soon irritation gave way to amusement, and he and Alice spent many an odd minute giggling over the excesses of his undeclared admirer. Indeed, it would have been difficult to be other than amused by some of the antics the love-lorn lady got up to in her attempts to engineer an "accidental" meeting with her beloved. Popping out from the shelter of some doorway as he came by; lurking in the nearby telephone box watching for him to come out into the front garden so that she could happen to walk past and say "Hello," in the tremulous expectation of hearing him say "Hello" back. Which, of course, he had to do; and though this was usually the extreme limit of the exchange, it seemed to suffice. On such insubstantial nourishment can an insubstantial passion thrive, Alice used to reflect, watching the ungainly figure fairly prancing down the road after one of these encounters, all lit up with unspeakable joy, with the sound of that perfunctory "Hello" still echoing in her ears.

Part of the fun was the way Alice would tease him about his "conquest"; and he in his turn would appeal to Alice, in mock-terror, for her protection.

"Go and have a dekko, darling," he would urge, with exaggerated wariness. "See if I can mow the front lawn this morning without getting raped!" And Alice, with barely suppressed giggles, would peer up and down the road and report that the coast was clear, or otherwise.

"She'll be writing you anonymous poems next!" Alice laughingly predicted one Saturday; and lo and behold, that was exactly what happened.

They would arrive by post, and Rodney and Alice would find themselves in fits of laughter, reading out to one another lines about love so true being spurned by you, or about hearts still yearning and passion burning.

"And stomachs turning," Alice remembered improvising, and together they had leaned back against the cushions and laughed until they cried.

Was this the last time—the very last time—that they had laughed together like this? Laughed in such an ecstasy of shared mockery that it was almost like an ecstasy of love?

It was hard to believe now that it was this same Rodney, this same beloved husband, who, not many months later, had been leaning back against those same cushions, explaining gravely to Alice that he was in love with Ivy, that she was a very wonderful person, and that he wanted to marry her.

CHAPTER 4

Oh, but it was cold, cold! The thin army blankets with which the bed was supplied seemed to help not at all. Even with her winter coat still on, even with her boots, the dank chill of the room was getting to her very bones. Draughts whistled in from the winter blackness outside, not only through the ill-fitting dormer window, but through mysterious cracks along the skirting-boards; the ancient bridal drapery over the motor-bike stirred and quivered, showing up the rusty stains of long ago.

Such cold was not to be endured. She must go down all those stairs and look for her landlady in the basement. Ask for more blankets. For a hot-water bottle. Some kind of heating—an electric fire, or something.

Oh, and a hot bath! How wonderful that would be! Mention had been made of a bathroom, albeit two or three floors down.

"A bath? But of course, dearie. Any time. As many baths as you like. The only thing is, Alice, the geyser seems to be in one of its moods this evening. It gets like that sometimes, it won't light straight away, and then you get this great big pop, makes you jump out of your skin . . . I'd better come up with you, dear, and see how it's doing. Sometimes, you know, it won't light at all, and then we have to wait for Brian to come in, he does something to it with a knife, and then it's all right for a bit . . . Mare-ee!" she yelled suddenly, turning towards the stairs. "Mare-ee! Where's Brian? Is he coming back tonight?"

A distant voice, incomprehensible to Alice, could be heard answering at somewhat greater length than the question would seem to war-

rant; and though Alice could not make out the words, the peevish tone
in which they were uttered was unmistakable.

"OK, dear, OK! I'm not trying to pry!" yelled back Hetty; and then
she turned with a sigh to Alice:

"No dice, never mind, we'll have a go at it ourselves"; and then, in a
lower voice as they set off up the stairs, "*I* don't mind who they have
up there, boy-friends and that, or who they don't. Love and let love is
what I say. But she's so touchy, that girl, you wouldn't believe. The
simplest question, and she jumps down your throat like you were accusing her of murder. Never mind, let's see what we can do—" and continuing on the way up the stairs, she pushed open the bathroom door,
revealing an untidy barn of a room containing an ironing board, several suitcases and a roll of carpet, as well as a bath.

"You stay there—over by the door, dear," Hetty warned; and herself
tiptoed warily across the floor towards the ancient geyser, like a cat
stalking a rather large rat.

"Pilot's off, I'm afraid, Alice," was her verdict, straightening up after
a prolonged inspection of the thing's internal organs. "I daren't light it
myself, not without Brian here, I just daren't. I've known the flame
jump three feet into the room, I'm not exaggerating, and I wouldn't
like that to happen to you, dear. Not your first night."

Alice felt that she could do without it on other nights too; but she
tried not to seem hyper-critical.

"Well, never mind," she said, clutching her coat yet more tightly
about her. Then, "Do you think—perhaps—if there *is* an electric fire
to spare? If I could have it up in my room? Just for tonight? I'd pay, of
course."

"*Of course,* darling!" cried Hetty, in tones of such impassioned liber-
ality that one could only assume the words related to the request for
the fire, and not at all to the offer to pay. "*Of course,* darling, you *must*
have a fire, it's terrible up there, a night like this, all those draughts.
The only thing is—" Here she cast her eyes anxiously up and down the
stairway, as if hoping that an electric fire just might spring out from
somewhere, come hopping and rattling to their feet, and thus solve the
problem. "The only thing is . . . We want one that *works,* you see.
That's the problem . . ."

That this was indeed a major consideration Alice could not but
agree, and she watched in suspense while her landlady frowned and bit
her knuckles.

"*I* know!" Suddenly Hetty's face cleared. "We'll take the one from

Brian's room, that's sure to work, everything of Brian's always does. I don't know how he does it, I really don't. And his eiderdown too, you could do with that, I'm sure, those miserable blankets you've got up there wouldn't keep a rabbit warm."

"But won't . . . this Brian . . . won't he mind . . . ?" Alice began, but Hetty interrupted her.

"Mind? Of course he won't mind. He's out. I told you," and lumbering gamely on up the next flight of stairs, she launched herself against one of the doors opening onto the landing just below Alice's attic floor.

"Hell! He's locked it! And he probably won't be in till all hours! I *wish* he wouldn't do that, I've asked him no end of times, but he doesn't seem to understand how inconvenient it can be." Here she rattled the handle again impatiently. "It's funny," she continued. "Because he's such a nice boy really, but he does have this possessive streak about his things. I don't know what he thinks might happen to them, I'm sure.

"Oh well. Never mind, I'll give you the one from the kitchen, nobody'll be using the kitchen this late, and if they do they can light up the oven and give themselves a good warm with their feet in it. I'll give you a hot-water bottle too, Alice, that'll make a difference, won't it, and then tomorrow we'll get you rigged up right and proper, blankets, pillows and all sorts. Oh, and what about something to eat, my darling? You must be starving. Come on down, and I'll see what I can find for you. Then, tomorrow, we must think where to fit you in, for cooking and that."

Sitting at the scrubbed wooden table, gratefully consuming the remains of a still-warm shepherd's pie, Alice listened attentively while Hetty expounded the system by which she apportioned the use of her kitchen among her various tenants.

The core and essence of the system, it soon became clear, consisted in not upsetting one Miss Dorinda.

"She's in the beauty business, you see," Hetty explained. "She likes everything to be just so; and so when she comes in at six-thirty she has to have the kitchen entirely to herself until she's finished. The best part of an hour it can be, all her bits and pieces and stirring up little messes on the cooker. She's into health, you know, and that takes up a lot of space, no use anyone trying to do anything else while she's there, so we all just keep out of her way till she's done. Or before she starts, of course, before six-thirty. But if you choose the before six-thirty time,

Alice, do for goodness sake get yourself cleared up before she gets in! If there's so much as a teaspoon left on the draining-board at six-thirty, she'll go through the roof! Actually right through it, I'm not exaggerating . . ."

While Alice's tired mind grappled feebly with this vision of the unknown Miss Dorinda, Hetty continued (aware, perhaps, that she had slightly over-stated her case) in a more sober vein:

"It's the nature of her work, you see," she explained. "She's manageress at the hair and beauty salon in the high street. Just beyond Marks —you'll see it when you go to the shops, Alice, you can't miss it, nearly opposite Tesco's, on the corner. They get like that in the beauty business," she went on reflectively, "I've seen it no end of times. I had a manicure young lady once, and she was the same . . . It's beauty, you see, it brings out a funny streak in them somehow, and that's the truth . . ."

Beauty is truth, truth beauty . . . Alice realised she was almost falling asleep; she roused herself with an effort.

"What about the others?" she asked. "There was a 'Brian' you mentioned—and 'Mary'—Do they have an hour each too?"

"An *hour?* My goodness, no! Listen, my dear, if everyone in this house had an hour to themselves like Miss Dorinda has, there'd be no end to it, the clatter and the clutter, and in-ings and the out-ings, the smells and the boilings-over and the clutter-up round the sink. It'd be midnight before I could set foot in my own kitchen. No, they fit in as best they can, the rest of them. They don't make a fuss, you see, not like Miss Dorinda does . . . Not fair? . . . Listen, dear, one thing I have learnt in this job is always to give in, straight away, to the fusspots, let them have everything exactly the way they want it right from the beginning, and you save yourself no end of bother. The others will always fit in somehow. Like Brian, I mean, he's a sweetie, no trouble at all, just brings in his take-aways and pops them in the oven, and is off up to his room with them before you hardly know he's there . . ."

Here she paused, glancing speculatively at her new lodger; and for an uneasy moment Alice felt herself being weighed in the balance: was she going to rate as a fuss-pot, and thus entitled to extra privilege? Or as a sweetie, who could be relied on to be in and out of the kitchen before you hardly knew she was there?

To postpone this issue, she continued with her queries:

"And the girl—Mary—when does she eat?"

At this Hetty shook her head sadly. "That's one of my worries, you know. The truth is, she hardly eats a thing—just a bit of toast and a cup of tea, and not always that. I'm quite bothered about that girl, Alice, I really am. She eats like a sparrow, and always in bed by ten. Such a pretty girl, too, can't be much over twenty—she ought to be out gallivanting till all hours. I always say, if someone in their twenties is getting enough sleep, then what on earth are they going to be like at forty?"

A difficult question; and one on which Alice felt unable to comment just now. Weariness was once again overcoming her, she felt almost light-headed with tiredness, and so she ventured, as politely as she could, to draw her landlady's attention to the urgent matters which had originally brought her down to the kitchen. Blankets. An electric fire. A hot-water bottle.

Hetty was all compunction. *Of course* Alice must have these things. Heaving herself from her chair, she began to pound around the kitchen and adjoining scullery, assembling such adjuncts to Alice's comfort as she could lay hands on. Then, carrying some of the load, she accompanied Alice up the first flights of stairs, switching lights on as they went, and apologising for the speed at which they switched themselves off again. You'd have to be one of those Olympic chappies to beat them to it, and one day Brian was going to do something about it, when he'd finished his cantata. Cantata? Oh yes, he was a musician, Brian was, a composer, though that wasn't how he made a living, my goodness no. He taught at the Adult Education Centre most days, and the odd private pupil too, evenings and weekends. It was nice to hear the old piano tinkle-tonking away, Hetty felt, kind of cosy, a bit of life going on; but unfortunately Miss Dorinda didn't see it that way, and so on and off there could be a bit of trouble. Artistic in her way, Miss Dorinda was, but just not the tinkle-tonk type, if Alice took her meaning. Well, there you are, dear, you'll be all right now, won't you. I'll be getting on down, if you don't mind, I've got things to see to . . .

By the time she reached her attic room, Alice was feeling quite bemused with cold and tiredness. Thankfully she dumped the hot-water bottle under the meagre blankets, plugged in the electric fire and, cowering close in front of it, began to undress. The fire glowed red, the growing warmth playing on her bare shoulders, and then, with a sudden "phut!" it spat at her like a furious cat. The brief warmth died, trickled away and became one with the icy draughts whistling in from every shadowy corner.

Alice gave up. Huddling most of her clothes back on again, she crawled into the chilly bed, pulled the thin blankets over her, and her winter coat as well. She did not expect to sleep. She lay there clutching the hot-water bottle against her, waiting, with abject resignation, for it to start leaking.

CHAPTER 5

Her eyes opened on the great red ball of the winter sun. Through the small high window it filled the room with rosy light, and she realised to her astonishment that she must have slept solidly the whole night through, a thing that hadn't happened to her in weeks. And the hot-water bottle *hadn't* leaked; it still lay faintly warm against her body where she had been clutching it last night. With a hot-water bottle that didn't leak, and with the mighty crimson globe of the sun welcoming her back to consciousness, Alice felt herself momentarily filled with new strength, new hope.

But strength to perform what task? Hope for what sort of a future? These weighty questions, like a pair of over-full suitcases, brought her brief optimism to a standstill. Before they could drag her all the way back into last night's depression, she resolved to do, one by one, the things you can do anyway, whether you are depressed or not.

Like getting out of bed. Like going down all those stairs to the bathroom, and then on to the kitchen in the basement.

It lay deserted now in the half-light of the winter dawn, and silent too—until, with a sudden peremptory rattle from the scullery, a large tabby cat appeared and planted herself, with stern expectancy, right in her path, fixing her with a gold, unblinking gaze. Evidently, the first person who came down in the morning was expected to do something about the animal.

But what? There was no telling. "Sorry, Puss, you'll have to wait for Hetty," she apologised, and with a vague idea of making herself a cup of coffee, moved in the direction of the cooker.

A small, agonised sound stopped her in her tracks. Not exactly a "meow"—the situation was too desperate for that—more a sort of tortured hiccup, the last gasp of a soul in torment. Glancing down, Alice was confronted by a look of such absolute outrage in those golden eyes that she almost shrank away. Obviously, she was doing the wrong thing. She tried moving in a new direction, and this time, it seemed, she was doing better . . . getting warmer . . . warmer . . . for the creature was now purring on a high, frantic note, coiling and weaving itself about her ankles as she moved.

The refrigerator. Of course. Led there unerringly by her expert guide, Alice opened the door and peered inside. No fewer than nine bottles of milk confronted her, all of them opened, and most more than half empty. One carried round its neck a sort of paper collar bearing the message "Hands Off!" and another, very neat and black, the initials "DD"—Miss Dorinda, presumably, who liked everything to be just so; certainly, she must leave that one alone. A third, looking as if it had seen better days, carried the initials "WX"; and the last in the line, more cryptically still, bore the inscription "Yesterday Only."

But she couldn't puzzle over these symbols for long. The single-minded intensity of desire that radiated knee-high from where the cat coiled and writhed in serpentine rapture was too much for her, and grabbing the "Yesterday" bottle she rapidly poured half of it into a pie-dish, set it on the floor and then stood back, contemplating the full glory of her achievement; the creation, single-handed, of absolute contentment, of that peace which passeth all understanding, of a whole tiny universe at harmony with itself, pulsing to the rhythm of a pink, darting tongue.

She couldn't find any coffee (she must buy some for herself this morning), and so made do with boiling up some water and adding a spoonful of sugar and a dash of the "Yesterday Only" milk. A label like that seemed to put it outside the conventional morality of Mine and Thine. It wasn't bad—it was better than nothing—and after carrying it up to her bleak and fireless attic, she sat on the edge of the bed and sipped it slowly, trying, now that it was full daylight, to take in more clearly the extent and nature of her new domain.

You could look at the room in two ways really. You could see it as so awful that hours and hours of daunting effort—not to mention Herculean physical strength—would be required to make it even half-way habitable. Or, on the other hand, you could see it as so awful that nothing could be done, and therefore nothing need be. You could see yourself sinking into the chaos, as one more item landing up in this graveyard of failed, unwanted, unworkable appliances. You could give up. Go to pieces. Lots of discarded wives do.

There was, though, a third option. You could walk out. Tell the landlady how sorry you were, how much you would have enjoyed living here, but unfortunately this, that and the other and so forth . . .

Thinking on these lines last night, Alice had resolved to leave the final decision till this morning, when she would apply herself to it with a fresh mind and a sheet of paper—well, the back of an old envelope, anyway—setting out in two columns the fors and againsts: "Quiet road, not much traffic; No rent at the moment; No references required; Kindly, easy-going landlady" in one column, and in the other, "Sloppy, incompetent landlady; No heating; Extreme discomfort; No space; No hot water"—that sort of thing. She would work out a points system for all these items, and then add up the totals. Easy.

She found an old envelope all right. She even found a pencil. But by this time the whole scheme had quietly and imperceptibly become obsolete, for she knew already that she was going to stay. She wasn't quite sure why, or where the decision had come from, but there it was. In the last few minutes the room had become hers. It was as if a marriage ceremony had been taking place inside her head, and without really noticing it she had said "I will"—and was now confronted (like any bride) with the necessity of making the best of her new acquisition; working out the minimum alterations necessary to render life tolerable.

Her first problem, she realised, was that she did not know what, if any, were her rights over her new domain. Was she entitled to get rid of anything she wished—and was physically able to carry down to the dustbins—or was her rôle that of reluctant curator on behalf of shadowy battalions of claimants, past and present? Looking around, it seemed to Alice highly unlikely that anyone in his right mind could possibly be going to claim any of it; but, on the other hand, if Hetty, the rightful householder, had felt hesitant about throwing anything away, then certainly Alice, the interloper, must feel even more hesitant.

But all the same, things could be stacked up a bit better to give more floor space. Those crates of china or whatever could be pushed further in under the beams, and the bits of rolled-up carpet could go on top of them . . . and all those cardboard boxes, crammed to overflowing with old journals and newspapers and such—they could be piled one on top of the other to take less space . . . Within a few minutes, Alice was bent double, pushing and pulling at the heavy, cumbersome things.

But as she did so, a better idea came to her. Instead of trying to get these boxes stacked up as much out of the way as possible, could she not build them into some useful piece of furniture? A sort of sofa, for example, with its back made of two sets of three boxes piled on top of each other against the wall, and then another three in front to form the seat? Such a seat would be quite a comfortable height—Alice tried it—and quite firm and steady, crammed as most of them were with tight-packed papers.

Some of them, though, were a bit *too* crammed, their tattered contents toppling lopsidedly well above the level of the lid; others were only sparsely filled, so that if you tried to sit on them you would sink slowly into a welter of collapsing cardboard. After a brief struggle with her conscience, Alice decided that although she mustn't throw anything away, she would be within her rights in transferring an armful of *this* into a vacant space among *that*, and so rendering the boxes homogeneous enough for her purposes.

Old colour-supplements; antediluvian sets of Lilliputs . . . newspaper cuttings going back to the *News Chronicle*, and even the *Daily Graphic* . . . the hoarder of all this must surely be in his grave this many a year? Yanking from one of the over-full boxes a yellowing armful of agriculture and fishery bulletins, Alice was slightly surprised to discover a set of exercise-books—a dozen or more of them—neatly stacked, and looking much more recent than most of the stuff she had come across.

Someone's amateur attempt at a novel, it seemed to be. A thriller, presumably, for opening one of the little books at random her eyes fell on a highly-coloured passage describing in fulsome—though probably inaccurate—detail the collapse of some character from a gunshot wound:

> His fall was like that of an ancient tree, sinking gently to the ground, settling there, without protest, arms outstretched like branches . . .

Not bad, in a way, thought Alice, reverting momentarily to her schoolteaching persona. Spelling, grammar, punctuation all beyond reproach—though 5 out of 10 for handwriting would be generous. Sad, really, that the author—someone very young, she felt sure—should have abandoned his task to this limbo. Fed up with it, perhaps? In despair of ever getting it published? At a loss how to end it?

She flipped through a few more of the volumes, smiling a little.

There seemed to be a death, or the aftermath of a death, on almost every page . . . a very amateur writer, obviously, who had not yet learned that by piling on the thrills you take all the thrill out of them. Here and there, loose among the text, were old newspaper cuttings and magazine pictures—presumably to stir the creative process. One in particular caught Alice's attention—a page from some magazine, a colour-supplement, probably—on which was reproduced a photograph of an autumn landscape: a hill-side dotted with rowan trees in full glory of scarlet berries. Emerging from behind one of the trees, with wings outspread, appeared an enormous bat. But enormous—for one mad second one could have taken it for a pterodactyl photographed in full flight. A clever piece of trick photography, of course, a picture of a bat somehow superimposed on the tranquil autumn landscape. Looking at the caption below, "Flittermouse Hill in Autumn," Alice saw that the cleverness had indeed been appreciated—a ten-pound prize had been awarded in a Junior Photographic Competition to Julian somebody, aged fourteen, from Medley Green Comprehensive.

Enough! If she stopped to read and examine every intriguing snippet she might come across, she'd never get anything done at all. Replacing the exercise-books, and piling in above them the requisite thickness of *National Geographic* magazines from a neighbouring pile, Alice gave her attention again to the construction of her sofa. Or divan. Or whatever.

The basic structure was soon in place. Now, if she could dig out from all that lumber behind the motor-bike some of those bits of material she'd noticed—old curtains or something—cretonne, it looked like, with a faded, pinky-yellowy pattern . . .

Yes, here it was. Crumpled and dusty indeed, but after being properly washed and ironed . . . Bending lower still under the sloping roof, she tugged at the pieces of material, trying to ease them from under a length of garden trellis, whose projecting slats threatened to catch on the stuff and tear it . . .

"Christ!"

At the suddenness of the exclamation, Alice sprang to her feet—or rather tried to. In fact, she banged her head with considerable violence against the low beam that spanned that part of the roof; and so it was through a whirl of dizzying pain and flashing lights that she first looked at her unexpected visitor. A slight figure—wearing something bluish—standing in the doorway . . . and as the effects of the blow subsided, and normal vision was restored, Alice found herself able to take in that the visitor was a young girl wearing jeans and a washed-out blouse. Her

light brown hair was cropped short, and her eyes, startlingly blue, were
darting from object to object in the disordered room. In ordinary circumstances she would have been outstandingly pretty, Alice guessed,
but at the moment her face was pinched with outrage.

"What are you *doing?*" The girl's voice was shrill. "What the *hell* are
you doing? And who are you, anyway? What are you looking for?"

The better to cope with this unexpected onslaught, Alice clambered
slowly out from her uncomfortable perch under the low ceiling, cir-
cumnavigated as best she could the motor-bike handlebars which stuck
up like horns, and faced her inquisitor. The pain was beginning to
subside now, and she felt more able to hold her own.

"Doing? Getting my room in order, of course. Trying to . . . If it
comes to that, what are *you* doing? Barging in like this," she added for
good measure, trying to turn the tables vaguely in her own direction.

The girl still stared at her accusingly, but some of the shock had
subsided from her face.

"What do you mean, *your* room!" she asked now. "It can't be your
room, it isn't anybody's room, it's all of us's. It's a—well, it's where we
all dump our stuff. Hetty told us we could. 'Liberty Lumber-room,
that's what that room is,' she told me when I came, and that's how
everyone has always been using it. As you can see. Right back to the
year dot. So it *can't* be yours."

Well, it *is* mine, I'm renting it, Alice would like to have said, but of
course, she wasn't, not yet. She wasn't paying anything so far, and that
put her at rather a disadvantage in the argument.

"Well," she said, "I'm sorry, there seems to be some sort of misun-
derstanding, we'll have to talk to Hetty . . ."

But the girl seemed now to be hardly listening. Her eyes were travelling round the room anxiously, as if she was trying to make mental
notes of everything in it.

"It's not *fair!*" she burst out after a minute. "She might at least have
warned me—warned us, I mean . . ."

Her protest faltered to an uneasy halt, and Alice broke in hastily,
trying to be reassuring.

"Look," she said, "I don't see why we need quarrel about this. This
is to be my room, it's all arranged, but I don't see that it need affect
you. You can go on storing your things here just as long as you like. I'm
not trying to throw anything out, I'm just stacking things up neatly so
as to give myself a bit of space." And then, trying to be friendly, she
added, "I'm Alice, by the way. You're Mary, aren't you?"

"How do you know? Who told you?"

The voice was sharp with suspicion, and Alice was momentarily quite thrown. What was the matter with the girl?

"Why . . . I suppose . . . well, Hetty told me," she stammered, feeling absurdly apologetic under the impact of that accusing stare. "She was just telling me—you know—about the rest of you who live here. I mean, we're all going to be sharing the kitchen and everything, and so I suppose . . ."

"What else did she tell you?"

Alice no longer felt apologetic. Annoyance mounted under this ludicrous inquisition.

"Nothing," she snapped. "Just that you were Mary, and someone called Brian was Brian, and someone else was Miss Dorinda— I hadn't even *met* any of these people, and so I don't see what she could possibly . . ."

"No, of course not. I—I'm sorry, Alice—" The girl was half-heartedly trying to make amends for her rudeness. "I'm sorry, but it was kind of a shock finding you up here, and I thought for a moment that Hetty must have . . ." She stopped; then continued, at something of a tangent:

"You'll like Hetty, Alice, she's as kind as can be, as I expect you've discovered. She just loves people with problems. Do you have a problem, Alice? A real, juicy humdinger of a disaster? If so, you're *in!* No wonder she's letting you have the bloody room! You'll be Landlady's Pet, and the rest of us will have our noses out of joint, even Brian!"

She gave a short, hard laugh, and turned to leave the room; then paused, and turning back continued, more gently, "I'm sorry, Alice, don't take too much notice of me, I'm in a bad mood. I shouldn't be saying nasty things about poor Hetty, she really is terribly good-natured. It's just that—well, it's not so much that she pokes her nose into other people's business, it's that she takes for granted that everything *is* her business. She's a marvellous person if you ever need help with your troubles—but a right pain in the neck if you don't!"

With which double-edged tribute Mary whisked around and clattered off down the wooden stairs. Alice heard a door on the third-floor landing slam shut, and then there was silence, broken only by a faint gurgle of water-pipes from somewhere across the landing. By now, it seemed like the voice of an old friend.

CHAPTER 6

The gurgle of the water-pipes was in Mary's ears, too, as she lay face-down on her bed, cursing herself for every kind of a fool.

She had made another enemy. No, enemy was an exaggeration; all she had done, actually, was to discourage a possible friend, to slap down Alice's kindly overtures before they became any kind of a threat.

Why did she keep doing this? With everyone? Surely she, with her star record as a psychology student, should be able to analyse it? Should have sufficient insight to diagnose her own case and suggest a cure?

The diagnosis was easy; but all the psychology textbooks in the world weren't going to come up with a cure. Advice on how to win friends—in books, articles and agony columns—must run into millions and millions of words by now, but of what use are all these words when, in your particular case, friends are more dangerous than enemies? When kindness, concern and sympathy present a bigger threat than the most virulent hostility?

The fog was thickening outside her window, and she was getting cold, very cold. She did not bother to go across the room and switch on her electric fire; only one bar of it was working, and it made scarcely any difference to this big draughty room with its ill-fitting door and windows. Instead, she slipped off her shoes and crawled back into the bed, properly under the bedclothes this time, and with the shabby eiderdown pulled up to her chin. This way, with her eyes closed, and with the slow build-up of warmth generated by her own body inside its cocoon of bedclothes, she would be able to withdraw from the wintry chill of this room, this house, this street, and travel back, back to the place where it was always summer, and the soft, sweet air was always warm. Flittermouse Hill.

It had been a wonderful place for children—for anyone, really, but not many people came, because the rutted tracks that led to it were almost impossible for cars. But to Mary and Julian it had been a sort of paradise during their growing years. A short cycle-ride from their home in Medley Green, it was their favourite haunt during school holidays, for it had everything. It was part of an unspoiled stretch of the Downs from which, on a clear day, you could see away and away across the rolling green distances to the glitter of the sea itself. Being up there felt not merely like being on top of the world, it felt like owning it, as a god might own it. She remembered how they'd talked about this, she and Julian (about twelve and ten they must have been) as they stood on the summit one noonday, the sun blazing down and the breeze of the high hills blowing about their heads. In her class at school, a few days back, they'd been doing the Temptation in the Wilderness for a Scripture lesson, and the teacher had been trying to impress the children with the hugeness of temptation that Jesus had faced:

"Just fancy. He was promised the *whole world* if He did what the devil said! The *whole world*—just imagine it," she had urged the children. "Just imagine owning the whole world!"

The words had come back to her as she stood amid the golden gorse and golden sunshine at the topmost point of Flittermouse Hill, and she was puzzled. In what sense *don't* I own it? she wondered. Here it *is*. Here I am, seeing it, knowing it, being right in the centre of it, as far as I can see. How is this not owning it? How can owning it be a temptation, when you've already got it?

She put the problem to Julian—he loved philosophical problems, even at that age. He thought about it gravely, his fairish hair blown about by the wind, and his eyes scouring the blue distances wherein the problem had its being.

"It must have been different for Jesus," he said at last. "I don't think He bothered about things being beautiful. Look at the way He blasted that tree. I'm glad He's not alive now."

This was blasphemy. Mary shuddered in delighted awe, as she often did at Julian's more outlandish thoughts. She wondered what her Scripture teacher would have said if she had heard him?

"Oh, but Julian, do you think one should . . . ?" she began; but already his thoughts were elsewhere, his small wiry body suddenly taut and braced for challenge:

"C'mon, Midge! Race you!" he cried; and they were off. He never *did* succeed in racing her during these early years, his legs were too much shorter than hers; but likewise he never gave up the hope that, this time, he just might. She heard his breath, gasping with determination, close behind her as she ran: in and out among the clumps of gorse, scrambling through thick bracken, and landing up at the entrance to one of the caves which were a feature of these upper slopes. Mary (or Midge, as she was then) had often, when she was younger, wanted to continue their games inside one or other of the caves—turning it into a wizard's castle, or a pirates' hide-away or something, but Julian would not allow it. It would disturb the bats, he said. This was their bedroom, he explained, where they rested all day to be ready for their night's hunting, and it would upset them terribly to have pirates and wizards and things charging in and out while they were trying to sleep. Mary had acquiesced—as she nearly always did to Julian's pronouncements. Although he was nearly two years younger, he always seemed to know more than she did about almost everything; it was this, maybe, that made them such close companions all through the years of their child-hood. The age-gap seemed to be nil; it was almost as if they were twins.

Julian's fascination with the bats, and their near-miraculous way of life, had grown and grown; but it was not until they were both in their teens that their parents had allowed them to stay out on the hill-side late enough for successful bat-watching; and even then, it still pro-voked a good deal of parental unease.

"There might be nasty men . . ." their mother had anxiously spec-ulated, not realising (for how could she?) how ironic were these fears, in view of what was to come.

By the time they were—what? Fourteen? Fifteen?—the ban had been lifted, albeit reluctantly, and they would set off to Flittermouse Hill on their bicycles in the late afternoon, sometimes with sandwiches, some-times with just a bar of chocolate and settle themselves outside the caves—at a fair distance from the openings, in accordance with Julian's assessment of the bats' peace of mind as they made their exit. There they would lie, sometimes talking, sometimes in silence, waiting for the sun to go down and for evening to spread over the hill. The air would be shimmering still with late-afternoon heat when they arrived, and Mary recalled the peace of it, the solitude, and the feel of the hot, blissful turn against her bare legs as she and Julian flopped down, breathless after their cycle ride followed by the long, up-hill scramble through gorse and bracken to reach their chosen eyrie.

Often, as they lay there side by side on the dry, sun-baked grass, waiting for dusk to fall, Julian would start telling her about bats. Each time, he would have learned something new about them, something fascinating, and almost incredible. That they steered themselves not by sight, but by echo-location, was of course one of the first things that Mary learned; and although much of what he told her during subsequent sessions was beyond her grasp, it still held a magic for her which did not depend on understanding. About reflected sound, for example, radiating away from the object in an expanding spherical wave-front; and how the volume of the sound decays according to the square of the distance from the object, so that by the time the echo of his own voice comes back to him, the bat, like a tiny mathematician, can calculate from the loudness or softness of it how far away the object must have been.

And as time went on, with practice, she did begin to understand more and more of what he told her; and fascinating it was, sometimes almost beyond belief. How, at cruising speed, they emit sounds at the rate of ten per second, rising to two hundred per second when they are closing in on their prey—a moth, maybe, or some other night-flying insect. And how their voices are high-pitched far beyond the range of human ears because the very short wave-lengths of very high-pitched sounds are necessary for conveying accurate information about very tiny objects at varying distances. These tiny objects have to be located, and then re-located, in fractions of a second, because they are fast-moving, as insects always are . . .

"You can't really imagine it, Midge," he said, his voice half-choked with the effort of trying to convey something quite beyond her—or anyone else's—experience. "You see, most of the noises they make are so far beyond the range of our hearing that they are higher than the highest note anyone can possibly imagine," he told her; "And that's jolly lucky, in a way," he added, "Because as well as being so high, they are also incredibly loud—they have to be, for the echo to come back loud enough. They are actually shouting and yelling at this high frequency—if we *could* hear them, we'd be almost deafened. No one would be able to sleep through it, even with their windows shut!"

Thus would he talk, and tell her things; and thus would she lie listening, in absolute contentment, and occasionally asking a question, while above them the blue of the sky grew pale and paler, changing to the green and lemon of sunset, and then to the slow, encroaching violet of the coming night. And presently his voice would cease, and

with one accord they would fall silent, or almost silent. "Venus!" one
of them might whisper as the silvery point of light first flickered into
visibility in the western sky; or, "Look, a new moon!" as the pale,
gleaming thread of a crescent first detached itself from the pale gleaming background of the dying light.

But that was all; for by now it was necessary to be absolutely quiet.
The time had arrived for the coming of the bats.

Rarely did they manage to observe them actually emerging from the
mouth of a cave. They came out for their night's hunting intermit-
tently, it seemed, in ones and twos, not at all in the spectacular dark
mass, like starlings, that Mary had at first envisaged. The first she and
Julian saw of them, usually, would be a single one, darting in zig-zag
flight across the darkening sky, changing direction at angles as sharp
and clear as a diagram in a geometry textbook. And then there would
be another . . . and another . . . flashing this way and that across
the sky like dark lightning. More and more of them would come, until
the sky was alive with them; it was like watching a firework display, all
in black, only more amazing, more incomprehensible, than any firework display ever devised by man.

Sometimes, lying there, Mary fancied that she heard the magically
high-pitched cries, as they shouted and yelled across the night sky, but
Julian assured her that she couldn't have. There are some species of
bats where you just might, he said—the Rousettus fruit-bats, for example; but these were mouse-eared bats, and their echo-location system
was such that . . .

This, of course, was on the way home. They never talked while they
were watching the bats, even though the bats almost certainly couldn't
have heard them. Their silence was like the silence of a religious gathering, in a church or a cathedral; to both of them it would have seemed
wrong to break it, as though something of the spectacle would have
been destroyed by a human voice.

Sometimes, though, without speaking, they would take a more posi-
tive part in the bats' hunting rituals. They would bring pellets of bread
with them, and little dry bits from the cake-tin, and fling them into the
air as high as they could, watching the bats swoop unerringly to snatch
each crumb out of the empty sky. It was like watching Wimbledon
tennis, only a thousand times swifter and more exact—the same reli-
ance on perfect timing and unerring pace.

And then home again—later than expected—their mother anxious and waiting, hurrying them into hot baths, and cooking them bacon and eggs at nearly midnight, so thankful was she that they'd arrived home safe, and hadn't encountered any Nasty Men.

CHAPTER 7

There was a haze gathering over the brightness of the sun now. By afternoon a fog would have come down, so Alice decided to go out straight away and buy essentials for the weekend. Bread. Coffee. Sausages. A pint of milk—which presumably must have "A" slung around its neck before it joined its down-at-heel companions in Hetty's fridge. First of all, though, she must go to the post office and draw out some money. Luckily—or rather prudently, albeit guiltily—she had brought her post office savings book with her: an action somewhat at variance with her current self-image of having walked out with nothing, but justifiable (she told herself) on the grounds that the savings therein were indisputably hers, her own earnings, nothing to do with the joint bank account which she was treating as untouchable, a monument to pride and ex-wifely renunciation.

The shops were near, and pleasantly various, and for a little while she just wandered along, getting the feel of her new neighbourhood, and seeking vaguely for some good and sufficient reason for patronising one rather than another of the supermarkets that seemed to abound in this area. Suddenly catching sight of her meandering self in a large plate-glass window, she stopped and examined the rather sparse window-display, consisting of a yellow chiffon scarf on a pole and two very large, very succulent cacti with spiky leaves. She glanced upwards, and —yes, just opposite Tesco's, as she'd been apprised—she read the words "Dorinda's Hair Fashions" in large gold letters. Lower down, in smaller and merely black letters, was a list of the wonderful things that could be done for you within, at a price—or, rather, a whole list of prices, starting with manicure and ending with cold-perm and semi-permanent highlighting.

Curiosity mildly aroused, she peered more closely through the glass, and on the other side of a flutter of gauzy curtaining she could just make out the shapes of the Young Ladies employed here (they didn't have to be young, of course, merely perfect to the last eyelash.) In their pink beauty-parlour overalls, they glided back and forth among the shadowy hunks of customers who crouched like untidy bundles of washing under the various machines—a totally different species, one might have supposed, from the glittering lovelies who ministered to them.

And which of the lovelies, Alice wondered, pressing her face yet closer against the glass, was going to prove to be the redoubtable Miss Dorinda with whom she was destined to share the rather patchy amenities of Number 17 Beckford Road? It would be a daunting prospect, the encountering of such elegance, such flawless grooming, on the dark stairways first thing in the morning, as you stumbled up from the bathroom in dressing-gown and slippers, hair still a mess.

Perhaps, though, Miss Dorinda, being the manageress, no longer had to be perfect? Maybe she had by now attained the exalted status of being able to bite her nails, wear woolly cardigans and leave her hair untinted? Maybe she would right now be sitting over a gas-fire in a cosy cubby-hole somewhere at the back, smoking a cigarette, reading a tattered copy of *Woman's Dream*, and only emerging when she felt like it to reprove one of those glittering underlings, in a super-posh accent, for some small neglect of one of those hunched-up shapes who paid the money that kept the whole thing going . . . ?

At this point in her speculations, Alice became aware of one of the pink shapes gliding purposefully in her direction. Realising suddenly that her rudely-staring face must be clearly visible from inside, she backed hastily away and moved on along the pavement, praying that it wasn't Miss Dorinda herself who had spotted her unmannerly curiosity. Not that the lady would know who Alice was, of course; she probably didn't even know of her existence yet, so no harm had been done. Putting the little incident from her mind, Alice took her list from her handbag and applied herself seriously to shopping.

By the time she got back to Beckford Road, the sun was quite gone, and the damp misty air was fast thickening into fog. She stood on the top step, her plastic carrier-bags strewn around her feet, while she struggled with the key Hetty had supplied her with, trying to make it

open the door. Was it the wrong key? Hetty had fished it out of her
sewing-basket with great aplomb last night, but of course keys that find
their way to the bottom of sewing-baskets are bound to be slightly
suspect, however encouraging the assurances with which they are
handed over.

Alice gave another twist to the thing, still to no avail. It seemed to go
in all right, but after that nothing happened; and by now her right
hand, from which she had removed the glove the better to cope with
the whole manoeuvre, was growing numb with cold and clumsy.

Perhaps it wasn't the key that was at fault at all? Perhaps the lock was
in a mood this morning, like the geyser? Reluctant though she was to
be a nuisance on this her first morning in her new home, to which her
entitlement was still slightly precarious, Alice gave up and pressed the
bell. Which didn't work either. By now really annoyed, and quite
pleased at the idea of being a nuisance, Alice raised the knocker and
brought it down with a resounding thump—at which the door burst
effortlessly open. It hadn't been locked at all, apparently, merely swollen and stuck with damp. In the whole episode Alice felt herself
recognising yet another example of her landlady's special brand of off-
beat logic: it's all right to give people keys that quite likely won't work,
so long as you also have a front door that quite likely won't be locked.

Wisps of fog seemed to follow her indoors as she gathered up her
scattered packages and moved into the cluttered hallway. Edging her
way past the bicycle, and the awesome array of empties waiting for
someone to take them to the bottle-bank, Alice made it to the foot of
the stairs, where she became aware of lovely strains of music floating
down towards her. One of the Schubert piano sonatas—beautiful! As
if she were really entering a concert hall, late and shamefaced, Alice
tiptoed up the stairs, clutching her parcels, until she came to the source
of the sounds on the third landing. Here, from behind one of the doors
with its dark chipped paint, the music poured out, and Alice stood
entranced, quite awed by the performance. Brian it must be, the young
musician of whom Hetty had generously declared that she quite liked
to hear his tinkle-tonking, it gave the place a bit of life.

The third movement was starting now, and Alice found herself
scarcely conscious any longer of the dark, shabby stairway, of her cold
hands or her heavy parcels. She was in a kind of dream, totally lost in
the music, when she was abruptly and disconcertingly brought to earth
by the sound of a door opening behind her. Swivelling round, she
found herself confronted for the second time that morning by the

sharp, suspicious gaze of the girl, Mary. The blue eyes, wary and hostile, bored into her own for a moment, and then, without a word, the girl withdrew once more, closing the door quietly behind her.

At the same moment, the music ceased abruptly, and the door facing Alice burst open, revealing a sturdy, dark young man with horn-rimmed glasses and a mop of very thick black hair, and wearing a heavy fisherman's jersey and corduroy trousers. But the most noticeable thing about him at the moment was the look of almost comical disappointment that flashed across his face as he caught sight of Alice.

"*Oh!*" he exclaimed, in tones of unflattering dismay. "*Oh*, I thought it was Mary . . . I thought I heard her door opening . . ." and then, recovering himself and remembering his manners, "I'm sorry—I don't think we've met before . . . How do you do? I'm Brian."

"How do you do?" responded Alice, taking the proffered hand. She noticed that the strong, flexible pianist's fingers were somewhat ink-stained, and that they were beautifully warm to the touch despite the coldness of the room in which he was working. "I'm Alice," she continued, "Alice Saunders"; and then, with a little laugh, "I'm sorry I'm not Mary—she was here only a moment ago, though. She's in her room, if you want her—" and she stepped aside, leaving him space to cross the landing to Mary's door opposite.

He made no move to do so. Simply stood where he was, looking as if he had been slapped in the face—though whether by Mary herself, or by the malignant fate which had placed Alice, and not Mary, on this third-floor landing at just this moment, was unclear. In an effort to lighten an obviously fraught moment, Alice changed the subject.

"I thought you were playing the Schubert piece just beautifully! Hetty told me you were a musician, but she never told me you were as good as that! Is it a grand you've got in there?"

To her relief, his face brightened. He was even smiling, and he spoke eagerly:

"How wonderful to have someone in this house at last who recognises something I'm playing!" he exclaimed. "All most people notice about my playing is whether it's at some time when I'm not allowed to, like before nine in the morning or after ten at night. Not Hetty, of course; she's a darling, she doesn't mind *when* I play, or how loud, or anything. Except she likes it best when it's a tune, she says, so that she can dance to it as she tidies round, if she happens to be in the mood. Apparently she can dance to the 'Moonlight Sonata,' but alas, I've never seen her doing so. I'd love to see how it works out."

He laughed, and so did Alice, and a minute later she was in his room, picking her way across piles of music and miscellaneous garments towards the piano, whose virtues he was anxious to display.

"Not a grand—I wish it was—but just listen to the tone! I fixed the new felts myself, the old ones were all rotted away to nothing, and it's made all the difference—listen!"

He played a few bars of some piece with which Alice was unfamiliar, and the tone was indeed superb, though whether it was the new felts or the pianist himself who deserved credit for this, it was hard to say.

"Lovely," Alice approved. "You've got a smashing career ahead of you, I'd guess. Concert pianist, I presume? Though Hetty did say something about you being a composer as well?"

He shrugged, grimaced wryly.

"Pie-in-the-sky, I'm afraid. Or rather two pies, each one further out of reach than the other. Trouble is with me, I want *everything*. I used to think it was because I was young, and young people do have this idea that nothing is out of reach, you merely need to bash away till you get there. But it's just the same now, I'm afraid. I'm *thirty*, you know, and I *still* want everything. Which is crazier, actually, with every passing year, because really I should have got somewhere by now, if I'm ever going to . . ."

He paused, waiting with touching confidence for Alice to contradict this melancholy diagnosis; which of course she did, racking her brains for examples of famous musicians who had had their big breakthrough well after the age of thirty.

"It's not as if you were trying to be a pop-star," she pointed out. "I imagine they *do* have to be practically in their teens still if they're to hit the big time. But *you* are a serious musician with a serious career in prospect. Maturity can only be an asset."

He demurred, though obviously pleased by this confirmation of his own secret and ineradicable confidence in his own talent: that confidence without which no one ever gets anywhere, and Alice was glad to see that he possessed it.

"Oh, well," he said. "Never say die—and I suppose I never do. Meantime, I keep myself busy starving in a garret."

"*I'm* the one in the garret, actually," Alice pointed out, "though I've no intention of starving there. I bought some sausages today." And then, impulsively, "Why don't you share them with me? I've got a whole pound, much too much for just me, and I'm going to fry them this evening. At least, I hope I am. If I can work out where I 'fit in,' as Hetty puts it."

"Fit in with the cooking, you mean? Oh, you don't want to worry about that. We all just muck in really—all except Dorrie that is—Miss Dorinda. She's into health, you see, and so we have to leave the kitchen clear for her to do her polyunsaturated this and thats. Or is it saturated? Anyway, it's what sausages *aren't*, I'm sure, so we'll have to wait till she's finished and safely back in her room.

"Look, shall I make some coffee? I'm sorry it's so bloody cold in here, but Hetty seems to have pinched my fire. To give to you, I dare say. She does that sort of thing: she must have reckoned that your need is greater than mine. But I've only got to go down and show her my poor blue fingers and my chattering teeth, and I'll get it back, and then *you'll* be the unlucky one. And so we go on.

"However. Coffee. Let me move the debris off the armchair, and then you can sit down. Lucky me, I've got a gas-ring in here: how about you? No? Well, I might be able to rig you one up if we can find the fittings for it behind all that junk you've got up there. A bit of rubber tubing may be all we need. I'll come up presently, if you like, and see what I can do . . ."

No such fittings were revealed, but nevertheless Brian proved himself an invaluable assistant in all sorts of ways. He applied himself enthusiastically to stacking out of sight—more or less—the dauntingly heavy objects which had so far defeated Alice: the rusty refrigerator door, the old-fashioned mangle, and the various defunct television sets. An oblong monstrosity the size and weight of a cabin-trunk gave him pause for thought. It was, he assured her, an early tape-recorder. Forties vintage probably. "A museum-piece, really," he opined, running his finger through the thick dust that obscured all marks of identification. "If only we knew someone who . . ."

"But we don't," Alice hastily interposed, fearful lest some plan should come into being other than making the damn thing disappear as completely as possible behind or beneath other damn things. "I'm trying to make this place *not* be a museum, I want to *live* in it, see?" At which he shrugged good-naturedly and concurred, dragging the thing towards long oblivion in accordance with her wishes.

He really was a singularly good-natured fellow. Too good-natured, perhaps, Alice mused, to be likely to succeed in "getting somewhere" in the fiercely competitive musical world. Not that she knew anything about this world, but it was common sense that a streak of ruthless determination, even of savagery, would be needed in the process of clawing one's way up, however outstanding one's talent. Savagery was certainly no part of Brian's nature; on being ushered into Alice's domain, and finding that his three-bar electric fire had not only found its way up here, as he had surmised, but had also, in the kindness of Hetty's heart, been switched full on, all three bars—he had merely laughed.

"She *is* a nice old stick, isn't she?" he commented. *"This* ought to knock the damp for six, Alice, if anything could. This is a hell-hole for damp, you know, especially under the eaves. I tried keeping my old college notes up here—you know, in boxes. I'd been dragging them about with me for years, ever since my parents got divorced and ceased to provide a convenient dumping-ground. I fancied I'd be needing them—the notes I mean, not the parents—but I might just as well have let them go down the chute with the rest of the happy home, because when I came to look at them they were glued together with mould, right through. Mind you, I could have won a prize or two at art exhibitions, if I'd thought of it, because they were wonderful moulds, a kind of pink and green tracery, some like trees, some like diagrams in a medical book. Each page different, like a set of Rorschach blots. They'd have been a wow in the art world, ending up on television, probably, illustrating some grievance or other about Arts Council grants. Still, one can't think of everything . . ."

By the time darkness came down, the room had been transformed. Brian had dragged out the various bits of rolled-up carpet from their various hiding places, and unrolled them one by one for Alice's inspection. Most of them were too worn and tattered to be worth considering, but one, of intricate Persian design, had only a couple of easily-mendable tears in it; spread out over the bare boards alongside the divan, it gave a wonderful air of luxury to the room, a glow of pink and orange and copper which toned rather than clashed with the multi-coloured pinkish cretonne already covering the improvised sofa. The final and most useful task performed by Brian was the raising of the motor-bike from its prone position, in which it took up a couple of square yards of precious floor-space, and up-ending it against one of the beams. Tossing aside the lace bed-cover with which Hetty had swathed its ugliness, Brian stood back to admire his handiwork.

"You should never cover things up just because they're ugly," he pronounced. "You should feature them—make something of them. Just as you should with your own failing and failures. Don't hide them

from the world—stand forth boldly and say, 'Here I am, the chap who
fails at everything! The chap who gets doors slammed in his face by
pretty girls, publishers, concert-promoters—the lot!' Look, Alice, I've
got an idea! Why don't we *paint* the motor-bike—scarlet, gold, blue—
that sort of thing! Make it the central feature of your décor! We could
start now—I've got the remains of some red paint downstairs, and we
could buy the blue and the gold—just small tins—tomorrow. No, Monday—those sort of shops won't be open on Sunday. Anyway, let's get
going with the red—just a sec—"

In less than a minute he was back, with not only the tin of paint but
a couple of relatively un-congealed paint brushes, and they set to work.
The rims of the wheels scarlet, they thought, and the antler-like handlebars too. The hubs of the wheels should be gold, and so should its
mysterious broken insides . . . with touches of deep blue here and
there to add depth.

"And significance, too," Brian insisted. "You must go a bundle on
significance, Alice, if you're going to live in a place like this," and with
swift, deft strokes he set about outlining in scarlet the lopsided rim of
the back wheel, while Alice, with a damp rag, prepared the front one
for a similarly glorious new career.

CHAPTER 8

The sausage supper didn't turn out quite as Alice had anticipated. Hetty had agreed without protest to her request to be allowed some time after seven-thirty to fry her sausages, but nevertheless seemed a little crestfallen at the proposal. The reason for this soon became clear. It happened that Hetty had, that very day, come into possession of a nice big bacon joint—a real butcher's joint, with the bone still in, none of your boneless rubbish from the supermarket all done up in plastic. It had been simmering all afternoon with carrots, swedes and a couple of bay leaves, and it had occurred to Hetty that it would make a nice hot supper for everybody, it being such a cold, miserable sort of a night. Especially if she popped a few nice large potatoes into the oven, which it happened she had already done.

It sounded most inviting; but what about the sausages? "Besides," continued Alice, "I can't keep sponging on you for meals. I had that delicious shepherd's pie last night, remember."

Sponging? Oh no, that's not how Hetty saw it at all. "It's helping me out, really," she explained. "I do like a cut off a nice big joint now and again, and how can I have it if I'm just cooking only for myself? I'd be finishing up cold meat day in and day out until my stomach turned. But I'll tell you what, love, why don't we be devils and have your sausages as well? Sausages and bacon—it doesn't go too badly, does it? Sausage and bacon—bacon and sausage—you only have to say it out loud and you can hear how it kind of *belongs*, if you know what I mean. Our Brian, he's going to be over the moon when I tell him we're having *both*. He does enjoy his food, that boy does, it's a pleasure to watch his knife and fork going. I only wish I could say the same of

Mary; so picky that girl is, it's not true! Still, I'll try to get her to come down this evening; maybe if I tell her Brian's coming too . . ."

Clearly this inducement (if indeed it had been an inducement, which Alice doubted after witnessing the little scene on the landing this morning) had failed, for when the little party gathered round the large scrubbed kitchen table, Mary was conspicuous by her absence. In her place, however—much to Alice's surprise, after all she had heard—was Miss Dorinda, the lady who liked everything just so, and who was supposed to enjoy special privileges each evening for cooking her own carefully-balanced meals. Alice had already met Miss Dorinda earlier in the evening—on the stairs, in fact, exactly as she'd envisaged it, and her first impression had indeed been of someone intimidatingly smart: bleached up-swept hair, a svelte and slender figure, and painfully high heels teetering round the ill-lit bend of the stairway. Not so ill-lit, however, as to obscure the cool-thumbs-down glance which seemed to take in Alice from top to toe—from her no-bother hair-style, that is, to her discreditably comfortable shoes.

But now, seated directly under the glare of one of Hetty's 150-watt bulbs, Miss Dorinda seemed both smaller and less imposing. Lines of tiredness, clearly visible now under the make-up, softened the rigid pink-and-white perfection of her enamelled cheeks. Her eye-shadow was reassuringly smudged after its long day's service in the salon, and even her slimness was somehow modified by the eager glint in her eyes as she watched the steaming slices of bacon sliding one after another from under Hetty's expertly-wielded knife. You felt, watching her, that here was somebody who *should* have been comfortably plump. "Inside every fat woman there is a thin one struggling to get out," they say. Well, this one had got out, and here she was. Alas for the plump, comfortable one that had been left behind!

"Good God! *Dorrie!*" exclaimed Brian, taking his place opposite her. "Whatever on earth are *you* doing among the carnivores? I thought you were supposed to be vegetarian?"

"Well, yes, I am . . ." Miss Dorinda looked both confused and affronted, marshalling her arguments. "But—well, this isn't *meat*, exactly, is it? This is *bacon* . . ." and she reached out hungrily for the lavishly-filled plate that Hetty was passing her.

"Of course it's meat!" Brian insisted, ignoring Hetty's protesting glances and shake of the head. "Whatever do you mean, it's not meat? It's meat from a *pig*. A pig is just as much an animal as a cow or a sheep is—and a lot more intelligent, actually. Do you know, a pig can work out how to lift a latch and open a gate. I remember, when I was a kid, the pig they had just up the lane from us, it used to—"

"Hush, Brian, do hush!" Hetty could contain herself no longer. "You're spoiling Miss Dorinda's meal for her! I don't think it's nice, it's not nice at all, to talk about pigs while we are eating bacon. Just get on with your food, Brian, and let us get on with ours."

"OK, OK." Brian shrugged. "I don't want to spoil Dorrie's meal, I just want her to be logical. If she would only be logical, she would enjoy it more, not less, because she'd realise it was no more cruel to eat a pig than to eat a slice of bread. How many mice, and squirrels, and rabbits does she think have had to be killed in order to preserve for humans the grain which goes into bread? And Muesli, too, and All-Bran—all those health foods she's so—"

"*Brian!* If you aren't careful, I won't invite you down anymore. You know what I was planning for Sunday lunch? A nice roast chicken, with bread sauce, and roast potatoes, and sprouts. But of course I won't be doing it now, not if it's going to start all this argy-bargy . . ."

"Argy-bargy about whether a chicken is a vegetable?" Brian was beginning; and it seemed to Alice that it was time someone changed the subject.

"What a pity Mary couldn't be here," she said, rather at random. "I don't know how she could resist all these delicious smells. I suppose she has a date this evening . . . ?"

She was aware, as she spoke, of a slight tension to her left. Brian had paused in his eating, and with fork poised half-way to his mouth, was listening with painful intentness. She realised that she had tactlessly blundered from one awkward topic right into another.

"A date? Not on your life!" declared Hetty, beginning to apply herself to the carving of second helpings. "That girl never has dates. I wish she did. It really worries me, you know, the way she stays up there evening after evening. Sometimes she doesn't even have the light on. What does she *do*, I wonder?"

"Perhaps she has to go to bed early," suggested Alice, trying to render innocuous this topic she had so inadvertently raised. "Perhaps her job . . . ?"

"And that's another thing," continued Hetty. "A job. She hasn't got a job. Of course, I know it's difficult these days, unemployment and that; but so far as I can see she's not even looking for one. It makes me really unhappy, you know, the way that girl's wasting her life. No dates. No proper meals. And if I invite her down, like this evening, when I happen to have done a bit of cooking, what do I get? Such a look she gives me, like she wouldn't demean herself. 'Thank you, Mrs. Harman,' she says, 'But I'm not hungry.' Kind of uppity, you know, as if not being hungry was the in-thing for top people, and the rest of us too uneducated to know it! It makes me really annoyed sometimes, I feel I want to put her in her place good and proper. But then again, I can't help worrying—after all, she's only young. There's something wrong. I know there is. Something badly wrong. But what can I do? I can't keep asking questions and interfering, can I? It's not my business. Do you think she's maybe got that illness they've been on about lately on TV —Anna-something?"

"Anorexia?" supplied Alice. "Well, I suppose she might have. Though she's a bit past the usual age, I should think—it's more a thing with teenagers." And then, in a vague attempt to reassure Brian, who was still sitting unwontedly tense and silent at her side, "Perhaps she eats more than you think she does? Like now—for all we know she might be out getting fish and chips at this very moment."

But Hetty shook her head. "I'd have noticed," she asserted. "I'd have heard her. I've got so I listen for her, I'm that worried. Like I say, she stops in nearly all the time. Five weeks she's been here, and never once has she gone out in the evening . . ."

"And can you wonder?" broke in Miss Dorinda here, dabbing her lips delicately and laying down her fork. "*I* don't go out in the evening either, not on my own. You hear of such dreadful things happening nowadays, the rapes and the muggings . . ."

"I don't think it's as common as all that," Alice was beginning, but Miss Dorinda interrupted, full of indignation, as people tend to be at any suggestion that something isn't as dreadful as they thought it was.

"It's all very well to talk like that, if you'll excuse my saying so! You wouldn't talk like that if you'd been one of the victims! Suppose you'd been attacked by the Yorkshire Ripper? Or the Cambridge Rapist? Or the Flittermouse Fiend? He was a vampire, too, as well as a murderer. That's what Flittermouse means, it means a vampire . . ."

"No it doesn't, it just means a bat," interposed Brian, roused from his dark mood by the prospect of controversy. "It's simply the old English word for 'bat'—"

"Well, and that's just what I've been saying!" retorted Miss Dorinda triumphantly. "A vampire *is* a bat. It's a huge, savage bat that sucks human blood! Didn't you ever see the Dracula film? Those awful yellow

fangs, and claws dripping with blood? The Flittermouse Fiend must
have been . . ."

They all heard it. A soft scuffling from beyond the closed door; light
footsteps racing up the stairs; and then the slam of a door, high up in
the old house. Brian's chair scraped back with a violent shudder, and
he was across the room, out of the door and racing up the stairs.

The three women, struck silent, were left facing each other, but not
for long. In less than a minute, Brian could be heard thundering down
the stairs, and he burst into the kitchen, wild-eyed, his whole body
grown somehow loose and disjointed with shock.

"Something terrible has happened!" he gasped. "Her door—Mary's
door, it's all over blood! I can't get it open! A hammer, Hetty—an axe
—something to smash it down with . . . !"

"All over blood" was an exaggeration. The door-handle, as Alice
bent to examine it, was indeed stained with red, and there were smears
of red here and there on the panels. Alice bent lower—sniffed—and
burst into hysterical laughter.

"Brian! You idiot! It's not blood at all—it's paint! Red paint! The
wretched girl's been mucking about in my room, and she's got the
motor-bike paint all over her. That's what it is!" And her anxiety
abruptly transferred itself from Mary's safety to the fate of her new
décor.

The delicately outlined rim of scarlet was indeed smudged and
spoiled, and the whole contraption had been dragged a few inches out
of position as if to allow space—but only just—for a slender figure to
creep in behind it. By now, Brian had joined in her mirth, though still
with the residue of shock jerking somewhere in his lungs; and together
they stood contemplating, with relief and bewilderment, their now
somewhat blemished handiwork. Behind them, agog for their fair share
in this happening, whatever it might prove to be, stood Hetty and Miss
Dorinda.

Hetty, despite the inconclusive nature of the data so far, was already
able to discern a bright side.

"It's a mercy," she pointed out, "that I couldn't remember where
that axe had got put. It hasn't been used since that sculpture fellow was
here trying to turn the outside lav into a studio. It must still be out
there somewhere, and if I'd been able to lay hands on it, Brian, like you
yelled at me to, then we'd have had this door in splinters all to no
purpose! And then, oh dear me, men in and out for days repairing it,
and most likely telling me I've got dry-rot into the bargain; you know

what they are, these builder chappies. And then the insurance—I don't know what they'd make of a story like this, I really don't . . . a fuss, anyway, it's surprising the fuss they can make, every tiny thing . . . Never mind. All's well that ends well."

If indeed it had ended. After the others had gone downstairs, Alice knocked, and knocked again; but inside the room was absolute silence, and she had to desist. After all, Mary had a right to her privacy. All the same, Alice went to bed feeling uneasy, and half-afraid; which was no doubt why, just before dawn, she had such a very horrid dream. She dreamed she was back in her old job, sitting at her desk correcting a set of exercises, when she came upon one written in red ink, making it difficult for her to mark corrections. She spoke to the girl in question, pointing out the problem and asking her to use a black biro next time; but the girl shook her head sadly. "Oh no," she said, "I can't write in black anymore, from now on I have to write everything in blood—look!" and pushing up the sleeve of her blouse, she displayed a nasty jagged wound into which she must dip her pen.

Alice woke, shaken with horror, and then with relief at knowing it was only a dream. But for a few moments she was quite disorientated in the darkness, and in her still unfamiliar surroundings. By the time she had located the small square of the window and recovered her bearings, and the sense of where she was, the dream had already begun to fade. She could no longer recall whether the girl in the dream had actually resembled Mary, or whether she had been a mere faceless ghost, of the sort that habitually drift through dreams.

Not that it mattered. The shocks and alarms of last night were quite enough to account for such a dream, and there was no point at all in looking for anything subtle in the way of interpretation; and so Alice settled back on her pillow, and tried to sleep. Already, it was nearly morning.

CHAPTER 9

"I'm *sorry*," Mary was sulkily repeating. "I'm sorry, I'm sorry, I'm *sorry!* But how could I know you'd painted the bloody thing? You *said* I could have my stuff whenever I liked, and then you set a trap like that to catch me!"

"Don't be ridiculous!" Alice retorted. "It *wasn't* a trap, and of course I wasn't trying to 'catch' you, why should I? Catch you at what, anyway? All we were doing—Brian and I—we were trying to brighten the place up with a bit of colour. Don't you think it looks better already? You saw the ghastly mess it was yesterday: look at all the extra space we've made just by stacking things up tidily."

Alice was trying to turn the conversation—which had started as an altercation about the wet paint, and whose fault it was that Mary had got it all over her hands last night—into something more amiable. "Don't you think it looks nice?" she persisted, when her companion remained silent. "And see that couch affair, with the cretonne cover? Cardboard boxes it's made of! All those boxes crammed with ancient papers . . ."

"What papers?"

Alice was somewhat thrown by this sudden twist to the conversation, and found herself stammering.

"I—I . . . Well, I don't . . . I don't know really. Magazines and things—you know. Newspapers . . ."

"What newspapers?"

The inquisition was relentless. Alice found annoyance coming to her aid, and she spoke briskly.

"Look, Mary, why don't you just tell me what you want—what you were looking for last night? Perhaps I can help you find it?"

"Help me find it! That's rich—that really is! First you muck up the whole room, dragging everything about so that no one can find anything ever again, and then you say . . . you say . . ."

Abruptly, the girl turned and darted out of the room, but not before Alice had glimpsed the tears suddenly welling in the hostile blue eyes, and heard the choking of the young voice.

"Mary! Wait!" she cried, full of compunction, running out to the landing, leaning over the banisters.

But it was too late. Mary's door had closed with that curious, controlled savagery which she had noticed before, and which she recognised now as a substitute for a resounding slam.

Again! I've done it again! Mary lay face downward on her bed, listening while Alice rattled on the door, calling her name. Listening as Alice rattled again . . . and yet again; and listening still as the tiresome woman gave up, and retreated slowly up the stairs.

As the sounds faded, as the impending danger of sympathy, of caring, of compassion began to recede, Mary's tension relaxed a little, and she found herself able to think again, to try and assess this new and terrifying onslaught on her privacy. How could she have guessed that the attic lumber-room, which by all accounts—and indeed by all appearances—had lain untouched and neglected for goodness knows how many years, should suddenly, within twenty-four hours, become subject to all this upheaval? It had seemed to secure a hiding-place at the beginning. The worst that could happen to her dreadful secret—so she'd thought—was that it might be overlaid by daunting piles of fresh rubbish, chucked in pell-mell on top of the existing strata. The possibility that someone in this sloppy, down-at-heel household should suddenly take it into their head to *tidy* the place—this had seemed too remote to consider. That darkest, dustiest, most inaccessible corner, under the low beam, behind the almost immovable barrier of the motor-bike, and underneath a pile of ancient curtains and mysterious rags of carpeting—this had seemed as safe a place as one could ever hope to find. Safer, certainly, than the sparsely-furnished barn of a room that she, Mary, had been allotted, and which offered almost no hiding-places at all. A huge wardrobe, with a door that wouldn't stay shut even when you wedged it; a rickety chest-of-drawers with drawers that stuck and groaned and jerked when you tried to shut them; and—as a last resort—the dusty, fluff-ridden space under the bed, already occupied by the many discarded shoes of some previous incumbent and the remains of a huge garden-party hat, pale straw and tattered artificial roses. It wouldn't take a person so much as five minutes to search through these meagre and obvious hiding-places, especially if they knew what they were looking for. And the people she was afraid of *would* know what they were looking for.

Was this Alice woman one of them? Or not? How could one tell? What clues should one look for? That a person might seem, on the face of it, to be quite pleasant and ordinary proved nothing—nothing. As Mary knew only too well.

If only she could have locked her door! But Hetty, maddeningly, "didn't hold with" locks and keys. How smug can you get, you people who can afford not to "hold with" locks and keys?

Besides, a locked door (she was beginning to learn) does little but attract the very things it is supposed to fend off—namely, interference, prying and suspicion.

Last night, for instance, if she hadn't panicked and wedged the door with a chair-back under the handle, there would never have been a fraction of the fuss and upset that had in fact been aroused. Brian would presumably have walked in and instantly noticed her paint-stained hands and jersey, and the whole thing would have passed off as a tiresome mishap, quite funny really, and the rest of the household would never have been alerted at all.

Or—going only a few minutes further back—if only she'd boldly marched in on the supper-party and asked Hetty openly for a bottle of turpentine-substitute, explaining what she wanted it for—then the disturbance would have been minimal. Instead of which, by hanging about outside the door, hesitating, while the paint congealed on her hands—and then, when she heard what they were talking about, taking to her heels—all this had simply been a recipe for stirring up maximum curiosity, maximum interference and questioning.

Part of the trouble, of course, was that when she went downstairs she'd still been in a state of shock from touching the newly-painted motor-bike. For one mad moment, she had imagined that the wet red stains on her hands were indeed blood: that somehow, by some weird and virulent magic, her secret had come horribly alive during the hours of darkness and had crawled out from under the beams . . .

Absurd! Almost at once she had realised that the stuff was only paint, but it was only her mind that knew this: her body thought it knew better, and it wouldn't stop trembling . . .

There was a lesson in all this somewhere, and already she could see, more or less, what it was. She *must not* panic. If she hadn't panicked on discovering that this new woman had actually taken up residence in the room that concealed her secret; and if she hadn't given way to further panic when she found that the hiding-place itself had been dismantled . . .

Now, reflecting on the episode more calmly, Mary realised how damagingly she had over-reacted. She could see, now, that the Alice woman probably hadn't been searching for anything, but, exactly as she'd said, was simply trying to clear the room. This was a perfectly viable hypothesis, consistent with all the facts. But all the same, the shock of discovering that her terrible secret had simply disappeared from its accustomed hiding-place . . . that she had no idea, now, where it might be, or even whether Alice had in fact seen it, examined it, and already drawn the inescapable inference—all this had been too much for Mary's self-control, and she had burst out into pointless but uncontrollable rudeness towards this devastating interloper who had—albeit unintentionally—upset the precarious balance on which Mary's existence here was poised. The fact that it was unintentional made it worse, in a way—more alarming. It was like being a tightrope-walker, with the rope juddering hideously beneath you on account of someone blandly hanging out their washing on the far end, totally unaware of your predicament. How can you *not* scream at such a person? And thereby make an enemy? One more unnecessary enemy to add to the growing list . . .

The sense of enemies moving in on her, more and more of them, from every direction, gripped her yet again. So powerful it was, closing in on her rational faculties, crushing them as if with an iron fist, rendering them incapable of ordinary common-sense reasoning. And the irony was that she knew very well the correct name for this feeling of hers; it was paranoia. Only a couple of years ago, in the unimaginably blissful days of not yet knowing anything about it, she had been given an "A" for an essay on this very subject. Her innocent, book-learned dissertation on the malady had impressed her tutor, and had helped, via Continuous Assessment, to bring her the coveted First Year Prize for Outstanding Achievement.

What a triumph! What rejoicings there had been! Parents delighted;

Julian delighted too, it seemed, teasing her with brotherly incredulity about her success.

"They must be potty, these examiners of yours," he'd jeered admiringly. "All that psychology has warped their tiny minds! Still, it's a jolly good happening to have happened to you, Midge, so let's celebrate . . ."

Had the clouds already begun to gather, and did Julian already know it? Was it with monstrous irony, or with helplessness in the grip of the dark gods, that he'd suggested they should go for a celebratory picnic, just the two of them, champagne and all, to their favourite picnic spot on Flittermouse Hill? Such games they'd played there as children, long ago, sometimes with friends, sometimes on their own. Traditional games like Cops and Robbers, Cowboys and Indians; and many another, invented by themselves. Lying there on that hot June day, almost the last day of unclouded happiness she would ever know, she and Julian had laughed, and reminisced, and stared up through the rowan boughs at the blue, incredible sky. She recalled, now, how she had noticed the beginnings of colour just lightly tinging the clusters of nascent berries which, by September, would be a glory of scarlet.

She had not known, of course, that she was looking at this scene for the last time. By next summer, the bulldozers would have moved in.

Dusk was falling. The shadows and smudges of the stained and faded wall-paper were changing, growing palely luminous in the last of the silver-grey light, and Mary rolled slowly off the bed, blinking and rubbing her eyes as though waking from a deep sleep; but this was an illusion. She didn't sleep deeply anymore, neither by night nor by day. Peering closely into the small, specked mirror, badly placed, she wondered how much it showed.

CHAPTER 10

"What you want," said Brian, with the kindly condescension of experienced youth towards helpless middle-age, "What you want is to stop looking at advertisements for jobs vacant, and start advertising for yourself. Not in the local paper, that's a dead loss as well as costing a bomb, but on the boards outside newsagents, among the baby-sitters and the handy-men and the house-trained kittens. That way, you get the impulse-clients. That's my experience, anyway. What happens, you see, they're standing there looking to see if their own notice about a wardrobe for sale has gone up yet, and—yet presto—they catch sight of my ad about piano lessons, with its pretty picture of notes and staves. And they think, well, why not? I may never get shot of Aunt Agatha's bloody wardrobe, but at least I might be able to put her bloody piano to use. Or my kid might, it'll give him something to do after school besides teasing his sister, and who knows, he might turn out to be a genius?

"That's the thought-process, roughly, and that's what you want to cash in on. I'll help you with the wording if you like, I've had a lot of experience, and if we *can* work in a funny illustration, it does help . . . It's coaching you're after, isn't it? Private coaching in—well, something or other? You say you've been a teacher up to now—well, you must know *something* . . ."

Good thinking. So I must. Aloud, Alice said:

"That's the trouble, really. My subjects—no one wants them anymore. Latin and Greek—they're the extinct dinosaurs of education nowadays. My last job—I was amazingly lucky that in the very town where my husband worked there was this old-fashioned all-girls school where they still went in for that sort of thing. Not so much now, though—it was some years ago when I got the job, and it went on ticking over in a sort of a way, though lately I've found myself teaching French as well, and Religious Studies, because there weren't enough girls opting for Classics. I don't think there'd be the slightest chance of a full-time job in Classics now—even if it wasn't for my age, and—well —the way I left. Rather sudden. Normally, you'd never leave a teaching job until you'd got yourself fixed up for another one: it'll look funny on my record . . ."

"But it's *coaching* we're talking about," Brian interrupted briskly. "Not a full-blown job. *Everyone* doing coaching has a record that looks funny, else they wouldn't be doing it, would they? Now, let's get down to it. A picture—that's the first thing. You have to have a picture to catch the eye—to compete with the kittens . . ."

He pulled a large brown envelope out of the wastepaper basket at his side, and in a few swift lines sketched a lively caricature of a very small boy with very large spectacles bending over an enormous tome, open to reveal an imaginary script hitherto unknown to linguists.

"Now for the caption—" Brian's face was alight with creative fervour as he sucked his pencil and stared at the wall for inspiration. "I know!" And in large imposing capitals he quickly printed under the sketch: "IT'S GREEK TO ME!"

"There—that'll get 'em looking. Everyone loves a code. Or you can make it actual Greek if you like, in case they know some already. Underneath all that—and in much smaller letters—you can get in the serious stuff for the parents about what you are actually going to teach, and why it's going to turn their kid into a paragon of all the virtues as well as equipping him to knock hell out of his little friends in life's rat-race . . .

"*Something* like that. Or—and from what you say this might be a better bet—you could highlight the sheer uselessness of your subject. 'An antidote to the crass materialism which is currently destroying the world'—that sort of thing. Everyone likes the idea of everyone else being crassly materialistic; and of course the lure of the useless is irresistible. Always has been. Look at the pyramids, and the sacred cows, and the cathedrals. Not to mention crinolines, crossword-puzzles and space-travel.

"We'll soon knock something out. Indian ink, of course, for the pic —I've got some somewhere . . ."

And so, a couple of hours later, with four spectacular postcard-size notices lurking in her handbag, Alice found herself slinking past the hair and beauty salon like a criminal, irrationally fearful lest Miss Dorinda should be glancing out of the display window at just that moment, and should somehow guess at her embarrassing errand. For embarrassing it was: not because there is anything inherently disgraceful about offering to the public your skills, whatever they may be, but because she had never done it before, and couldn't as yet slot it into her self-image. Moreover, Brian's flamboyant style of advertisement was very much not Alice's own style. Something much more sober and low-key would have evolved if she had designed the notices on her own— that is, if she had nerved herself to embark on the project at all.

That was the point. Brian's enthusiasm, his flair for the eye-catching, had supplied the impetus which Alice lacked, and so she had gone along with it. Also, it would have seemed most ungracious, even snubbing, to have turned down his so-eagerly-proffered help. Lastly, of course, it might work.

What's more, it did. Before the week was out, she had received three phone calls: one from a retired postman who had spent the first years of his retirement in the local library reading Homer, Plato and most of the plays in translation, and had been fired with the ambition to read them in the original before he died; a second from a lady who thought that those enormously large round spectacles would suit her a lot better than the National Health ones she had at present, and could Alice tell her where they could be obtained? A third was from the mother of a twelve-year-old boy called Cyril, about whose wish to learn Greek she was almost insultingly apologetic, but nevertheless contemplated an interview "just to talk about it."

Excitedly, Alice found herself with quite a time-table to organise. The postman, a small wiry man with a lined, rosy face, a slight limp and a freckled balding skull, wanted to come on Wednesdays and Saturdays. Alice tried to explain that she might be coaching school-children who would only have Saturdays free; but this distressed him greatly. Although (he had to agree) he wasn't a school-child, he nevertheless did have other engagements, and these Greek lessons would have to be fitted in with his classes at the local institute. Drama, Car-Maintenance, the History of Art: Saturday it would have to be. He knew the Greek alphabet already, he told her; he'd learned it by himself, and now couldn't wait to go further, in particular to read Alcestis right through in the original.

Alice tried, without being too discouraging, to give her prospective pupil some idea of the vast tracts of grammar and vocabulary that lay between knowing the alphabet and reading Alcestis in the original; but he was undeterred.

"If I make up my mind to a thing, then I keep going until I get there," he told her; and to substantiate this self-assessment, he told her how he had had polio as a boy and had been told that he'd have to settle for a desk job, as his leg would never be up to very much walking.

" 'Very much walking!' Tens of thousands of miles I reckon I've walked on my rounds—five times round the world, just about! Forty-seven years, and never a day off sick, bar just the one winter, a bad go of pleurisy . . ."

As a qualification for embarking on a study of ancient Greek, walking five times round the world might seem to some teachers irrelevant; but not to Alice. She took Mr. Bates on with alacrity, and after discussing terms and the books he would need, they parted with a sense of happy anticipation on both sides.

Cyril proved a little more complicated to enroll. For one thing, the negotiations had to be primarily with his parents, not with him; and for another, Alice was to be expected to travel to his home for the lessons, and not he to hers. The distance was not great—less than a mile—but the elegance of the suburban road in which he lived was in itself intimidating, with its large and well-kept late-Victorian houses set well back from the road behind wrought-iron gates and barriers of smugly evergreen shrubs that looked as if they had lived there for a hundred years.

Walking up the short gravel drive to her preliminary interview with the Bensons, Alice felt her heart thudding uncomfortably, and her brain (even more uncomfortably) emptying itself of suitable sentences with which to advocate the claims of both herself and her outdated subject.

Both were necessary. The beautifully-proportioned pale grey drawing-room, with its floor-length velvet curtains and its silver vases of out-of-season roses, formed a setting singularly unkind to Alice's one and only winter coat and her scuffed suede boots. Not that Mrs. Benson, an anxious and well-preserved blonde of about Alice's own age, showed any signs of being overtly snobbish about this. On the contrary, you could see her deciding after a single glance that one can't go by appearances, and that anyway in this new high-speed age, with which it was so important to keep up, class didn't count for anything. Though of course if this woman who was proposing to coach her son had actually had an *accent* . . .

Mercifully, Alice hadn't. As soon as she began to speak, she could see her prospective employer's face clear, and knew she was over the first hurdle. The second was more difficult.

"You see," Mrs. Benson was saying, crossing her shapely legs and settling herself more securely against her discreetly-positioned back-support cushion, "You see, without meaning to disparage your qualifications in *any* way, Mrs. Saunders, I'm sure they are excellent, but we *are* a little unhappy, my husband and I, about the whole idea of our boy spending time—valuable homework time—on studying an out-dated language that no one is ever going to speak. Where will it get him?"

Where would it? This was the question that was bound to arise. Alice had prepared for it.

"I think," she began, "and this is simply my experience as a teacher —I think that in educating a child one has to look beyond the immedi-ate practical qualifications that he—"

Mrs. Benson was onto it in a flash. "Why 'he'?" she demanded. "Why not 'she'? I hope, I do hope, Mrs. Saunders, that you haven't a *sexist* attitude? I wouldn't like Cyril to—well . . ."

She paused, perhaps a little uncertain herself exactly what it was that she wouldn't like Cyril to do, or be, or have, or become as a result of Alice's instruction in elementary Greek syntax; so Alice intervened to help her out.

"Of course not," she said. "I was just using the word 'he' in a general sense. If you'd got a daughter I was to teach, I'd naturally have said . . ."

"I *have* got a daughter actually," interrupted Mrs. Benson, with a touch of reproof at the implied accusation of not having one. "But she's only six, and so . . . But anyway"—here she changed tack slightly—"I must be frank with you. If it was a daughter of mine who wanted to learn Greek, I'd be even more worried than I am about Cyril. I feel it is *so* important for girls, just as much as for boys, to learn science and technology and . . . and . . . well, technology. Wouldn't you agree? And that's what worries me about Cyril. We—his father and I—we naturally want him to do maths and science, and this whim of his to learn Greek—naturally we find it rather upsetting. But, on the other hand, if we oppose him about it, if we forbid him to have lessons, it might just drive it underground. What do *you* think? As a teacher?"

"Well," Alice was beginning, "it does seem to me . . ."

"Exactly!" exclaimed Mrs. Benson in tones of relief. "Just what we were saying, his father and I. I thought you'd agree. And so, for the moment . . . You see, there *are* signs that he may be already learning, in secret. Only last week, I was going through his clothes, and in his sock drawer I found a book called *The Republic*. At first I thought it was just politics—you know, Peace Studies, that sort of thing—but when I opened it, I saw it was all in *Greek!* Mind you, I don't suppose for a moment that he can read it, but all the same, there's no knowing how it will end if we don't handle it right at this stage."

She sounded like a mother who has come across a secret hoard of drugs in her son's bedroom. Her face, under its neat and superbly-styled cap of shining straw-blonde hair, was puckered with concern; and Alice, partly to change the subject and partly because she felt it was high time, suggested that she should be introduced to the boy himself. "I can't really judge the situation until I've met him," she pointed out. "And in case we *do* decide on the lessons, I'd like to know how far he's already got. You know, for books and things."

After a half-hearted flutter of demur, in deference to maths and science and the modern high-speed age, the boy was summoned from upstairs, and Alice had the few moments before his arrival to wonder what he would be like. Boys of twelve come in two main categories: tall, half-formed young men, loose-limbed, with voices already broken; or they can be children still, little boys with scraped knees, scrubbed innocent faces and high, piping voices.

Cyril at first sight was decidedly in the latter category; not exactly small for his age, but compact and wiry, with the innocent inquiring face and agile body of the pre-pubescent child. Beneath a mop of fairish hair the wide-spaced grey eyes, alert and inquisitive, sparkled out at the newcomer, assessing her, measuring her up against some inscrutable yardstick of childhood judgement.

He was polite enough, though, shook hands nicely, smiled a neat smile, and did not interrupt while his mother launched into a long— and by now surely familiar?—dissertation on the demerits of a classical education. He spoke only when she at last turned to him with a direct question:

"So why *do* you want to learn Greek, Cyril? See if you can explain to

Mrs. Saunders. Because we all know, don't we, that science and maths are—"

" 'The essential qualifications for the new technological age,' " he quoted in a clear childish treble, whose innocent tone very nearly can-celled out the underlying impertinence of the interruption. " 'Science and maths are the gateway to tomorrow's world.' " Here he stopped quoting, looked straight at Alice and spoke in his own, slightly less child-like voice:

"But you see I don't specially want to live in tomorrow's world. I don't think I'm going to like it. But I *do* like Greek, especially Plato and Herodotus, and I want to learn to read them properly."

CHAPTER 11

"So I've got *two* jobs!" Alice announced that evening as she, Brian and Hetty gathered round the kitchen table for a midnight feast of doughnuts and the remains of a jumbo packet of crisps; this washed down by the much-stewed pot of tea with which Hetty had been regaling all comers ever since ten o'clock. "And pretty well paid, too," Alice continued. "At least one of them is. It's funny, you know, the mother doesn't really seem to approve of the boy learning Greek at all, and yet she's quite happy to pay the earth for it."

"It figures, though, doesn't it?" Brian suggested. "I've had mothers like that too. Having tin ears themselves, they have no idea of what music is for, or why anyone should want to spend time on it, but on the other hand they're dead scared that their kid might miss out on something, or be traumatised by the sound of the word 'No'—that kind of thing. So what they can't provide in understanding and intelligent support, they fall over themselves to provide in money. Paying off their own guilt-feelings. Inadequacy-feelings, rather. For lots of people it's the same thing.

"Anyway, congratulations, Alice! Long may Mrs. What's-it's guilt-feelings screw her up, and long may Master What's-it—"

"Cyril, actually," Alice interposed. "Rather a prissy name, isn't it, for nowadays, but then they're rather prissy people, what I've seen of them. Anyway, I start this Saturday as ever. Oh, and I've got a dear old chap as well, not so much money, of course, but he's dead keen. He's coming to me, thank goodness, so if you run into a slightly Worzel Gummidge sort of figure on the stairs on Wednesdays and Saturdays—"

"Which reminds me," Hetty broke in. "Figures on the stairs, I mean. There's a piece of good news! This fellow—quite a nice-looking fellow actually, well, not too bad, anyway. A bit yellow, perhaps, unless it was the light; that one without a shade, you know at the turn of the landing, puts years on anyone, that light does. So maybe he was fairly young, really; on the *old* side of fairly young, if you know what I mean; and anyway, I've always said that an age difference doesn't really matter all that much, provided there's common interests . . . Presentable he was, anyway, quite neat and all that. A bit on the small side maybe, still, you mustn't go by that, there's plenty of short men who—"

"Hetty, darling, the suspense is terrible!" Brian interrupted. "This yellow dwarf in his natty suiting—what *about* him? You've told us everything, in splendid detail, except what the hell you're talking about."

"I was just coming to that, and just you keep your mouth shut, young Brian, and let me tell it my own way. It's a boy-friend, I do believe! A boy-friend for our Mary at last! You know how worried I've been about that girl, how she never goes out, never has anyone in— Well, it's happened at last! I'm so relieved! And I don't think it can be his first visit, either, because when he got up as far as her room, he just pushed the door open and walked in. Well, you wouldn't do that, would you, if it was a first visit. You'd knock on the door, wouldn't you? And he didn't: nothing like that. I know he didn't, because I was watching up through the banisters."

"And what happened?" Brian had quite dropped his bantering tone. "Did Mary—I mean, did she say anything? Did you hear how she sounded?"

Hetty bridled, putting on what Alice thought of as her "tut-tut" look.

"Really, Brian! How should I know how she sounded? I didn't stay to listen, what do you take me for? I just hurried off down the stairs as fast as I could go to leave them their privacy. All I do know is that everything seemed very quiet up there, and I really began to hope—you know—that they might be . . . Well, I mean, it would do her a power of good, wouldn't it, poor child? Just what she needs to cure her of the megrims."

"*When* was all this? Is he still there?"

Brian was leaning forward over the table, poised as if to spring to his feet at Hetty's lightest word. But Hetty merely flapped her hand at him.

"Relax, boy, relax! Hours ago it happened, not long after lunch it must have been. He wasn't here above half an hour, I heard the door go when he left. Still, it's something isn't it, to know that she's got a friend at all. It could be the start of something. And Brian, don't look like that. You've no call to look like that, all the chances you've had up there on the same landing all these weeks, and you've never taken advantage . . . Oh no you haven't, Brian, *I* can tell, you can't deceive me . . . And so now when another chap comes along— Well, you've brought it on yourself, is all I can say. Right dog-in-the-manger, I'd call it if you start complaining now."

"I'm *not* complaining!" He sounded quite angry. "I'm just simply worried: is she *all right*? Have you seen her since? I mean, you don't know if she knew him at all. He might have been a total stranger. A rapist! A murderer! Anything! This leaving the front door swinging open day and night is all very fine and dandy, but—"

" 'Swinging open' is a lie, and well you know it. Just I put the latch up now and again, that's all, and so would you if you were the one who had to be up and down all day long answering the bell to every Tom, Dick and Harry—"

"Seeing that the bell doesn't even work," Brain retorted, "I don't see how—"

"And whose fault is that, I'd like to know!" Hetty crowed triumphantly, delighted at being dealt so unsolicited a trump card. "Who promised he'd fix it? Days ago it was! And the geyser, too! All these tepid baths, I'm just about fed up with it, and so is Miss Dorinda. And Alice too, aren't you, Alice? We all are. And the fridge as well, while we're on the subject, the funny noise it makes when you shut the door too hard, and the light inside has gone on the blink too. All those bits of milk going sour, or will do if you don't get on with it. And it's no good saying give them to Hengist, he won't touch sour milk, as you well know—"

"That cat won't touch anything except best steak and breast of chicken—if you ask me," Brian retorted, recovering something of his usual tone under the reassuring onslaught of familiar reproaches. "Ever tried giving him the chips from a fish-and-chips parcel? The look he gives you fairly burns a hole in the paper!" And then, turning to Alice, "Look, Alice, couldn't you come up with me and check that Mary's all right? I know it's late, but you could just peep round the door, see if she's safe in bed sort of thing? Obviously, I can't because we aren't—I mean she doesn't—"

Alice got the point, and together they set off up the stairs. On the third landing Brian retreated tactfully into his room, leaving Alice alone outside Mary's door.

A minute later she rejoined him, shaking her head.

"Her door's wedged on the inside again," she reported. "And there's no light under it. But at least it means she must be *there*. I mean, wedging her door—she's always doing that, isn't she? It doesn't mean anything's wrong."

So there's nothing to worry about, Alice would like to have added, but it wouldn't have been true. There *was* something to worry about. She knew it, and so did Brian.

He was having trouble with his voice. His habitual, jokey style had collided head-on with something beyond its scope.

"*Why the hell* can't she *tell* me!" he burst out at last, in a sort of whispered shout. "She *knows* how I care about her, she *must* know. I could help her, I know I could. *Whatever* it is, I'd fix it for her . . . I'd go to the ends of the earth . . . I'd fight whoever it is . . . Little bloody yellow dwarfs . . . the lot! If only she'd *tell* me! Oh, Alice, she's in some dreadful trouble, I *know* she is. How can I find out . . . ? She's so cold . . . so distant . . . it's like I'm her worst enemy . . . Why? Why?"

"Me too. She's like that with all of us, not just you," Alice pointed out reassuringly—aware even while she spoke of how totally non-reassuring the fact actually was. Then, on a sudden impulse, "Look," she said. "We've got to get to know her better. In general, I mean; not delving into her secrets, whatever they are. Bring her into things; get her to join in a bit of harmless fun sometimes. There's not much *you* can do, Brian, the way things are between you, it'd be misinterpreted. But why don't *I* give a little party? Up in my room, for the whole household? A sort of attic-warming? Now that we've finished painting the motor-bike—I did the gold this afternoon, you know, you haven't seen it yet, it looks kind of splendid with the dark blue spokes. We'll have candles instead of that awful glaring light, and I'll bring in some pork pies and some beer . . ."

"*I'll* bring the beer!" exclaimed Brian, his spirits miraculously reviving at the prospect of some action. "And Hetty can bring up the rest of that long-life bacon joint she's been on at us to finish, it can go out in a blaze of glory. That's a super idea, Alice. But we must make sure Mary knows it's a *party*, not any kind of a tête à tête, which would frighten her off, I'm sure. Let's get out some invitation cards and push them

under everyone's door. 'JUNK ROOM GALA NIGHT'—something
like that? With a picture of a motor-bike sitting in an armchair holding
a beer-glass in one handlebar and a pork pie in the other. Look—I'll
show you. Pass me that old envelope—no, the big one . . ."

CHAPTER 12

The danger seemed to be over, for the time being. All the same, Mary lingered just inside her door to make sure that her barricade was securely in position under the handle; then she tiptoed warily back to the bed on which she spent so many of the long days, and even longer nights.

Just as if she was ill.

Well, a shock *is* an illness, of a sort, especially a bad shock like the one she'd had this afternoon. It would have been a shock to anyone, however normal. A man, a perfectly strange man marching into one's room as if he had a right to do so. For a moment, she'd thought he was a plain-clothes policeman; and then, even more terrifyingly, that he wasn't, that he must be bent on darker business. It had happened at last! She'd been sussed out, hunted down, finally cornered, in spite of all her desperate precautions . . .

What a fool he must have thought her! Standing in the doorway, blocking his path, choking and stammering, bracing herself to lie and lie, to fend off his questions with one fabrication after another—when all he wanted, actually, was to find Alice! He'd mistaken the room . . . was full of apologies for intruding . . .

Her relief at finding that the visitor wasn't for her at all had been so overwhelming that she'd been barely able to speak; had simply waved him on up the further flight of stairs, and then slammed the door in his face. Well, that was what it amounted to. And then she had listened, as she always seemed to be listening; had heard him stumbling about up there, first into the cistern loft, and then—yes, she heard him cross the bare boards of that attic landing towards Alice's room. This time, he'd knocked—presumably having learned his lesson—and then had knocked again; but whether Alice was out, or simply not answering the door, of course she could not tell.

And here it suddenly occurred to Mary that maybe the man's visit was giving Alice just as big a fright as Mary herself had suffered! Well, and serve her right too! And really, it was quite likely. It seemed obvious, by now, that this new lodger had something to hide. Why else would a well-heeled, well-educated young woman, barely middle-aged, be fetching up in a dump like this?

But *what* was she hiding? This was what concerned Mary. The irrational conviction that it must be something that had to do with herself once more took over, obliterating any sensible weighing-up of probabilities. In her over-stretched imagination, the scenario grew more and more horribly clear the more she allowed herself to dwell on it. It went like this: the strange man had tried Mary's door first not because he'd made a mistake, as he'd alleged, but because he'd wanted to make sure that she was indeed living here, before going on upstairs to discuss with Alice their next move. They were in league together, the two of them, of course they were. Alice had been planted here as a spy to watch over Mary's movements, to note her comings and goings, to record her every careless word. And above all, to search for the thing hidden in the attic. On the pretext of "arranging the room," this Alice woman had given herself an excuse for searching every nook and cranny. She would find it in the end. She was bound to. Had she, indeed, already found it? Was this why she had sent for this man, her fellow-conspirator—to share the revelation? Were they, at this very moment, staring wild-eyed at the dreadful secret . . . ?

The absolute silence from above had been hardly in keeping with this scenario. Nor, come to that, were the stranger's footsteps tramping heavily down the stairs barely five minutes later, right past Mary's door without a break in their rhythm, on and on, down and down, until the slam of the front door betokened final departure.

Lying on her bed with eyes tight closed against the outside world, Mary weighed up all these bits of data and could see that they were reassuring. But something inside her refused to be reassured. "The Impact on Paranoia of the Rational Assessment of Data"—this would have been a good essay title once. To do well in that exam, to qualify in psychology, you had to know absolutely everything about feelings, except what they felt like.

CHAPTER 13

When Alice found the note from her estranged husband propped against her Jane Austens, her first reaction was one of amazement. Not so much at the fact that Rodney had taken the trouble to track her down—though this was indeed surprising—but at the wholly unexpected feelings that the sight of his handwriting aroused in her. Not grief; not hope of reconciliation; but simple, uncomplicated relief that the note was merely from him, and not from one of her prospective pupils cancelling the lessons.

Did she already care more about her new life than about the old? And if so, was this an indication that . . . ?

And then she read the letter, and at once the more-to-be expected feelings took over, and she found herself trembling, mostly with anger.

It was the word "we" that got through to her; the reiteration of those cruel little mini-syllables, "we" and "us," with which a new partnership can so effortlessly (and often unconsciously?) torture the discarded member of the old.

"We've been worrying about you, Alice . . . you should have left an address, you really should . . . We wanted to make sure you were all right . . ."

What lies! How could Ivy possibly be wanting to make sure that the discarded wife was "all right"? Surely Ivy's cup of joy would only be completely full if she could learn that her rival was *not* all right at all? That she had taken to drink . . . had let herself go . . . was shuffling around in slippers all day, hair all over the place, egg-stains down the front of her dressing-gown? Isn't this the secret dream of almost any woman in Ivy's triumphant but still slightly precarious position?

"We want to help you as much as we can, if only you will let us," the letter went on. "To start with, we'd like to take you out to dinner one evening soon . . . Talk it all over in a sensible, friendly way . . ."

Yes, Ivy *would* like that, very possibly. To glide across a restaurant on Rodney's arm, while Alice walked a pace or two behind, the guest, the third party; to discuss with Rodney how to seat the three of them, playing hostess to Alice's gooseberry . . . Well, of course she'd like it. She'd be disappointed—genuinely disappointed—if it didn't happen.

As it bloody wouldn't.

Refolding the note, Alice noticed a P.S. scribbled on the back:

"Really, Alice, you must get those bells at the front door to *work!!* And label them properly; 'Top Floor' is pretty ambiguous, you know, to anyone who doesn't know the house. I found myself barging into the room of a perfectly strange young lady who wasn't *at all* pleased to see me!"

So *that* had been Hetty's strange man. And now Alice's emotions made another U-turn, and she was flooded with protective tenderness towards her errant husband. "Not too bad . . . a bit yellow perhaps . . . a bit on the small side." How dared she describe him thus! Rodney wasn't tall, certainly; not quite as tall as Ivy, actually (as Alice had noticed quite early on); but this was only because Ivy was so large, as well as so ungainly. And as to *yellow*—what a way to describe Rodney's healthily sallow complexion! Anger boiled in her; and then she remembered that tomorrow she was due to go to the Bensons for her first coaching session with Cyril, and that she ought to be making some sort of preparation for it. But what sort? Not for the first time, she thought longingly of her well-stocked shelves of classics "at home," including several elementary textbooks for beginners. To go back there and help herself was of course out of the question. She would have to ring on her own front-door bell, be ushered into her own house as a visitor, and have Rodney cordially giving her permission (as he certainly would) to help herself to her own property. And Ivy would be there too, of course, backing him up, and falling over her lumpy self to show what a tolerant, what a magnanimous Other Woman she was.

"Take anything you want," she would say sweetly, making generous gestures with her plump wrists towards the books that weren't hers and of which she couldn't even read the titles.

No. She would manage somehow.

And actually it wasn't too difficult. Once ensconced with Cyril in the lofty and elegant drawing-room, and once Mrs. Benson had stopped teetering in and out, ostensibly to make sure that Alice had everything she needed, but in fact consumed by a shadowy and unfocussed anxiety at the idea of her son being exposed to something beyond his mother's ken— Once this was over, and teacher and pupil were on their own, it soon became clear that Cyril had every intention of directing operations himself. He had come equipped with the books he wanted to study—a lexicon, a Goodwin's *Greek Grammar*, and Book I of Herodotus's histories.

"I hope you don't mind starting with Chapter 109," he apologised. "But you see I'm specially interested in Cyrus, and how he founded the Persian Empire. Absolutely single-handed, just by being brave enough, because to start with he didn't know he was a king's son at all, he just felt like one. Anyway, I've got to where Cyrus as a baby was to be put out to die on a hillside. Do you mind if we go on from there?"

Far from minding, Alice was thankful to have so many decisions taken out of her hands, and the relevant books so efficiently supplied. At first, when he began translating, she wondered how far he was really following the text, and how far he simply knew the story already in detail; but a few searching questions about specific words soon elicited the fact that he was in the habit of making systematic lists of all the words he had needed to look up; and as to his proficiency in grammar, she had no sooner queried the tense of a certain irregular verb than he treated her to such an exhaustive lecture on the Ionic form of the Optative as compared with the Attic, that she decided then and there to leave grammar alone in sheer self-defence. What on earth was she going to be able to teach him that he didn't already know?

Plenty, as it turned out. As with any self-taught amateur, Cyril's knowledge was patchy, startlingly extensive in some directions, and with incongruously elementary gaps in others. He was quick, though, attentive, and deeply interested. The session flew by, and Alice was both surprised and disappointed when Mrs. Benson came into the room to announce with an air of quite disproportionate relief (apparently at finding her son still alive) that the hour was up.

"Satisfactory?" she asked, with an air of unease; but when Alice began assuring her that the lesson had indeed been satisfactory, and that Cyril was proving a most apt pupil, Mrs. Benson's attention began almost at once to wander. Her eyes drifted round the room as if in search of something, and she interrupted Alice in mid-sentence:

"Cyril hear, have you seen Sophy's new toy? You know—the toy tractor Daddy bought for her? She's been looking for it everywhere. I thought I saw it in here this morning?"

"Yes, here it is." Cyril reached down beside the sofa, and pulled out a sizeable toy tractor of a bright metallic grey with touches of green, and very shiny. "Here you are. You'd left it on the table, but it was a bit in the way, and so I—"

His mother's face cleared. She looked really happy for the first time since Alice had made her acquaintance.

"You see?" she exclaimed, turning to Alice with an air of quiet triumph. "We don't believe in sex-stereotyping when it comes to children's toys. We give Sophy exactly the same kind of toys as we used to give to Cyril. We're so very anxious not to brainwash her into the traditional 'feminine' rôle, you see, as happens to so many little girls. She's never had a doll in her whole life!" she added proudly; "And you can see the results already; she takes to the traditionally 'masculine' toys every bit as eagerly as any boy. She just loves this model tractor—it's her very favourite toy. Isn't it, darling?"

Here she turned to the sturdy little figure who was lurking behind her, peering warily and with provisional disapproval at Alice's unfamiliar presence. "Here you are, Sophy darling, here's your tractor, it was here all the time. Why don't you wind it up and show Mrs. Saunders how well it goes, even on the carpet? It has three speeds, you know," she continued, turning to Alice again, "and a reversing lever, so she can—"

By this time Sophy had reached out eagerly for the proffered toy, and was clutching it to her breast.

"No," she said firmly. "No, Tracty's tired. He's not to be wound up, not no more today, it's his bedtime"; and wrapping the awkwardly shaped vehicle in a loose woolly garment and hugging it close to her, she marched out of the room, crooning gently: "Tracty go bye-byes, then. Tracty be a good Tracty, come with Mummy and go bye-byes . . ."

For a moment, Mrs. Benson looked as if she was going to cry; then, with an effort, she controlled herself.

"Oh, well. Anyway," she said.

To which Alice could find nothing to add.

It was only after she had reached home, and was about to settle down to preparing tomorrow's lesson with Mr. Bates, that Alice discovered that her reading-glasses were missing. Hell! She must have left them at the Bensons', departing as she had in a hurry, somewhat embarrassed by Mrs. Benson's discomfiture over the Tracty episode.

A phone call confirmed that the glasses had indeed been found, and Alice set off at once to recover them.

The rain had stopped, but the air was still heavy with damp, and the pavements glistened wetly under the occasional street lights, few and far between in this rather down-at-heel neighbourhood. She walked briskly, pulling her coat collar up over her ears against the encroaching chill; which was perhaps why she did not at first hear the footsteps following steadily at a short distance behind her. Didn't notice them, anyway—well, why should she, it was a public highway—until, reaching the bus-stop in the high road, and pausing to see if a bus were just coming (if so, it would be worth jumping on it to save herself the last half-mile or so), it came to her that the footsteps behind her had also stopped. Turning quickly, with a twinge of uneasiness, she looked back along the way she had come; but no one seemed to be watching her, or furtively lurking. Indeed, few people were in sight at all. A busy shopping-centre by day, the high road was almost empty at this hour of the evening—empty of pedestrians, that is; as always, there were plenty of cars passing.

For a few moments, she lingered at the stop, peering into the moving maze of headlights, hoping to discern among them the looming, lit-up oblong of an approaching bus. But no; and so, shrugging even deeper into her coat, she continued on her way.

No more footsteps. Or maybe it was the noise of the passing traffic that had drowned them? Because less than a minute after she had turned into the broad, leafy avenue where the Bensons lived, she became aware of them again—the same steady, purposeful pad-pad that she had heard before. Whoever it was must be wearing trainers or something of the sort—the characteristic footwear, according to Miss Dorinda, of the muggers, rapists and murderers who infested the London streets when darkness fell.

It was the thought of Miss Dorinda that prevented Alice looking behind her now. I'm *not* going to be like her, she thought: letting herself be turned into a bag of nerves by all the hyped-up horrors she watches on TV each night, imagining them to be commonplace when in fact they are once-in-a-lifetime rarities. After all, if they were common, they would no longer be news, would they? Alice remembered carefully making this point to Miss Dorinda one evening recently, but totally without success. Now she made this same point to herself, even more carefully, and strode forward boldly, albeit slightly increasing her pace. Only a hundred yards or so now, and she would be safe inside the Bensons' front garden . . . she chided herself for using the word "safe" even in her own mind, for wasn't she safe anyway? Statistics were massively on her side—a woman living in London is likely to be raped or mugged once every five hundred years, she had read somewhere.

This broad, prosperous suburban road, flanked by the shrubs and ornamental trees of the well-screened front gardens, was silent, and absolutely deserted. No cars, even, were passing. Big well-curtained windows, set well back beyond lawns and flower beds, showed an occasional crack of light, but the houses here were too well-built, too painstakingly double-glazed, for any sound of life to emerge into the outside world. All was quiet except for the pad-pad-pad behind her, and also the sound, suddenly preternaturally loud, of Alice's own boots as she hurried towards safety.

Yes, safety. She was no longer bothering to vet her own inner vocabulary.

Number 11 . . . Number 13. Number 21 could only be a few gates away . . . Yes, here she was, and as she paused, fiddling with the icy latch of the ornamental iron-work gate, she was aware of a sudden rush of sound from behind; then the man was upon her, grabbing her arm and holding it in a relentless grip. Sheer panic, strangely mingled with a detached and cool determination not to admit any of this to Miss Dorinda, blurred her reactions for a moment, and she stood limply in the man's grasp.

"Good evening," he said; and only now did she take in that her assailant was not the unkempt teenager of the stereotype, but a man approaching middle-age, heavily built, and with a lined, pallid face under the harsh street lighting.

"Good evening," he repeated. "I'm sorry if I've alarmed you, Mrs. Harman, but I wanted our interview to take place well away from Number 17 Beckford Road. I've been watching for you to come out on your own, and this seemed a good chance . . ."

Mrs. Harman? Mrs. Harman? Oh, he means Hetty, of course. Hetty Harman.

"I'm sorry," she said stiffly, "I'm afraid you're making a mistake. I'm not Mrs. Harman, she's the landlady. I'm just one of the tenants, I . . ."

"Oh, but that's all right, that's fine! It wasn't Mrs. Harman herself that I wanted to see; the person I am trying to contact is a young lady residing at that address; I'm sure you'll be able to help me. A blonde young lady. You know her, I take it? I wonder if you could be very kind, and tell me what her name is? The name she is using?"

"But . . ." Alice was aware of the grip on her arm tightening. "But, if you don't even know who she is, how can you . . . ?"

"I didn't say I didn't know who she is. I said I didn't know . . . Now, look, madam, it's a very simple question I'm asking you—simply the name of a fellow-tenant of yours. You *must* know it."

Alice's wariness deepened. I'm *not* going to tell him, she resolved. No way. I don't know what he's after, and I don't care, but I know—I absolutely know—that Mary won't want anything to do with it.

"I'm sorry," she said, "I'm afraid I can't help you. There is no such person as you describe at our address. And now, if you'll excuse me—" She made to open the gate with her free hand, but his hold on her arm tightened again.

"Now now, madam, not in such a hurry! Perhaps I should tell you that my business could be greatly to the young lady's advantage, should she care to co-operate. You will be doing her a great service, I promise you, if you will tell me . . . Now, come along, madam! Just a simple answer!"

He paused, scrutinizing Alice's face in the half-light. Then, "Look, I'll make it worth your while . . ." and here he pulled out a wallet, and from it took a thick bundle of notes, which he fingered encouragingly.

If Alice had had any doubts about the rightness of her decision, this settled it.

"No!" she cried, "Absolutely no!" and seizing her chance—for her interlocutor had had to release her arm in order to get at his wallet— she wrenched the gate open, raced across the garden and up the steps, ringing a frantic peal on the bell.

It was Cyril who answered—still up, though it was nearly ten—and he led her into the drawing-room where his parents were watching television. They were polite and pleasant about the whole thing, not a word was said about the demerits of classical studies; she was even invited to stay for a cup of coffee, after which Mr. Benson insisted on driving her home. For which she was profoundly thankful; the thought of walking back alone up this deserted road, never knowing behind which bush her inquisitor might be lurking, had been weighing heavily on her.

CHAPTER 14

The most awful thing about getting old is watching yourself getting worse at things. Every year from now on my body is going to work a little bit less efficiently than it does now in all sorts of ways, and every year I'll enjoy my favourite things less, and be less good at them. My friends will be getting less good at things too, because of course they are getting old just as fast as I am, so that one by one we will be giving up the things we do together. It's awful the way I can see it coming.

People laugh when I talk like this, they think it's funny. They don't seem to realise that twelve *is* old. Already, at twelve, your muscle-weight ratio is not quite as good as it was when you were eight and nine. You don't fall so well, and if you jump off a roof you're more likely to break a bone than you were then. Your hearing is deteriorating too, especially in the high registers. I've noticed that myself. A few years ago I could hear bats squeaking, and already I can't anymore, they dart past in silence, and from now on they always will.

I was saying this to Mrs. Saunders—Alice, I usually call her now —about the high-frequency loss of hearing, and not hearing bats anymore, but, alas, she didn't seem to get my point. "Who told you that?" she asked, which was silly, really, because surely it is common knowledge. "What made you think of bats suddenly?" she asked me then, and when I told her it was the picture she'd got stuck up on her wall for all to see, she seemed to be quite bothered; so I decided to shut up. Perhaps she has a phobia, or something? "Nucteriphobia" it should be, if there is such a word. I must look it up sometime.

Still, I quite like going there for my lessons, it's much nicer than having them at home. We're going quite fast, we've got to the bit where Cyrus is only ten and thinks he is a poor shepherd's son, but of course he isn't, he is really the son of the Great King. I like that bit, because I've felt like that myself sometimes, though of course in my case it's pure fantasy, because Daddy isn't a poor shepherd, he's in the City and jolly well off, and anyway there aren't such things as Great Kings anymore. This is one of the reasons why I like reading Herodotus; he writes about a time when it was possible to be glorious and powerful without its being Right Wing, and Reactionary, and all that sort of thing.

Also, I've added nearly 200 words to my vocab. since starting, mostly nouns, and sometimes Alice asks me to stay for supper, which is quite fun, especially when Hetty does a fry-up. Hetty is the landlady, and she says she gets fed up with all the things her lodgers buy and put in the fridge and then forget to eat, and so every so often she takes the whole lot out and fries them all together with masses of onions, and invites everyone down. Sometimes there is a fuss about the smell from someone called Miss Dorinda, but in general they like it. I certainly do.

I wish Christmas wasn't looming. Really, I wish there wasn't such a festival. This is one more deterioration I've noticed in myself with advancing age. I used to love Christmas, like Sophy still does because she's only six, and so there's lots of things she still wants. There's nothing I really want anymore, at least nothing I could get as a present, and that makes it very sad opening my parcels. I used to love opening my parcels, even if it was some silly toy, but that's all gone now. I'm merely bored, the way adults are bored, which just goes to show how old I'm getting. Soon, I'll be bored with everything. And quite soon my brain-cells will start dying off, they start doing it in your middle teens, so I read recently.

Growing up is like a slow terminal illness; the time is coming when you won't even *want* to run about anymore, or jump over things. Have you ever watched an adult trying to run for a bus? Or to jump over some obstacle? See what I mean?

Mind you, it's not only humans that experience this deterioration as they reach maturity. Both sea-squirts and oysters have a lively existence for a few weeks as larvae, swimming about all over the place and foraging; then, once they are mature, they settle down to immobility for the rest of their lives. Barnacles too, I believe.

So it's not only humans. But it still seems a shame, especially if you are one.

Yawning, stretching his cramped fingers, Cyril closed the school project book, whose many untouched pages he was using up as a diary. No one ever looked at project work anymore, not since the strikes, and so it seemed sensible to use up the blank pages in any way he chose. He leaned back in his chair—or, rather, leaned the chair itself back, as far as it would go, balancing it on its back legs at about forty-five degrees, a wonderfully precarious feeling.

Outside his bedroom window he could see the sky beginning to fade from the brilliant blue of a sunny mid-winter day to the pallor of evening. The year was already on the turn; even before Christmas, the days would be drawing out. All at once, he was stirred by a sharp restlessness. The chair clattered back into its correct quadripedal position as Cyril jumped to his feet; and throwing his anorak round his shoulders he was downstairs and off into the cold, clear twilight. With the perfunctory information "Out!" in response to the vague babble of concerned enquiry emanating from his mother's room, he was slamming the front door behind him and leaping down the steps, four at a time. He *could* do six; but that left only two for the second leap, which was a bit pointless.

Park Rise Estate was his destination, for several of his school friends lived in the flats there; in particular his very best friend, Winston, who was not only black, and therefore a member of the Top Gang, but had also invented the wonderful new game they called the Bike Run. The joys and terrors of this game were right now half-choking Cyril with anticipation and excitement as he raced along, darting across busy streets regardless of little red men and little green men, his speed and agility making a mockery of these dreary traffic regulations—regulations which the lumbering, slavish adults were obliged to observe. There they stood, huddled in their coats and scarves, patient as cows, waiting meekly for the signal that they might blunder across with their briefcases, their shoppers and their bad legs, while Cyril, member of a different species altogether, could skip and skim and dodge among the slow-moving traffic, making rings round the lot of them, as the early

small mammals had once made rings round the slow, doomed dinosaurs.

Running, running, running! The air, the wind was like silver moonlight in his lungs . . . and with a final spring he was on the parapet at
the foot of the stairway used for the Bike Run. The gang wasn't there
yet, nor was the bicycle; but Winston was, all ready with his wide
welcoming grin, the whites of his eyes brilliant, alight with mischief in
his black face.

"Gitcher!" he yelled: and "Gitcher!" yelled back Cyril, and instantly
—because after all they had to pass the time somehow until the bicycle
gang had gathered—they were both tearing up the sloping pedway that
led to the bridge between the two neighbouring tower blocks; Cyril a
few yards ahead and Winston in furious pursuit.

It was like flying, it was like swooping to the seventh heaven on
wings of light, powered by the joy of racing blood pounding through
veins dilated with the ecstasy of the chase. Hunter or hunted? Which
was which? How little it mattered as your legs flashed over the cement
floors like scissored lightning, and your whole soul leaped to the challenge of speed . . . and speed . . . and then more speed . . .

Up the slanting pedways, over the bridges, down the darkling stairways, taking the steps four, six, eight at a time—bounding out into the
evening light once more . . . Turn . . . dodge . . . wild, bouncing
kangaroo-springs up the stairway once again, back onto the bridge
where the ground flickered beneath you, and your lungs filled with a
glittering ecstasy of wind and winning . . .

"No running on the pedways!" snarled an angry voice from behind a
lace curtain which twitched and dipped with righteous resentment; a
lace curtain with the law solidly on its side, because was there not a
notice at the entrance to the block: "NO RUNNING ON THE
PEDWAYS. NO BALL GAMES. NO PLAYING ON THE STAIRS."

By now, the lined and bespectacled face had made itself visible from
behind the curtain, and was mouthing through the glass the all-too-
familiar phrases:

" 'Ooligans! Bloody 'ooligans, the lot o' yer!" was roughly what it
conveyed before the curtains quivered back, consigning it to the dark
and cluttered anonymity from which it had come. But now another
voice took up the complaint, a gentle voice this time, civilised, and
using no bad language at all, but effectively delivering exactly the same
message. A little more consideration—surely not too much to ask?
Suppose there had been an old person there, you could have knocked

right into them, they could have been badly injured, a broken hip quite likely. Or suppose someone blind . . . deaf . . . using crutches . . . ? Or someone whose nerves were bad, think of the shock . . .

The two boys hung their heads, listening attentively, taking in the message. The message that the whole world is a geriatric ward into which the young and the strong are admitted on sufferance provided they observe the post-operative rules of moving slowly and with due circumspection. They don't actually have to use crutches themselves so long as they behave as if they did, recognising the fact that nearly everything is dangerous and to be avoided, and that fun and laughter may disturb someone who has a headache; and, in general, that being ill and miserable is a much more worthy and important state than being happy and well, and must therefore be ministered to assiduously at all times; whereas happiness doesn't matter at all, and can be damped down and trodden into the ground with impunity.

Oh, well. There was still the Bike Run. The others would be there by now, and since it took place at the back of the flats, behind the garages, with no windows overlooking them, there would—hopefully—be no interruptions. The people with the headaches and the crutches and the bad nerves never came that far, especially not when dusk was falling, as it was now.

Yes, there they were—Steve, Biko, Gus and Errol, all waiting—and Winston and Cyril were given a hero's welcome, especially Winston.

"Hi, nigger!" the two black boys yelled to him cheerily—they, of course, were the only ones allowed to use this intimate form of address; for a white boy to use it would have been bad form, arrogating to himself a privilege which didn't belong to him by right. There was nothing unfriendly about the distinction, but still, it was one more small factor in the prestige accorded to black gangs on the Estate. All the boys yearned to get into a black gang, but it was something of an honour, not accorded to all and sundry, and Cyril had been thrilled to the very core at finding himself accepted by this lot—albeit largely on account of being Winston's best friend.

Winston was the unquestioned Master of Ceremonies for the Bike Run. He it was who had produced the bicycle, a full adult-size, too large for most of them, but all the most exciting for that. Although still in working order, the machine was badly battered—but this was all to the good, really, as it was assuredly going to get more battered still.

The staircase used for this sport was dark and shadowy, lit only by a 40-watt bulb in the window of a warehouse behind the garages. It consisted of eighteen concrete steps, which were never swept, because why should the caretaker drag himself over to this part of the Estate where no one ever went, not unless they were up to no good, anyway, and why should he bother with the likes of *those*? Let them clear away their own beer cans and such if they'd a mind to, who cared?

As it happened, the bicycle gang *did* care, they had to, because the game was dangerous enough as it was, without the odd beer can getting in front of your wheel; and so the first thing they did—quietly, though with much hoarse whispering—was to sweep the steps with an old hearth-brush, also produced by the resourceful Winston.

"Whose turn?" . . . "No, mind" . . . "No, it's Biko's" was roughly the burden of the whispering; and when the steps were clear, the one whose turn it was—Steve on this occasion—humped the bicycle up to whatever height he dared, mounted it while clinging with one hand to the rail, and then— Whee-ee . . . ! This was where you had to let go, and come bouncing down, struggling to keep the machine upright, and above all *not*, absolutely *not* grabbing at the rail for support when you felt yourself out of control. If you did—and Cyril nervously thanked his stars that he had never disgraced himself thus—if you did, you lost *all* your points gained over the previous weeks, as well as being shamed in front of the whole gang. Points, of course, were scored by the number of steps you could descend before crashing.

So far, the highest step from which anyone had ever descended successfully was fifteen. It was Winston of course who had achieved this, though Biko was not far behind with a near-successful descent from fourteen; he had only crashed on the very last step, with the front wheel already on the ground, and the gang had unanimously agreed to award him full points for a successful descent, just as if he hadn't crashed at all.

Cyril yearned, with an aching of the soul quite beyond the power of words to describe, to be the first one to attempt sixteen; but so far he was light-years away from any such triumph. One of the rules of the game was that you had to go up step by step. Until you had managed at least one successful descent from, say, nine, you weren't allowed to go on to ten; and nine, it so happened, was exactly where Cyril had got to. So there were six more stages to be achieved, each of them harder than the last, and goodness knew that had been hard enough. Eight times he had crashed—once bruising his shoulder so badly that it was all he could do to prevent his family or the school finding out—before his final success, only a week ago. How they had cheered him (in whispers, of course, which was the way it had to be) as he arrived on the ground with a final fearsome jolt that felt as if it had knocked his spine right adrift from his ribs; but—joy of joys!—with the bicycle still upright. The fact that it had skidded immediately from under him detracted nothing from the achievement, for the front wheel had got itself beyond the bottom step, and that was what counted.

"Bloody marvellous!" they'd hissed generously in *sotto voce* approbation, even though they had all—all except Steve, that is—got themselves well beyond step nine. They knew it was harder for the white boys, they somehow bashed up more easily, there was some knack they hadn't quite got. The proud possessors of this knack could obviously afford to be generous.

"C'mon, Silly!"—there was nothing insulting about the nickname, it just seemed more friendly than "Cyril"—"C'mon, Silly, s'your go! Ten, you're on. Hey, watch, Silly's on ten. C'mon, Silly . . ."

The previous incumbent—Errol, as it happened—handed over the bike even before dusting himself down from his unfortunate spill between steps four and five, and Cyril clutched the handlebars as if they were straws and he drowning. His hands were sweaty, his knees jumping with nerves and happiness, as he slowly mounted the steps, the voices chanting behind him in whispered unison: "One . . . Two . . . Three . . . *Ten.* There y'are, Silly. *Ten.*"

It was important to let go of the rail at the exact moment when you felt the bicycle steady into exact equilibrium beneath you; a moment's delay, and the equilibrium would be lost . . . not to mention losing points in the most disgraceful way possible, by hanging on too long. He took a deep breath, felt the machine right itself at its perilous angle, and—*let go* . . .

It was like a thunderstorm in your spine. It was like an untamed stallion trying to throw you, and of course it *did* throw him, because after all this was his first go from ten. Still, he didn't come off till between two and three—jolly good, really, and his friends evidently thought so too—jolly good for a white boy, anyway; and they jumped up and down and hugged him with congratulatory squeals.

CHAPTER 15

Alice was delighted by the new arrangement that Cyril should come to her for his lessons instead of her going to his home. Not only would this save her the longish walk, of which she had had quite enough lately, but she would also be relieved of the vague miasma of anxious disapproval which was liable to bedevil the sessions in the Bensons' drawing-room.

"It'll be Christmas, you see," Mrs. Benson had explained, in vague apology for this welcome change: "Visitors and so on."

Fair enough; but Alice couldn't help wondering whether the carefully non-brainwashed Sophy might have something to do with the decision. The child's evident propensity for raising single-handed the ugly head of sexism under the very eyes of any random outsider was maybe a risk not to be taken more than necessary. Who could guarantee that the next time Alice arrived she would not find Tracty sitting up at table with a bib on, having raisins fed into his carburettor?

Anyway, whatever the motive, it left Alice feeling lucky as well as rich. Buoyant with sudden extravagance engendered by the feel of just-earned cash actually in her purse, she turned her steps towards the main shopping street, where she plunged recklessly into purchases for this party that she and Brian had so impulsively thought up. Candles: blue, yellow and red. Weird packets of edibles called things like Snack-Bits and King Pops. Decorations, too. Crazy, really, but the day they had fixed on was the Saturday before Christmas. Before that, Brian had explained, he would be tied up with pupils and with playing the piano for end-of-term dance displays, carol concerts, Open Days, and fifth-form productions of *Oliver*. This was the ego-trip season, he told her, for parents and children alike, and it extended from about December 9 to December 21; then stopping as suddenly as it had begun, as if wiped out by a mighty hand.

"It's almost enough to make you actually *believe* in Peace on Earth," he said. "Quite suddenly, you wake up one morning and find that nothing is happening. Total peace. No one crying about costumes not being finished; no one loosing off about their kid being only a shepherd and not Joseph. No one screaming hysterically down the phone about the pianist having flu and can I fill in for them, thumping my way through a vast and varied repertoire ranging from 'Dear Little Buttercup' to 'Hark the Herald Angels' . . . So you see," he'd concluded, "a party is just what I'll need," and he'd gone on to offer every possible kind of help with the preparations, but not yet.

Meantime, Alice could be getting on with the task of making the room look as festive and as upbeat as its many shortcomings allowed. Party or no, this was essential, for who knew when Rodney might be turning up again, unannounced. And inevitably, sooner or later, driven by an all-consuming curiosity, Ivy would be coming with him, all agog to cast her sharp Other-Womanly eyes over Alice's set-up, hungry for signs of squalor. Underclothes left on chairs. Dirty crockery. Dust, cigarette-ends. Smears, stains, spider-webs. All the familiar indications of a woman who has Let Herself Go.

Mind you, she would find some of the clues difficult to assess. Does a gaudily-painted motor-bike in a small bed-sitter indicate that the occupant has let herself go? Or that she hasn't? With a certain glee, Alice pictured her rival staring at it, planted on her stout legs in the centre of the room, and wondering what she ought to think.

Well, what ought she? Looking round at her now almost cosy domain, burgeoning with colour in every direction, Alice could not but feel a certain pride in her achievement. The new candles were in place now, cunningly disposed among the shadows, all ready to turn clutter and muddle into a dancing mystery of interlacing light. No one could describe this as the room of someone who has "let herself go." An eccentric, perhaps? An impractical fool? Maybe; but at least no one visiting here would be able to go away and talk about "Poor Alice!"

A daring thought occurred to her. It would be fun—or wouldn't it? —to invite Rodney and Ivy to this projected party? Show them that in barely three weeks Alice had contrived to start a new life, to amass a whole lot of new, amusing friends, and to have recovered the kind of self-confidence needed for giving a party. No longer a Poor Thing, by any stretch of the imagination. Poor Things don't give parties. Not even unsuccessful parties—if that, unfortunately, was how it should turn out.

And anyway, why should it be unsuccessful? She couldn't, it must be admitted, envisage Rodney—or, indeed, Ivy—getting on particularly well with the members of this oddly assorted household—but then, you never knew. Maybe they would? Maybe Ivy and Miss Dorinda would turn out to be soul-mates at some deep, hair-tinting sort of level? Maybe Rodney and Brian would engage in a man-to-man conversation on some innocuous topic like motorway pile-ups or nuclear fall-out? Though actually Rodney would be better employed—would he not?—in flirting mildly with poor Mary, on whose account (Alice now recollected) the whole project had first been mooted. Maybe a little male attention would do Mary good, and with any luck it would annoy Ivy at the same time.

Anyway, there was still much to be done. The kaleidoscope of clashing colours and eye-catching distractions only distracted just so far, and indeed served in a way to make the neglected bits of the room look even more neglected.

Pictures. Posters. Photos from glossy magazines. These were what she needed now . . . Only a few days ago, she'd come across a whole box of that sort of thing . . .

It was fun, and took quite a while, to pick out the brightest, most exciting pictures and to cut them out ready for their camouflage job on the grimy walls. Blu-Tack of course, was the next desideratum; Brian would be sure to have some . . .

Unfortunately, Brian didn't; or, rather, didn't want to search through all the places it might be just when he was trying to make fair copies of some of his compositions for a man who just might be able to get another man interested in them: but he'd only be interested if six copies could be made available by nine o'clock tomorrow morning before this other man—or was it the same man?—boarded his plane to New York.

Or something to that effect.

"Later on, Alice love, it's got to be somewhere," he assured her distractedly, looking, now that his deadline was upon him, more than ever like a real musician.

But "later on" wasn't good enough for Alice. Having cut out all these pictures and started to visualise them in position, she was consumed by impatience. She hurried on down to Hetty's domain where, sure enough, two half-used packets of Blu-Tack lay handily behind the bread-bin, in company with a packet of dried yeast and Hengist's supply of worm pills. Pointing out how similar all these packets were to one another (a brave attempt to instil some logic into the system of categorisation), Hetty found herself suddenly and forcibly reminded of Hengist's current problem. Would Alice—could she *possibly* . . . ? He should have had his second one on Tuesday, really, but it was difficult, you see, if, like Hetty, you only had two hands. One to hold him down, one to force his mouth open, and then—well, there you were, you see, with nothing with which to put the pill on the back of his tongue. Alice did see, didn't she?

Indeed she did; and since there seemed to be no acceptable way out of it, she resigned herself to her rôle, though with some reluctance. Hengist didn't like her much anyway, except when she was actually pouring out milk for him; at other times, he was inclined to walk out of the room with a nasty little twitch of the end of his tail as soon as she walked in. This was going to do nothing to improve the relationship.

Holding him on her lap with all her strength, one hand pressing down on his haunches and the other clutching the scruff of his neck, she thought, not about England, but about her own inability to say no to things, or at least to say it quickly enough. Or was it not so much her own inadequacy in this respect as Hetty's outstanding skills in so manipulating a situation as to make almost anything sound reasonable?

It was over at last, after three tries; and, as Hetty sadly pointed out, it was lucky in a way that Horsa wasn't still with them; with which sentiment Alice could only agree, from the bottom of her heart.

The episode ended with a necessary consolation prize for Hengist in the form of cream off the top of Alice's new bottle of Gold Top, which he lapped up greedily, though twitching his tail the while to show that he was still annoyed.

Hetty's thanks for assistance, and Alice's thanks for the Blu-Tack, criss-crossed amiably for a minute, and culminated in Hetty's ploughing her way upstairs in Alice's wake in order to admire Alice's transformation of the lumber-room.

Her admiration—as Alice had anticipated—was enthusiastic.

"My! . . . Oh my! . . . My goodness gracious!" fell from her lips in flattering profusion.

The only thing she wasn't sure whether to admire or not was the motor-bike; nothing in her experience or background rendered it easy for her to decide with any certainty whether it was quite nice to have a motor-bike so flaunted as part of the décor of a bed-sitting-room. Mightn't it have been more, well, you know, to have draped something decorously over the naked mechanism? An old curtain, or something?

The argument was short and quite without rancour. Hetty's deep-seated amiability, reinforced by the obvious bothersomeness of doing anything, soon won the day, and she settled herself on what was left of the improvised settee—the box of magazines being still in the middle of the floor, spilling its contents in all directions—to watch Alice Blu-Tacking her pictures to every available space on the grimy walls; after which the two of them repaired to the kitchen for a late-night cup of tea—which seemed to be something of a ritual in this household. They were joined on this occasion by Miss Dorinda, complaining bitterly about the lateness of the hour. She liked to be in bed by ten, she pointed out—though it was unclear who was preventing this—and also what about the geyser, which was in one of its moods again; the water was not merely tepid, but jerking out in a funny sort of way with nasty brown streaks in it, and there was a horrid popping sound somewhere up in the pipes.

The subject proved a fruitful one, branching out into a far-flung discussion of burst pipes, errant plumbers, and geysers of yester-year; which was how it came about that Mary had all the time in the world to creep upstairs to the attic and find out what they had been doing. For some time now she had been listening, in silent dread, to the noises which had come to her through the ceiling; thumpings, and bumpings, and a non-stop murmur of voices—though there was no way she could make out what they'd been saying, and could only guess what they'd been doing.

Not that she needed all the time in the world. Staring her in the face as she walked into the room was the picture of Flittermouse Hill as it had been in the golden days now blacked out for ever; and gaping open on the floor, the whole of her dark secret spilling horribly out of it, lay the box containing her brother's relics. "The Monster of Medley Green," as one headline had described him; "The Midnight Mad-man"; "The Fiend of Flittermouse Hell," as one sparky journalist had seen fit to mis-spell the magic haunt of her childhood. The devil incar-nate, who during one long hot summer had gunned down half a dozen innocent passers-by, and whose arrest and trial had filled the TV screens for weeks.

The Madman. The Monster. The Fiend. Julian.

CHAPTER 16

In the past Alice had sometimes vaguely wondered, reading of some terrible crime in the papers, what it must be like to be a close relative of the criminal? A mother? A sister? A wife? Utterly innocent, and yet irrevocably involved?

Now she had her answer. Hour after hour of it, punctuated by distant clocks chiming the hours and the half-hours all through the night. So dreadful were the revelations that there were moments when she felt that she ought not to be listening, that there was something wicked about even hearing such things: as if she was eavesdropping at the keyhole of hell.

Eavesdropping, anyway. She was hearing these revelations on false pretences; had it not been for Mary's instantaneous assumption, at the sight of the ransacked box, that all had been discovered, Alice would never have heard the story at all.

Or would she? During that long night of despairing tears and agonised reminiscence, Alice more and more got the impression that the girl had, by now, worked herself up to such a pitch of terror and anguish that confession to someone, somehow, had become a necessity. Alice's accidental and wholly innocent discovery of the fatal box had maybe been little more than a trigger.

It had started as soon as Alice returned from the kitchen to her attic room. As soon as she set foot through the door, she was greeted by violent, hysterical accusations from the hunched and frantic figure on the floor; and at first she could not make out what she was being accused of. What was so special about a box of old colour supplements? Oh, and right at the bottom, someone's amateurish attempt at a detective novel, absurdly melodramatic, with a fresh murder every few pages . . . ?

Well, it wasn't a novel; that was what was so special. It was a diary, a real-life account of real-life killings. That's why there were so many murders: because there *were* so many murders; it was not a failure in artistic judgement at all.

At first, Mary seemed unable to take in Alice's assurances of having known nothing. Her suspicion that Alice had planted herself here—or had been planted—with the express purpose of finding and exposing the damning document had grown over the days to such obsessional proportions that she simply couldn't envisage any innocent motive for ransacking the box of incriminating papers.

Incriminating because they were—look!—in Julian's own handwriting.

"Can't you *see?*" she cried—and it was in this utterly irrational appeal (because how could Alice possibly know anything about Julian's handwriting?) that Alice recognised the first hint of the change in her own rôle from arch-enemy to desperately needed confidante.

Julian's own handwriting. Incontrovertible evidence not only of his guilt, but of his calculating awareness of what he was doing: evidence which Mary had desperately kept from the police all through the months leading up to the trial, not so much as a coherent attempt to protect her brother from justice as in the wild irrational hope that if they couldn't *prove* he had done it, then somehow he wouldn't have. As if by sheer will-power she could make it not have happened, could beat the facts into pulp with her bare hands, and thus bring back into existence the happy companion of her childhood whom the media were so grotesquely changing, hour by hour, into a monster, a fiend, a devil, a creature of headlines, of Late Night Horror; not a reality at all.

But the facts had won in the end, as they were bound to do. Her tiny, struggling fantasy had been no match for their sledgehammer power, and she had had to face at last the knowledge that her beloved brother was indeed a monstrous and horrific killer. And even this was not the final twist of the knife: the truly intolerable thing was that *she,* Mary, was the *sister* of a monstrous and horrific killer. And for her there could be no reprieve; no remission for good behaviour. She would be the sister of a murderer for ever. No judge, however compassionate, no jury, however biased in her favour, would ever be able to reduce by a single hour her life-sentence. The sister of a murderer. For life.

Looking back, it was hard for her to pin-point the moment of full realisation. It had come upon her slowly, a little bit at a time, like the symptoms of a terminal illness; good days and bad days; small remissions burgeoning into monstrous, short-lived hopes; fantasies of finding, one day, that none of it had happened; that she was miraculously well again.

She had been at college, working hard for exams, when the thing first hit the headlines. At that stage, the police had no clue as to the identity of the attacker; and so, apart from the natural sense of shock at learning that these things had been happening quite near her home, she had given the matter only the attention normally accorded to suchlike horrific news items; disasters that pertain only to other people, outside one's personal horizon.

It had been a further shock, of course, when the police (it was the summer vacation by then) had arrived at the house, not, on this first occasion, with a search warrant; merely about who had been doing what on various nights. Her father, just out of hospital after his first heart-attack, had been away convalescing, and her mother with him; so the brunt of the questioning had fallen upon the young people at home. Mary remembered, afterwards, that she had wished Julian would be more forthcoming, less sulky and withdrawn in his manner. The police were being perfectly civil at this stage, a routine call, that's all; they were checking on all the households in the neighbourhood, con-. centrating, perhaps—though they didn't say so—on households which included young men in their teens or twenties. This was pure guesswork, at this stage of the investigation, for no definite clues of any sort had emerged as to the probable identity of the assailant.

This was after the first two shootings. The third one occurred two nights later, and this time the victim, though shot in the chest, had survived, and while recovering had been able to describe the experience to detectives at his bedside. He had been walking along the new, not yet made-up road that led from what had once been Flittermouse Hill (Medley Green Estate, it was now called) towards the town, when he had become aware of hasty footsteps behind him, as if someone was hurrying to catch him up. Before he had time to turn round, he experienced what felt like a violent blow on the shoulder. He remembered collapsing onto the ground . . . a sound of running footsteps . . . a vague sense of someone speaking . . . yes, a man's voice, a young man . . . and then had lost consciousness. He had woken up in hospital several hours later, having undergone an operation to remove the bullet from his ribs, to learn that he had been the third victim of the Monster of Medley Green, as the unknown person was by now being called.

Was Mary blinding herself to the hideously obvious that night? It had not seemed so at the time, but looking back she wondered how she could possibly have been deceived by the preposterous story which Julian had blurted out as he raced into the house, just before midnight, his anorak all smeared with blood.

"Out of the way, Midge—one of my nose-bleeds!" he'd gasped as he pushed past her and raced on upstairs to the bathroom.

"One of my nose-bleeds." As if it was part of a known family pattern that Julian should now and again have nose-bleeds.

But it wasn't. He'd never had one before—not to Mary's knowledge —through all the long years of their childhood. But somehow, something deep inside Mary had accepted it—or, rather, had refused to query it; and, amazingly, had *still* failed to query it even when the news of the new attack took pride of place in all the media the very next morning.

Another visit from the police. Her father back in hospital again— She had wondered, since, whether he already suspected what she, Mary, ought by now to have suspected; and whether this had hastened his death. He never spoke about it if it was so—but then, neither did she.

Julian sulky and withdrawn again, answering the police questions— more probing this time—in monosyllables. She wished desperately that he wouldn't *be* like that, but somehow she still didn't suspect anything. After all, he was only eighteen—still a teenager, really—and what teenage boy doesn't sometimes react to adult questioning with sulks and withdrawal? Still, it was bound to give the police a bad impression; and sure enough, when they next interviewed her they asked her a lot of searching questions about her brother as well as about herself. Had he had any special worries lately? Had she noticed any changes in his personality? In his usual habits?

No, she'd said: and No, and No, and No. And in a way it was true, for the change had not been recent—which surely was what the police were asking about?—but had started more than a year ago. And there had been good reason for it, or so it had seemed to her, for that was the time when they began the destruction of Flittermouse Hill. He hadn't talked about it much, or even at all, after those first few shattering days; but sometimes she wondered if he'd ever really got over it; it was as if his childhood and youth had been shattered by the bulldozers as surely as the soft springy turf and the primroses that starred the edges of the copse at the foot of the hill.

"I'll *kill* them!" he'd said at the beginning, his eyes bright and harsh with the burning, difficult tears of adolescence. "I will! I'll *kill* them!"

But, of course, plenty of people talk like this in times of stress. No one dreams of taking it seriously. Pointless, certainly, to repeat such a wild and childish threat in the context of serious police enquiry nearly two years later.

It was after the fifth murder that the question of the diary came up. Someone—was it her father—in hospital once again with what proved to be his last heart-attack—who'd told them? Had he, either innocently, or from a grim sense of civic duty, revealed to them that his son, ever since the age of twelve, had kept a diary? A nature-diary it had been to begin with, full of data about Pimpernels, and Enchanter's Nightshade; a first sighting of a Bee Orchis, of a Purple Gromwell, with little sketch-maps about where to look for them among the brambles and short turf of the chalky slopes, or alongside the cool damp ditches that flanked the copses of silver birch. Butterflies, too, sightings of Yellow Brimstones and Chalk-Hill Blues. And the bats, of course. Pages and pages about the bats.

Later, though, as he became thirteen, fourteen, fifteen, the diary became more personal, more secret. Even his sister wasn't allowed to read it anymore. Still, she knew the special place where he kept it, and when the police asked her about it, some instinct—surely, by now, to be called suspicion?—warned her to deny all knowledge of it. By the time they came with their search-warrant, she had already made sure it was no longer in the house. She had packed it carefully in a suitcase and deposited it in the Left Luggage Office of a main-line station. It couldn't stay there for ever, of course; after three months it could come under suspicion—maybe in connection with some other murder hunt altogether. After three months, she would have to find some other hiding-place; but three months was a long time, and at least for that period it would be out of trouble.

Trouble? What trouble? Here she was, taking all these precautions, suppressing evidence, obstructing the police in the course of their duty, and all without any clear sense of why she was doing it. Was it to protect Julian? But she hadn't, as yet, admitted to herself that her brother needed any protection; hadn't, in her heart of hearts, admitted that any of it was really happening. It was only on the day they arrested him—no, the day after—that she realised just what it is that makes something really have happened; it's other people knowing about it.

Other people! Other people in their millions and their billions all over the world. Every newspaper, every TV screen, to the ends of the earth, were filled with his enormous face, his huge black name, and his terrible deeds. Between them, the TV and the newspapers were turning him, hour by hour, into a monster of evil. With their headlines, with their films and photographs, they were moulding him into a monster as purposefully and as inexorably as a sculptor moulds a lump of clay in accordance with his vision.

They were doing another moulding job, too, at the same time, working away at it on the sidelines: Sister of the Monster.

Think about it. Yesterday a bright intelligent girl, attractive, with lots of friends, doing well at college: today a totally new, totally unrecognisable creature: Sister of the Monster. Her father had died that very night, just before dawn, just in time to not hear the seven o'clock news; just in time to escape changing from himself into Father of the Monster. Well, she was thankful that it was just in time. The change from life to death was surely a lesser thing.

For Mary, there had been no such escape. Young, strong, healthy, her body would not dream of dying; it would not even collapse with illness, or anaesthetise her with a nervous breakdown. The onslaught of reporters, film crews, psychiatric social workers, friends, strangers, camera-men came at her in a single concerted attack, which nothing could withstand. For although the voices were various, ranging from heights of compassion to depths of revulsion, they all actually spoke in unison, conveying the same message:

"You will never be a normal person, ever again."

CHAPTER 17

During her years of teaching Alice had, of course, found herself at times the recipient of confidences from one or another of her pupils, and intractable though the problems could sometimes seem, she had always prided herself on being able to find *something* helpful or encouraging to say: some suggestion for a possible course of action; an idea, perhaps, for breaking a vicious circle; some new angle from which to view an impasse; a touch of humour, even, to put the problem more in proportion.

But among all the troubles that had been laid before her, there had never been anything like this. Her repertoire of appropriate responses was silenced. To a trouble of these dimensions nothing you could possibly say would be adequate; and yet you must say *something*. And quickly. A pause for thought, a few moments' silence, would come across as an embarrassed revulsion, and could close up the floodgates of confidences for ever. It was four o'clock in the morning; the girl's white, exhausted face poised above her thin shoulders looked almost middle-aged under the harsh ceiling light. Maybe it would have been better, less depressing, to have created a softer illumination for their vigil by lighting the candles; the bright, waiting candles newly purchased for a festive occasion which now could never be. But how heartless this could have seemed! *Candles!* There was no way of getting it right; none at all.

How thin Mary looked, poor child, in this cruel light, bones sticking up everywhere! How come she hadn't really noticed this before? And suddenly, without thinking about it at all, Alice found herself speaking, firmly and decisively:

"I've got some bacon," she said. "Downstairs in the fridge. I know it's early, but let's have some breakfast. With coffee. And toast."

"But . . . but . . ." A suggestion from such an unexpected angle had obviously given Mary a jolt. "I don't eat breakfast," was all she could come up with.

"I know you don't. And you don't have lunch, either. Or any supper to speak of—Hetty's been worrying about it for weeks. What are you trying to do? How is starving yourself going to help? Or *is* that what you're trying to do? Literally to starve yourself? It won't work, you know, it takes weeks and weeks to get anywhere remotely like dying, and even then . . ."

"I'm *not* trying to starve myself!" Mary protested. "I was just trying to get thin so that I wouldn't be so recognisable—I used to be quite plump, you know, and it makes a lot of difference to your looks. That's the important thing, Alice—that no one shall ever, ever recognise me, as long as I live. I've cut my hair, I've changed my name, I've come to live in this grotty place, I've got thin and hideous—what more *can* I do? What *can* I?"

Well, what could she? What *did* families do, in this sort of terrible situation? You didn't hear much about it, really, in the news reports. About the wives and girl-friends, yes—but then that was different. These might indeed heroically insist on standing by the evil-doer through thick and thin; but all the time they had the option of not; of changing their minds, of ditching him, of shaking the past off completely, freeing themselves from it, and getting on with their lives; sooner or later becoming someone else's wife or lover.

But you couldn't opt for being someone else's sister. This was a blood tie which nothing could sever, not as long as you lived. Was Mary's solution perhaps the only possible one? To cut yourself off from everyone and everything you had ever known? To exile yourself into a world of lies, lie upon lie, a vast top-heavy structure of falsehood, for ever needing to be shored-up, for ever needing emergency repairs and alterations in panic response to this or that unforeseen occurrence in the outside world? Such tiny, everyday things would be able to set the whole contraption rocking; a chance encounter with a former acquaintance; a careless gap or inconsistency in the fictional life-story?

And yet, if this *wasn't* the answer—then what was? What could one say? And who was Alice to say it? It was Mary, not Alice, who was the expert in this grim speciality. How can one dare to give advice to someone enduring an ordeal which one has never faced, and never will have to face? Oh, there is always *something* you can say to people in appalling trouble: like, "Be thankful it's not *both* legs," or, "Lucky you're not going to be deaf as well." That sort of thing.

Alice drew a deep breath.

"Come on," she said, "Breakfast!" and reached out a hand to pull the girl to her feet.

"*Oh* . . . *!*" Mary pulled away, but seemed bewildered rather than antagonistic. "I can't, you know, Alice, I really can't. It's not that I'm still trying to get any thinner, it's that I *can't* eat now, I really can't. My stomach's shrunk up, or something. Like, yesterday Hetty was trying to get me to eat one of her rock-cakes, and I did try, just to please her, I'd had nothing all day, and they're not bad, you know, those cakes of hers. But I couldn't get it down, honestly, Alice, I just couldn't. My throat just wouldn't swallow it . . ."

"Bacon's different," declared Alice authoritatively. "Come on. When you smell it, sizzling away in the pan, and fried bread too, done in really hot fat so that it's all crisp and golden . . ."

It worked—at least to the extent that Mary consumed not just one rasher, but two, as well as a square of fried bread and a finger of toast. She even managed a watery smile when Hengist marched in, quite noisily as he sometimes did when he knew it wasn't a proper mealtime, and staked out his claim to some sort of share of whatever was going at this unaccustomed hour. No, not just *rinds*, for heaven's sake, a bit of proper bacon if you don't mind, and not all fat, either . . .

And then milk, of course. He established himself alongside his usual saucer, front paws neatly together, and stared at them, without blinking.

"Do tell me, Mary," Alice said, going to the fridge, "you've been here longer than I have; which of these milks is it all right to give to Hengist? There's so many of them, some with labels and some not, whose *are* they all? This one called 'Yesterday Only,' for instance . . . Who on earth?"

"Oh, that's Hetty," Mary explained. She laughed a little, and Alice secretly rejoiced that her ploy of raising a trivial domestic problem was turning out more than half-way successful; it was the first time ever that she had heard Mary laugh. There was colour in her cheeks; she was looking, for a moment, like any other twenty-year-old. "It's history really," she was explaining. "Once upon a time a note was left out for the milkman saying 'Yesterday only two pints were delivered, please leave extra today'—something like that. Most of the message got rained away, but Hetty kept what was left because she'd had such a lot of trouble threading the rubber band through it to attach it to the bottle, it seemed a shame to waste it, so she kept it for hers. It had to be hers, she said, because anyone else would make a fuss, having a label like that."

"Oh." Alice continued her researches. "And so what's this 'HH' one? I've been taking for granted it must be Hetty. 'Hetty Harman,' you know—"

"Oh no," said Mary. "That's Hengist's. You see, there used to be Horsa, too, until he disappeared, and Hetty's keeping it like this just in case he comes back." She laughed again. "Do you remember the rhyme, Alice—did they have it when you were at school?—'Hengist was coarser than Horsa/And Horsa was awfully coarse!' I forget how it goes on, something about 'And Horsa ate peas with a knife!' I remember Julian saying—"

And suddenly, without warning, she was in floods of tears, rushing out of the room and up the stairs. Before Alice had thought what to do, the distant door had slammed.

To interfere? Or to leave the girl to the solitude she seemed so urgently to be seeking? By the time she had decided on interfering, several minutes had passed. Pushing open Mary's door—for once it was not barricaded—she saw, to her relief, that the girl was already asleep. Sound asleep, dead asleep, her face rosy and untroubled in deep unconsciousness, like a tired child.

And no wonder, after the stress, and the misery, and the all-night vigil. Alice felt quite envious, she wished that she, too, might settle down to a day's sleeping, but this could not be. The day that was to dawn in a couple of hours' time was Saturday, the day when both her pupils were due to come for their respective lessons, and there was quite a lot of preparation that she must do.

On top of which, she was going to have to explain to Brian that the party must be cancelled, at least for the time being. The explanation was going to be difficult, because Mary had sworn her to secrecy; adding, in addition to this:

"*Whatever* happens, Alice, don't let Brian find out! Don't let him suspect anything! *Promise* me, Alice, that you won't let him suspect a thing!"

CHAPTER 18

Cyril arrived at Alice's for his Greek lesson slightly late and in a state of extraordinary euphoria. Funny, that, because he hadn't actually succeeded in the descent from step eleven, which was where he was at now. In fact, he had failed quite dramatically—his elbow was still hurting fairly badly from this failure. The feeling of triumph wasn't to do with success, then—it must be to do with having had a go; and as he and Alice began to work their way through Cyrus's various tribulations and set-backs on his way towards supreme power, it occurred to Cyril that he and the Great King were linked by something more than the common derivation of their names. Ascending the throne of the mighty Persian Empire to the cheers of your victorious army . . . Ascending to step eleven behind the garages of Park Rise Estate to the cheers (whispered) of your special gang—it was the same thing really. People didn't understand this sort of thing nowadays, because "glory" had become a bad word; but Cyrus would have understood. As a child, he'd gloried in excelling at boys' games—they'd recently been reading a splendid chapter about this. He'd have taken part in the Bike Run like a shot, Cyrus would, if he'd happened to have been born nowadays instead of two and a half thousand years ago. And would have won it hands down, too, he'd have been at step eighteen already, beating even Winston. But of course none of this, nowadays, would lead to becoming a Great King. In order to attain power nowadays, he'd have to start by getting into local politics and being for or against things like housing subsidies . . .

"So why is the verb in the infinitive?" Alice was asking; and Cyril quickly turned his mind back to the text in front of him. In a way, he liked her being pernickety like this, even though it slowed things down rather irritatingly and interrupted the progress of the story. All the same, he did want to understand the twists and turns of this fascinating language, and this was the only way. He listened carefully to her explanation of the whole passage being in indirect speech because of Herodotus having been told the story by some chap, starting pages and pages back so that you'd almost forgotten; but the infinitive made it clear that it was still indirect speech, and therefore the chap must be still talking. What an ingenious system! You couldn't do that in English. Greek was a wonderful language.

"When we've finished Herodotus," he said, "I'd like to go on to Homer. He uses the Ionic forms too, doesn't he? Can we do that?"

Alice was slightly taken aback. *Finish* Herodotus?

"You know, Cyril, there are *nine* books of the Histories," she pointed out, "and we're not a quarter through this one yet. I don't see how there will be time."

"Why—aren't you going to go on teaching me?" demanded Cyril, suddenly shocked. "Have you got another job, or something?"

"No—oh no—" Alice laughed uneasily. "Not so far, and even if I had I'm sure I could still fit you in all right. But you know, Cyril, I don't think your parents are going to want you to study Greek for ever. You've got all your school subjects, remember; and in a year or two you're going to have to start thinking about exams. What you're going to take for O-level. That sort of thing. I know your parents are expecting you to do maths and science—"

"Of course I'm going to do maths and science. They more or less make you, if you're at all bright. And I *am* bright, so there isn't much option, is there? I just wish people wouldn't go on about it, that's all. I don't want to have to think about it. It's depressing."

"Well . . ." Alice hesitated. It seemed a glum sort of way for a promising boy to be embarking on his special subjects; but on the other hand, a lifetime of teaching had ingrained in her the necessity for displaying a degree of solidarity with parents and their wishes. "Yes, well," she temporised, "they're anxious for your future, naturally they are, and they want you to have an education which will lead to a really good job. As you say, you are bright . . ."

Cyril did not dispute this; he had already admitted it, and certainly did not suffer from false modesty. But why was being bright made to seem so much like being crippled? Far from increasing your range of options, it drastically reduced them. The cleverer you were, the more

narrowly specialised would be your job, and the more certain to be
indoors, sitting down, for forty or fifty years. Not very different from
being confined to a wheelchair, when you thought about it.

"Well, we'll see," said Alice, meaninglessly, as befitted the intractabil-
ity of the problem. "Anyway, we'll keep on like this for the time being.
So long as your parents are happy about it. By the way, will they want
you to go on coming here after the holidays are over? Or will I be
coming to your house again?"

"Oh, *here!*" said Cyril emphatically. "Ma hasn't said, but I'm sure
that's what she'd rather. She doesn't really like Greek going on in the
drawing-room, where people might come in and out, you know, and
might think it's funny. Besides, I'd rather come here, much rather. It's
more fun. And I *love* this room . . ." He leaned back in his chair and
glanced round appreciatively. "All these funny things you've got . . .
Would you like a dried octopus? I could bring you one if you liked, and
you could hang it up somewhere."

The lesson had stretched well beyond the allotted hour, as it nearly
always did. Quite often, it ended with an invitation to Cyril to stay for
supper. On this occasion, though, they had to keep an eye on the time
as Cyril was expected home to baby-sit for his small sister while his
parents played bridge next door.

"No, I don't mind," he said, in answer to Alice's sympathetic query.
"I expect I'll let her stay up and play for a bit. She's trying to teach
Tracty the Greek alphabet, you know, and Ma worries about it, even
though she mostly gets it wrong. The only letters she really knows are
gamma and delta, and so now she wants to call our new hamster Gammerdelta; that's what's worrying my mother at the moment. She's
afraid that Sophy's catching the Greek bug from me, though I
wouldn't think myself that calling a hamster Gammerdelta showed a
tremendous leaning towards the classics, would you? It's partly because
of Sophy being a girl, my mother wants to bring her up in a very
Women's Lib sort of way to be interested in technology and things.
That's why they give her tractors and things to play with instead of
dolls, just to prove that girls are exactly the same as boys.

"Mind you, they're a bit illogical, it seems to me, because they never
forced *me* to play with dolls, which I would have thought would have
proved the point just as effectively . . . Hey, look, I've got to go, I'm
going to be late . . . !"

The whole house shook to Cyril's departure, as he sprang from
landing to half-landing almost in single bounds; and Alice waited on

tenterhooks for Miss Dorinda to launch herself into the hallway trembling with not unjustified protestations. One of these days that boy will have the ceiling down, she would point out, and it could well be true. Most of the ceilings had cracks spidering across them already—ever since the Blitz, according to Hetty; the bomb-damage people had gone off and kept saying they were coming back, but they never did. In a manner of speaking she, Hetty, was waiting for them still. No good crying over spilt milk, though, and it seemed to Hetty that the Blitz (here the metaphor began to get a little bit out of hand) was just about as spilt as anything can get, after all this time, didn't Alice agree?

Alice did; but all the same, she must have a word with Cyril before next time. Even if none of the ceilings *did* fall down, Miss Dorinda's would assuredly threaten to do so, and would rival the erratic geyser as a topic of conversation for weeks to come.

The slamming of the front door ended the suspense. All was quiet. Evidently Miss Dorinda wasn't back from her salon yet, and Alice relaxed. No one else would complain. Hetty wouldn't because she always liked the sound, however ear-splitting, of a bit of life around the house. Brian wouldn't, because no pianist ever ventures to complain of any sort of noise, ever, for fear of bringing on his own head an avalanche of tit-for-tat grievances about his practising. And Mary wouldn't complain because—well—she just wouldn't. She had too much to brood over for the house falling about her ears to make much impact on her.

How *was* Mary? Hadn't she been asleep for rather a long time now, even allowing for the sleepless night which had gone before? That is, if she *was* still asleep? Or was she just sitting in her room, moping, as had been her custom for so long? Was she, then, slipping back into her old habits just as if nothing had happened? Had the long night of talk and confidences made no difference for her at all?

Alice felt a little hurt—but also relieved. She had been wondering, on and off during the day, what she would do when Mary reappeared, perhaps desperate for further tête-à-têtes, and she, Alice, too busy to attend to her, maybe with one of the pupils just about to arrive. It would look heartless to give them priority over Mary's desperate need —and yet you couldn't cancel everything on account of someone else's tragedy. Life must go on, as the cliché has it. Though Mary herself seemed to have taken the opposite view—that life *mustn't* go on. It must come to a dead stop.

Well, as it happened, the conflict hadn't arisen. Alice had neither had to cancel any lessons, nor feel guilty about not having done so, for Mary hadn't appeared at all. The party she *had* cancelled, though, much to Brian's puzzlement and displeasure; for of course she had been debarred from giving him the real reason, and her invented excuses sounded feeble in the extreme, as well as there being too many of them. Two excuses are always less convincing than one, but it is difficult to remember this while in the throes of white-lying.

And on top of all this, Christmas was almost upon them. You can cancel a party, though maybe with some difficulty; but nobody can cancel Christmas.

CHAPTER 19

The gaping hollow gouged out of December by Christmas is never easy to fill; but it was made easier on this occasion by the fact that the other members of the household were all away, and Mary and Alice were left alone in the tall echoing house to talk and talk and talk all through the short darkening days and far into the night. In retrospect, it seemed to Alice less like a series of separate conversations than one single one, going on non-stop through blurred, yellowing afternoons as daylight merged into street lights; and then the lights from passing cars swept in procession across the smudgy walls of Alice's little room, flickering from poster to poster, from dried octopus to Jane Austen to motor-bike, like some avant-garde film without story-line, only some vague, inscrutable message about the Human Condition.

Rarely did they put the light on; Mary felt safer in the dark, she said. Not very safe, though. Every so often the discourse would be inter-rupted by a quick indrawn breath as the girl stopped in mid-sentence, tilted her head and listened, as a cat sometimes does when to other ears there is no sound. A creaking stair? A tapping of rain against a win-dow? The murmur of a door half-opening in the draught?

Sometimes Alice would tour the empty house, at Mary's urgent insis-tence, and would return, slightly breathless from all the flights of stairs, with reassuring news of a rattling window-frame; of the geyser softly hiccuping to itself as it sometimes did even when no one was using it. Or perhaps Hengist was prowling around his lonely kitchen, unnerv-ingly tidy and empty of unpremeditated snacks. He got his regular meals, of course, while Hetty was away—Alice saw to that—but he missed the odd remnant of chicken, the unfinished parcel of fish and chips, the half-eaten yoghurt pot left open and unattended on the table —all those things that were such a feature of life when everyone was in residence.

Reassured, temporarily, by these news items, Mary would relax, and the conversation would continue, though rarely from the same point at which it had broken off; and so it was only gradually, bit by bit, that Alice got a coherent picture of how it had been, and of how—in Mary's tortured mind—it still was.

To start with, her name wasn't Mary. Of course it wasn't. She'd seized on the name in a panic, as the most unremarkable name she could at the moment think of, but the trouble was, she just couldn't get used to it. She didn't feel like a Mary; she didn't know how Marys behave, or how they talk. Her real name was Imogen, but actually they'd always called her "Midge," and in a way, that made a good shortening—for Mary, too, didn't Alice think? But in any case, no one would ever call her Midge again, and so what? Yes, her mother was still alive, but finding it all as unendurable as Mary had found it, had fled to someone's hide-away home in Spain, just as Mary—Imogen—Midge— had fled to London. To get away from it all, only of course you couldn't. Or perhaps you could, in Spain—who could tell? They didn't write to each other about anything of that sort, well about anything at all, actually, because how could you? Everything was too awful to write about. Her mother had gone back to her maiden name; she knew that much, and felt vaguely envious because this was an escape-route denied to her.

And Julian? The once beloved brother? Julian had got a life-sentence. Had Alice really not heard this on the news—in the papers—at the time?

"I suppose it must have been happening just when my marriage was breaking up," Alice tried to explain. "I was too occupied with my own troubles. You see . . ."

But the explanation faltered to a stop under the impact of Mary's open-mouthed disbelief. The idea that anyone, anywhere in the world, could have been more concerned with their own problems than with Mary's appalling and much-publicised tragedy, seemed to be an entirely new one to her, and she went on with her confession as if Alice hadn't spoken.

Yes, Julian had got a life-sentence. Well, how could he not? There had been some talk at the trial of diminished responsibility, but nothing had come of it. If that had been the verdict, he would presumably have been sent to Broadmoor instead of the high-security place where he now was. So what? The place where Mary had been imprisoned, in disgrace for ever, would have been unchanged.

Had Mary—Midge—visited her brother in prison? *No!* The girl's voice was high with panic.

"No! No! I can't! I *can't*, Alice! I couldn't bear it! They can't make me! No! No!"

How *did* she feel about her brother, Alice wondered, though she dared not ask. How *do* you feel about someone you have once deeply loved, and who has now done something appalling beyond comprehension? So close they had been once, this brother and sister, through all the long years of their growing up, sharing a happy childhood, enjoying together a secure and loving home.

Had all that closeness, all that love, vanished totally and at once when she learned what he had done?

Mary knew the answer to that one, and suddenly—on December 25, it so happened—she came out with it. Love just isn't relevant, she said, when things are really awful. Love doesn't come into it anymore, one way or the other. It reminded her (she told Alice) of an incident in the school swimming bath, years ago, when she and her best friend, fooling about in the deep end, had somehow lost control—or balance—or something—and found their heads going under, each clutching frantically onto the other for support, somehow pushing one another down and down. She recalled the desperate, mindless struggle to be the one to clamber on top, to be the one to reach the sweet air, pushing the other down regardless.

"The fact that she was my best friend—that I loved her—it simply wasn't *there*. It was something totally irrelevant. The only thing that existed was myself struggling not to drown. She—my best friend—was just a lump of something to get a purchase on.

"That's how it was when I heard about Julian. It wasn't him at all I was thinking about, not for a moment: it was *me!* Me having to be the sister of a murderer—I couldn't bother about him *being* the murderer —it was me being the sister of one that mattered. Like the drowning, though of course that was all over in a couple of minutes, someone dragged us out, and afterwards we were as good friends as ever. But this isn't just for a couple of minutes; this is for *life*. No one is ever going to drag me out of it, I'm caught in it until I die. That's why I can't think about Julian, I can't think about him *at all*, just about me, that's all I can think of. That's what it's done to me. You ask me whether I still love him"—actually Alice hadn't, she wouldn't have dared—"and all I can say is, it isn't relevant anymore. Like I say, love *isn't* relevant once things are really bad. They say love makes the world go round—but it doesn't, you know. Love is a luxury, and you indulge in it when things are OK. As soon as they are bad—*really* bad—there just isn't a place for it anymore—no place where there could be room for it.

"And no, Alice, I don't love my mother anymore either, and she doesn't love me. We can't, it's too awful. We've both had to run away and never see each other again, because we couldn't bear it, neither of us could. The way we couldn't talk, just sat and looked at each other, and I was looking at the Mother of the Monster, and she was looking at the Sister of the Monster.

"No, you don't understand, it was impossible to talk, it really was, there was nothing either of us could say that wasn't even more awful than saying nothing.

" 'Where did I go wrong?' I could see her thinking, as she sat staring at the picture-rail; and she could see me thinking the same thing, because after all, I was the eldest, and perhaps if I'd . . .''

At this point (Alice remembered) she had felt compelled to intervene.

"That's something you must *never* feel, Mary!" she exclaimed. "That you could possibly have been to blame in any way: that it was something you did—or didn't do—that made him . . . well, that made him how he turned out. You were only a child, Mary, only a young teenager, when his character was being formed. It *couldn't* have been your fault. Nor your mother's either, I dare say. These things . . .''

Alice had meant her words as some sort of consolation or reassurance, and so was quite unprepared for the outburst they provoked.

"Oh, God, if only it *was* my fault! If only there was some *reason* why my life should be ruined like this! If only I'd bullied him—tortured him —locked him in dark cupboards—burnt him with lighted matches— told him he would go to hell if he didn't give me his pocket-money . . . ! Told him that masturbation would send him blind . . . that he was adopted from a lunatic asylum! If only *something* awful had happened to him in his childhood! If our father had been an alcoholic . . . our mother a battered wife! Or if he'd been a battered baby . . . !

"If only it *was* someone's fault, so that you could feel it wasn't really him, but merely something done to him—some damage from outside

. . . some awful trauma . . . But there was nothing like that at all, ever. We had a wonderful childhood—love—security—everything that every expert you've ever heard of has extolled in every child-psychology book you've ever read—we had it all.

"And so what is wrong with him is really *him*, and not any damage that he's suffered. Whatever it is is genetic, it has to be; and so now *I* can never marry, never have children. No man will ever let himself even fancy me once he knows who I am. He'll be thinking all the time about my horrible polluted genes, and the horrible polluted children he would get if he let himself care about me . . .

"I came here to start a new life, Alice. To be a new person, called Mary. But I'm *not* a new person, I've just got a new name that I don't even like. All the rest of it is still clinging round me, and it will go on clinging round me for ever. Whatever I do, wherever I go, for the rest of my life. You know what it's like, Alice? It's like that mediaeval punishment for murderers—I read about it once. Instead of hanging the murderer, they would chain the corpse to him, tightly, face to face, and then let him go. To go where he liked, and to do what he liked, but with this horrible rotting corpse fixed against his body, staring into his face with its horrible rotting eyes, bulging with decay and slowly dangling down its cheeks . . . That's what it's like, Alice. That's what I've got to offer to any man who ever falls for me. That's what he'll be taking about with him . . . out to dinner . . . to a film . . . then take it home to bed with him, a rotting corpse, lying there in the bed between us. Once he knows who I am, finds out my real name . . . Oh, Alice, *don't* ever tell anyone! Don't let Brian find out . . . Don't . . . ! Don't . . . !"

That had been the worst day. Or night, rather, for it had been far into the small hours when the confession reached this point. The candles Alice had lit at the beginning of the evening had guttered out and the room was in darkness except for the grey, starless square of the window. The street three storeys below was silent; not a footstep, not a car had passed for a very long time; and when Mary's voice ceased, Alice found herself yet again in the quandary with which she was becoming sickeningly familiar—that of being an ignorant interloper in a world of tragedy quite beyond her experience, and yet finding herself cast in the rôle of confidante and guide. It was like being parachute-dropped without a map into unknown territory, and having one of the natives coming up and asking the way to somewhere.

"I'm a stranger here myself," she felt like saying; but of course that wouldn't do. Through the darkness she could feel Mary's expectancy, her need, her hunger for—well, for what? For advice? For sympathy? For some sort of shock, even? Something to jolt her spirit out of the strait-jacket of fears in which it had become lodged? How about criticism, then? There are few souls so deeply sunk in despair that they don't rouse themselves, at least temporarily, to rebut an unfair accusation.

"Listen, Mary," she began, "Just listen to me. All this carry-on of yours, it's a cop-out. Or whatever the sociological jargon is, you should know, you're the sociology student. Listen to what you've been saying —how it sounds to an outsider. You have this secret to keep, and so you came to London to start a new life; and it's essential to this new life that you shouldn't be recognised— Right? Well, you *haven't* been recognised, have you—but you still haven't started the new life.

"It's all too difficult? OK, so it's all too difficult. But let's analyse this difficulty, pull it apart, and see what it consists of. As I see it, there are two main ingredients: one is the tragedy itself, and the other is keeping it secret. These are two quite separate things, of which the first is given, unalterable—it's happened, and you have no control over it. But the second thing—the secret—that's optional. It's something you've *chosen*, of your own free will, and so you *have* got control over it. I'm not saying it was a wrong choice—it may have been the best one open to you—but all the same, I think you should take another look at it now, and see where it's getting you. I think if you have a secret—if *anyone* has a secret, not just you—I think they should review that secret every now and then, take it out and have a look at it, see what purpose it is still serving. See if the keeping of it hasn't escalated into being half the problem. More than half. This is what I mean about it being a cop-out. You're hiding behind the part of the problem you *can't* alter—the tragedy—and using it as an excuse for not doing anything about the part that you *can*—the secrecy.

"Take *me*, for instance," Alice went on (by now they were well into Boxing Day, almost time to be thinking about breakfast). "Take *me*, and the way you've behaved to me. You spent days and days imagining that I'd somehow arrived here to spy on you; to catch you out, to show you up, to track you down, etcetera. And it was all wasted, because I wasn't. All that happened was that you worked yourself into a state of paranoia—yes, you did, I'm not misusing the word— There you were, prowling around my room at all hours, whenever I wasn't there; mess-ing things about; getting yourself covered in red paint; and all totally unnecessary, because if you'd simply told me in the first place what you were looking for, we could have found it in five minutes. And then there was all that panic when you met my husband—my ex-husband— on the stairs: *he* has to be in the plot, too! Soon, everyone will be, if you don't watch out . . .

"Can't you see what you're doing to yourself? All the while you keep this secret, you're going to be suspecting more and more people of having guessed it; and that's going to make you behave in a peculiar sort of way towards them, the way you did towards me . . . and then they really *will* begin to wonder about you, and to look at you in a suspicious way. The good old vicious circle. You don't need me to tell you that that's the way to turn yourself into a textbook case! Which gives me an idea. Why don't you look at the whole thing as if it *was* a textbook case? Let's assume that you're already qualified, a social worker, and you've been assigned this case of a young woman whose brother has been convicted of some horrible crime. What would you say to her?

"Go and hide yourself in some big city, would you say? Cut yourself off from everyone you ever knew—friends, acquaintances, colleagues, the lot. Make your life among strangers, don't speak to them more than you can help, and if anyone tries to be nice to you, bite their heads off in case they're getting at you in some way. Don't go out anywhere, in case someone in the street recognises you. Don't try to get a job, in case they find out your real name. Don't go anywhere, don't do anything, don't make any friends . . . Is that really what you'd advise? Honestly? And if not, why not?"

This, or roughly this, was the advice Alice remembered herself having given during that curious, out-of-time interlude while everyone else was experiencing Christmas, somewhere, with somebody; and though Mary had cried a lot, had denied a lot, and had indignantly refuted the charge that she'd bitten anyone's head off ever, or been disagreeable to anyone, or behaved oddly in any way, nevertheless her behaviour *did* change, gradually and unobtrusively over the next few days. She ventured out to the shops by daylight; she ate with increasing appetite the meals that Alice cooked for both of them; she would even, now and again, cook a proper meal herself. And when the others came back, weary from the holiday and laden with gifts that they'd now have to find storage space for until next Christmas, when they could give them to somebody else—one by one, as they came back, Mary greeted them with a smile, even with a pleasant word.

And then, at the beginning of January, the startling news burst upon the household:

"Mary's got a job!"

CHAPTER 20

Only a Saturday job, it was true, and only on the till at a local super-market, but all the same it was a big breakthrough. She'd at least gone out in broad daylight and *got* it, in spite of all her fears. She'd faced the ordeal of the interview at which, far from recognising her face from last summer's TV screens, the bored manageress hadn't even looked at her; just gave her a form to fill in with her imaginary name and the discreet omission of her four A-levels and suchlike over-qualifications. The managerial brows had been raised only at the section wherein Mary (after much deliberation) had admitted to O-level maths, on the as-sumption that, on a till, this might be reckoned an asset. She'd experi-enced a moment's panic at those raised brows, which seemed to imply that O-level maths was so singular a qualification as to arouse suspicion as to the applicant's true identity.

But no: all was well. No further questions were asked, and she got the job; the O-level maths must simply have been a surprise; or—as Brian was later to suggest—had maybe raised qualms as to whether this unnervingly egg-headed applicant might prove to have the wits to fid-dle the till. This, he declared, was what they actually meant by the term "Over-qualified."

This was at supper in Hetty's big kitchen. It was a celebration meal of a sort—as nearly as could be managed at such short notice, for it was already well after five when Mary had burst in, pale no longer but rosy with the cold, and actually noisy as she raced up and down the stairs looking for people to tell.

Although only Alice understood just what had been at stake, the whole household was aware that this was something of an event, and

all contributed what they had by them to the makeshift celebration
which Hetty immediately set herself to organise.

Based on spaghetti, of which it was possible to boil enough for a
dozen people in the old iron cooking pot which stood permanently on
the cooker since there was no shelf wide enough to accommodate it—
or, indeed, steady enough to bear its weight—the menu soon gathered
momentum as various ad-hoc contributions, together with a number of
ambitious but not very practical suggestions, poured in. Brian produced a sizeable remnant of Gorgonzola cheese and a couple of cans of
beer. Alice hard-boiled her last three eggs, and collected together the
bits and pieces purchased for the abortive party; also unearthed the
bottle of wine destined for that same non-occasion, while Miss Dorinda, peering into the simmering pot and shaking her head, proceeded
to explain just where it was that you could buy whole-wheat spaghetti;
at the far end of the high street, on the same side as Tesco's.

Hetty meantime had bethought herself of the two tired turkey wings
she'd brought back from her sister-in-law's—a kindly act, because even
though there were now only the two of them for Christmas dinner, the
sister-in-law still stuck to the tradition of a full-size turkey, with trim-
mings, and was thus left stranded with an awesome quantity of cold
remains. So appalling were the dimensions of the Boxing Day carcass
that it would have taken a far harder heart than Hetty's to refuse to
share at least part of the burden; so back the wings had come, to
languish in the freezing compartment of the fridge until this opportune
moment released them. The only problem now was to slice the meat
into thin enough strips as to render them indistinguishable from the
spaghetti with which they were to be blended, as otherwise Miss Dorinda might get upset. As Hetty said, although she wasn't a vegetarian
herself, she did believe in respecting the principles of others; and anyway, it was the least she could do when Miss Dorinda had not only
been so kind as to produce all those dehydrated Healthi-Grow Mushrooms, but had also refrained from uttering a word about Hengist's
stance on the dresser, alongside the bread-bin; from which vantage
point he was supervising the preparations with a golden and expert
eye, alert for any signs of relaxation of supervision over the tastier
morsels. Not spaghetti, of course, nor mushrooms. He had his eye
specially on the turkey, but that, alas, was to prove hopelessly inaccessible on account of the tiresome way Hetty was standing over it, trying to
keep her slicing operations hidden in order to spare Miss Dorinda's
feelings.

It was a joyous occasion, with Alice's bottle of white wine shared out into such tumblers and wine-glasses as could be mustered, and with Mary, for the first time ever, joining eagerly in the communal meal, enjoying the food, and praising Alice's wine. It was a delight to see her flushed and talkative as never before. Brian couldn't keep his eyes off her, Alice noted, as half-way into her second glass of wine she began to recount her adventures of the afternoon:

"And so after the interview, they took me down to the shop, and Mrs. Foulkes—the others call her Peggy, actually, but I don't know if I should, not yet—what do you think? Anyway, she took me down and showed me the list of prices, I've got to learn them by heart, about two hundred of them, though actually Sharon—that's the girl who does it weekdays—Sharon says there's no need, you just look at the prices as you take them out of the basket and clock them up as you go. It's pointless, she says, to try to learn them because they keep changing one day to the next. They only make you do it, she says, just to put you in your place, show you who's boss, kind of thing. It's awfully interesting really, you know . . . quite different from the kinds of things you get in the Business Studies part of the syllabus. Oh, and another thing she said—Sharon, I mean—she said not to worry about getting the money exactly right, no one does, no one can, they're never less than ten pounds out by the end of the day, on any of the tills. They turn a blind eye to it, they have to, with a turnover of thousands and thousands of pounds every day, what can they do? It was a big relief, I must say, because the way Mrs. Foulkes went on, it sounded like you had to make good any discrepancy out of your own pocket. But Sharon says no, it would be ridiculous, your whole pay packet for the whole day would hardly cover it. Still, she says, it pays to be as exact as you can, because if you *can* keep the discrepancy down to say two or three pounds, then you can keep the extra for yourself, up to about ten pounds. Not *exactly* ten pounds, of course, or they'd begin to suspect. Might do, anyway; they don't bother that much most of the time, she says. So I asked her, wasn't that kind of stealing, and she was kind of shocked, as if I'd used a rude word—which I had, of course, when I thought about it; I felt quite ashamed. Oh *no*, she told me, it's not *stealing*, no way, it's perks. It's what keeps us on the job, and they know it. Why else would we do it, for £1.80 an hour? *You'll* get more, of course, she told me, being Saturday, but all the same . . ."

Brian was by now grinning in boundless appreciation of all this—though his delight, Alice suspected, was less at the actual content of

Mary's recital than at the fact that she was talking at all, and with such uncomplicated zest and good-humour. Tossing back the final drops of wine at the bottom of his glass, he sought to enhance the rare and precious mood: "What am I waiting for?" he enquired of the company at large. "Why do I spend the golden hours of my youth slaving over a hot piano? I don't *have* to be a world-famous pianist, no one's twisting my arm, especially not the ten thousand other goons who are right now practising their guts out in order to pip me to the post. Do they have chaps, too, on these tills, Mary, or does it have to be girls?"

For the first time ever, Mary smiled at a sally of Brian's and forbore to snub him.

"Girls, I think," she said. "Well, so far as I could see—in this shop, anyway. I did notice one or two chaps, but they seemed to be more wandering about, up and down the aisles, and being brought cups of tea in the cubby-hole at the back. Supervisors and trainee managers: that sort of thing. *You* know . . ."

"It looks like we've got it made, Mary, love! *I've* got O-level maths too, believe it or not; not to mention A-level. So with you fiddling the till in the front, and me fiddling the books at the back, we'll soon . . ."

"*Brian!*" Miss Dorinda's voice was sharp with outrage. For some minutes now, Alice had watched her tightening her shoulders and sitting more and more stiffly upright, pursing her lips as the discourse plunged to ever-increasing depths of infamy; and Alice was praying that she would not burst out with some painful snub, thus quenching Mary's new-found (and probably still precarious) enthusiasm, and driving her back once again into withdrawal, suspicion and silence. The ethics of the discussion seemed to matter not at all in comparison with the resurgence of life, of hope, in that shattered, broken spirit.

But of course Miss Dorinda didn't know that the spirit across the table from her *had* been shattered and broken. All she had seen these past weeks was a sulky, ill-mannered young person making no visible attempt to find a proper full-time job, sponging off the State—off Miss Dorinda, that is, and the ever-escalating rates she paid for the salon; and now here was the idle, unprincipled young woman all set to sponge off her employer as well. Time she got her come-uppance!

"*Brian!*" she repeated indignantly, though everyone could tell that she was really addressing her remarks to Mary, "How dare you encourage such—such—*wickedness!*" As she chose the word and pronounced it, her glance stabbed across the table to where Mary was still smiling, and with lips already parted for some witty rejoinder—the first ever—to Brian's teasing. "Wickedness!" she said again, in case anyone had failed to hear her the first time. "Cheating . . . Stealing . . . And lying, too!" she spat out, warming to that sense of unassailable power which being in the right brings with it. *"Lying,* I tell you, that's what it is, you can tell your friend Sharon that from me! It's *lies* she's telling you! No one could run a business that way! *Of course* they check the discrepancies, you can take it from me they do. I've run a business for nearly twenty years, and I can assure you that not so much as a ten-penny piece goes missing at the end of the day! Not a ten-penny piece! Even the tips, I make my girls keep an exact record of the tips they get, so I know where I am: who's satisfying the customers and who isn't; all that sort of thing. And let me tell you, they respect me for it, my girls do. I'm strict, but I'm fair. I don't tolerate sloppiness in any form and they know it!"

In the teeth of this onslaught, Brian strove to restore the former bantering exchange—so delightful and so rare—between himself and Mary.

"But listen—from what Mary says, *her* bosses don't allow any sloppiness either; far from it. On the contrary, they seem to have a clear and well-established understanding with the girls that they are permitted to fiddle up to ten pounds a day, but no more. They allow for it in the accounts, I'm sure. It's a way of keeping the wages down and rewarding the brightest girls without incurring howls of wrath from the unions. It's a kind of under-the-counter merit award for the ones bright enough to fiddle the highest rake-off as a result of getting the actual money very nearly right. The ones too stupid to do this will find the whole of their possibly ten pounds mopped up by genuine mistakes and muddle. The management will notice this, you may be sure, and these girls won't get promotion. If you can't even fiddle the till, they'll reckon, then you'll never be much good in management."

He'd hoped to get a laugh; and from three of the company he did; but Miss Dorinda slowly turned a dull red.

"It's very, very wrong of you, Brian," she said. "Encouraging her in crime! That's what it is—*crime!*" Then, turning to Mary, "You'll be a very, very foolish girl, Mary, if you listen to a word he says—or to this Sharon girl either. It's lies, as well as being wicked. You'll get caught at once, I assure you, and then you'll go to prison! Yes, you will! *Prison!*"

Mary's face, bright with laughter only a few moments ago, had grown very still. Now, she burst out:

"I'd *love* to go to prison! I can't think of anything I'd like more! If only *I* was in prison too, it wouldn't seem so . . ."

She broke off. Too late she realised just what she was saying, and clapped her hand over her mouth. She glanced wildly round the table for a moment, meeting Alice's eye in desperate appeal, then lunged to her feet, almost upsetting the chair, which rocked to her departure. "Excuse me," she muttered, and with tears running down her face fled from the room; and once again with sinking hearts—even Miss Dorinda must have felt qualms at the startling effect of her admonitions— they heard the old familiar sound of Mary's feet pattering up the stairs in headlong flight, and the door of her room slamming shut behind her with all the old finality. As Hetty had once colourfully described it, it reminded her of the gates of hell clanging shut behind a scurrying lost soul.

CHAPTER 21

It looked as if they were back to square one. By next morning, however, Mary's panic seemed to have subsided somewhat. Knocking on Alice's door almost before it was light, she was soon seated on the improvised sofa and sipping the hot coffee that Alice had contrived to heat up on the up-ended electric fire—a practice that she had been told by someone sometime (maybe by Rodney himself, in the days when he still told her such things?) was dangerous. Whoever it was had also explained to her what the danger consisted of; but since she could no longer remember the explanation, she did not see why she should any longer heed the warning either; and certainly the practice saved many a long trek down to the basement and back.

"If only you didn't over-react so," she was now admonishing Mary. "No one—except me, of course—had the slightest idea what you were talking about, and so, in effect, they didn't really hear it. People don't, you know, when something is said which conveys nothing to them; it's pretty much as if it hadn't been said. If only, as soon as you realised you'd put your foot in it about prison—if only you'd just given a little laugh and gone on to some other subject, no one would have taken the slightest notice. They'd have vaguely assumed it to be some sort of over-subtle joke that they'd missed the point of: it's always happening in conversations.

"But there's more at stake, Mary, than just this one unlucky episode. It illustrates what I've been saying all along about your policy of keeping the whole thing such a desperate secret. You're going to be having to watch your tongue, day in and day out, for ever on the alert to cover-up for yourself every time you make the tiniest slip in casual conversation. And it's not as if you're any good at it, either, Mary; if you were, it might be different; but in fact you're just plumb rotten. I've told you before—if you're going to keep this wretched secret from everyone for evermore, then you're going to have to learn to be one hell of a lot better at it! *Of course* you're going to make slips now and again, like last night; in fact, you're going to make an awful lot of them if you're really planning to keep it up for the rest of your life, because life is a long time, all sorts of things are bound to happen that might catch you out. Tiny things. Your real name, for instance: one of these days, someone is going to shout 'Imogen!' to somebody across a crowded room, and you're going to jump out of your skin! I can just see it—spilling a glass of red wine down your dress, knocking into the waiter with his tray of canapés as you charge out of the room . . . slamming the front door so hard that a pane of glass falls out . . . Oh, yes, I can see it all!

"And that's just *one* little scenario, which happens to have come into my head at this moment. *Millions* of things are going to happen that we can't possibly think of in advance . . . every day, practically . . . and every time you're going to have to be a bloody good actress. Which you're not. You're bloody hopeless. Why, even *I* could do better! If it was *my* brother, I'd . . ."

She stopped. This could be going too far. Mary was sitting quietly with bent head, both hands clasped tightly round her mug of coffee as if she was warming them on it, though she hardly could be; the little low-ceilinged room was already stiflingly warm from the two-bar fire full on. Did her quiet, almost meek demeanour indicate some measure of acquiescence in Alice's strictures?

"So what *did* happen, Alice?" she asked. "Last night, I mean, after I'd gone? What did they say? . . . What did Brian say . . . ?"

"Brian? He jumped up too, nearly knocking his chair over just like you did! He's a rotten actor, too—that makes two of you! He was all set to rush after you, adding fuel to the general hysteria—but I stopped him. I told him you'd want to be alone—I hope that was right? I don't actually *know* what you want; and I sometimes wonder whether *you* do . . ."

Mary smiled weakly; reached out and helped herself to an Ovaltine rusk which she proceeded to nibble at with a sort of absent-minded intensity reminiscent of one of those hamsters resident in a primary-school classroom.

"What did they *say*, though?" she asked again. "The others, I mean . . . What I said about prison—did it make them suspect anything . . . ? What did they think I meant?"

"I don't think they thought you'd meant anything," said Alice crisply. "Like I've told you—when people have no idea what you're on about, they just give up, they don't bother, why should they? What did they all think, you ask me? They just thought you were being hysterical again, the way you often are. Have been, anyway. No, they didn't say anything much . . . let me see. Oh yes—the ice-pudding someone had brought in—Hetty asked hadn't she better put aside a helping of it for you, and did we think it should go in the freezing-compartment and get too hard, or onto the top shelf and get too melty?

"Oh, and Miss Dorinda started in about the young, the way she does. Not just you, my dear—the Young in general, how lazy they are, how ill-mannered, how undisciplined and inconsiderate. *I* was the one on the carpet, though, not you. Having been a schoolteacher most of my working life, I'm used to being counted vaguely responsible for vaguely everything, but she did rather hammer it in. I tried to get it across to her that I hadn't personally created a million unemployed teenagers, nor deliberately engineered the rising crime rate. Nor had I with my own hands . . ."

She stopped. She had been going to say, "committed each and every one of the three hundred or so murders we get each year," but she stopped just in time.

Or, rather, *not* just in time, for Mary had instantly guessed what the end of the sentence was going to be, and looked up sharply.

"I wish people wouldn't *do* that!" she exclaimed. "I mean, I wish they wouldn't tie themselves in knots right under my nose to avoid saying things that might upset me. That's what everyone was doing, and it was *awful.* It makes things worse, not better. It makes you feel more of a freak than ever. That's partly—well, it's a tiny bit of the reason—why I have to keep it a secret. If people don't know anything, then they don't know what subjects to avoid when they talk to me. They don't know what will upset me, and so they can't . . ."

But *everything* upsets you, Alice felt like protesting. I don't mean just this evening, I mean all the other times, ever since I've been here. How can you expect people to talk to you normally when absolutely anything may send you through the roof? I daren't even talk about the weather half the time in case it reminds you of something that once happened in just that kind of weather! Let me tell you something,

Mary; the surest way to get yourself treated like an outcast is to act like
one. You don't have to look far back in history to see . . .

But the little lecture never got delivered; for just then Mary looked
up, her tear-stained face suddenly bright with a new thought.

"Look," she said, "Alice, would you?—could you?—I mean, there's
something which really *would* be a help, if you'd do it for me. *Would*
you? Do you think you possibly could . . . ?"

By the age of forty, one has learned to resist the temptation to say
yes to this kind of no-holds-barred test of friendship. One has learned
to be mean-spirited, and cautious, ever mindful of the welter of un-
keepable promises and uncontrollable betrayals into which a more
heart-felt response can lead one. "Yes, within reason" is one possible
ploy; but the trouble here is that one person's reason is another person's arrant nonsense; and where can you go from there?

So, "What is it?" Alice asked, wishing she could make the chilly little
question sound less mean and cowardly than it did. She wanted to
sound warm and generous—she *felt* warm and generous—but into
what terrible course of action might she not be precipitating herself,
the nature of the whole problem being so intrinsically dreadful?

But it turned out to be nothing dreadful at all that was being asked
of her—or so it seemed at the time. It was the diary that Mary was
worrying about: her brother's tragic diary, which at the moment lay
hidden in the cardboard box which formed the bottom-left segment of
Alice's improvised sofa. It seemed that Mary wasn't satisfied with this
hiding place. Supposing someone, for some reason, was prying about in
Alice's attic, and should chance to . . .

"But that's nonsense!" Alice was beginning. "Why in the world
would anyone—"

"Oh, *please*, Alice!" Mary interrupted. She had set down her mug
with a little thump, and now clasped her hands beseechingly, the pale
fingers writhing in and out among themselves as if engaged in some
complex competitive game. "I want it out of the house, you see. I'll
never feel safe while it's here, never! So I was wondering—I mean, I
know your marriage is broken up, and all that, but after all, you still
have got your old home—lots of your things are still there—you told
me they were—books and things. And so couldn't you—couldn't you
possibly?—take the box along and pack it away there among all your
other stuff? No one would *dream* of looking for it there. Not the police
or—or anyone. Oh, *please* take it, Alice! Once I know it's somewhere
else—somewhere nothing to do with me . . . where I'll never see it

again . . . Well, I mean, I don't even know the address, do I, and I don't want you to tell me. Oh, *please*, Alice; it would make me feel so much safer! You *could* do it, couldn't you? It wouldn't be impossible?"

Impossible, no. But safe? Safer than here? Ivy was the one in residence now, and what more likely than that she would spend idle, inquisitive hours, now and again, going through Alice's abandoned belongings, impelled by natural curiosity and by equally natural Other-Womanly hope of unearthing something discreditable? Secret bank accounts, perhaps? Records of sexual misdemeanours? Something, anyway, to make a dent in her rival's hitherto unassailable probity. The diary, in this context, would be quite something: a detailed personal account of murder after murder would look like a revelation of misdemeanour beyond Ivy's wildest dreams . . .

It wouldn't happen like this. Of course it wouldn't. In any case, it would be perfectly possible to seal up the package in such a way as to be proof against idle curiosity.

But this wasn't the point, not really. The real point was—why did it matter so much that the diary should remain hidden? Now that the trial was over and done with, the sentence passed, there was nothing the diary could reveal, however horrendous, that could affect the unhappy young man one way or the other.

"No, but don't you see?" cried Mary. "It's not *him*—it's *me!* You see, I lied to the police. I told them there were no diaries, that they'd just been a childhood craze of his, and had all been thrown away long ago. I'd already hidden them, of course, like I told you; I'd already taken them to the Left Luggage place—don't you remember me telling you?"

"Yes—of course I remember. But, Mary—I wanted to ask you at the time, but somehow we didn't get around to it—*why* were you so anxious the police shouldn't see them? Your brother had admitted everything right from the start, you told me, and so there was no doubt that he had—well, that he was guilty of everything they'd accused him of, and so . . ."

Mary shook her head impatiently.

"No, no! I told you—that was *afterwards*. At the time when I hid them, that was while the police were still looking for evidence—*that* was when I lied to them. And if they were to find it out now—that that was what I'd done—suppressing evidence and all that— Oh, I couldn't *bear* it, Alice! It would start the whole thing up again, right from the beginning—you know it would! I couldn't—I *couldn't*—go through it all again . . ."

Fair enough. But, in that case:

"Well, then, Mary, why don't we just get rid of them? Straight away: burn them—shred them—something like that. Get it over with?"

But Mary once again shook her head. Shook it quite hard, as though to loosen from it some obstinate thought that had lodged there and could not be shifted.

"Alice, I'm too frightened! I daren't! I did think of it—but, you know, it's more difficult than you think. They find you out, you know, however clever you think you've been. They rake through the ashes of bonfires—they analyse the paper out of shredders—I've often read about it. Did you see, on *Crime Watch* one time, there was this man they'd managed to catch because of his fingerprints on a bottle at the bottle-bank? A *bottle-bank*, if you please! You wouldn't think anything *could* be more anonymous, would you? It was something to do with he was colour-blind, and this green bottle was in the container meant for brown ones . . . Something like that. Anyway, it shows how danger-ous it is trying to get rid of something. However cunning you are, they're cunninger still. They're trained to be cunning, you see, and you're not, you've had no practice, and so they're always going to be one jump ahead of you . . ."

Was this a fact? At the time of the murder-hunt, maybe. But after-wards? Months and months afterwards, like now?

But Mary would not be reassured. She shook her head obstinately. And then, suddenly, she burst into tears.

"I *can't* throw them away!" she sobbed. "I haven't read them! How can I throw them away without having read them? But I can't read them either—I don't dare—I can't bear to—I don't dare find out what's in them, I don't want to know! I don't want to know *anything*—not anything! It's Catch-22—I can't throw them away, and I can't *not* throw them away!

"Oh, Alice, help me! *Do* something!"

It was only afterwards that it occurred to Alice that in all this discus-sion about the diaries, the question of what Julian himself might have wished had just never been raised. Amid all the turmoil, he had be-come a non-person.

Or perhaps it didn't matter to him anymore, and never would? When he came out of prison, shrunken, brow-beaten, nearly fifty, thirty years away—a thousand years away—from his terrible youth, how could he still care?

Oh, Alice, help me! *Do* something! These were the words ringing in her ears right now. This was the plea to which she must find an answer.

CHAPTER 22

"Well, and so now you *have* read them; you *can* throw them away," said Alice wearily, "If that's what you want to do." Her eyes were sore and aching (as Mary's must be too) after all these hours of deciphering, page after page, notebook after notebook, of hasty, impassioned handwriting. At one point they'd found themselves struggling over their task in semi-darkness, both of them having omitted to switch the light on—or even to notice that daylight was fading as missing lunch slowly merged into missing tea as well.

Twice, Hetty had made her way up the long flights of stairs to enquire if they were all right. So quiet it had been all day, like not a mouse stirring nor even hotting up a bit of something in a pan (not that mice do normally hot things up in pans, but they got Hetty's point). She'd got a pot of tea on the go, as a matter of fact, wouldn't they like to come down and join her, have a bit of a break, like?

No, truly they wouldn't, not just now; and while Alice thanked her for the kind offer, Mary embarked on a hasty and quite unnecessary farrago of lies about what all these miscellaneous papers and newspaper cuttings were all about. Notes for a thesis, she babbled . . . sorting them . . . getting them back in order for the friend she'd borrowed them from, and who was in a hurry to have them back . . . would be calling for them . . . might be here any minute, really; you know, exams and things . . .

Hetty nodded uncomprehendingly, and then remarked on the sad aspect of Alice's sofa with one of its most crucial supports removed, and would they like one of the cardboard boxes from Mr. Singh's room to replace it: crammed up with papers his boxes were too, just like the ones here; Alice would never know the difference, once she'd got it in place. Nor would Mr. Singh know the difference; he wouldn't mind *what* they did, poor man, because it didn't look like he'd ever be coming back, did it? And if he *did* come back—well, that'd mean that his troubles were a bit sorted out, wouldn't it, the Home Office off his back, that sort of thing, he'd be so happy he wouldn't care about a box or two, now would he?

No; and no; and no. With due gratitude, but definite; and then they waited, as politely as possible, for her to go.

The light on this time, they returned to their joint task, Mary's own memories at this point supplementing those recorded by her brother through that last sweet spring on Flittermouse Hill; one of the loveliest springs in living memory, so green was the reviving grass, so lush the hedgerows at the base of the hill; the elders and wayfarer trees bursting into bud, huge pale clusters among the new leaves, already scenting the warm air, but never, now, to burst into flower. For before the spring had burgeoned into summer, the bright air had become heavy with threat, with the thud and jangle of machinery and of huge lorries. And before long, angry, protesting voices were to be heard too, as the hastily-daubed "SAVE FLITTERMOUSE HILL" banners tottered amateurishly against a blue incredible sky where, for just a little longer, the larks would be singing; before their nests, their eggs, their fledglings were mashed into the yellowish slimy ruts being gouged out of the hillside by the giant wheels.

For there had been a protest: of course there had. Mary herself had been on it, she told Alice, for she'd been home for the Easter vacation just then. She and Julian had stood shoulder to shoulder with a few dozen other stalwarts from Medley Green and the surrounding villages; taking turns to link arms and stand defiantly in the path of the bulldozers and other vehicles of destruction, daring the great cumbersome lorries to mow them down.

Of course, the lorries didn't. Of course, the police arrived, and the television cameras, and on the news that evening there was a twenty-second item showing the police breaking up the feeble little concourse, their banners skewed and flapping, and three of them—no, four—being carried away bodily. Julian, Mary explained, was in fact one of these, but happened to be off-camera at the moment, so his pluck—or obstinacy, or whatever—went unrecorded. Later in the evening, after the news, one of the protesters—a lady from the Medley Green Wild Flower Society—was given her say; but, inexperienced as she was in media-presentation, and not knowing that she was to have less than fifty seconds, she filled nearly all of it with a preamble consisting almost entirely of the correct botanical names of various species of wild flower that grow on chalk, and never got to her main point at all. The opposite point of view was presented, far more skilfully, by a town councillor who homed in at once on his two most telling points; the first, and most important one, concerning the number of jobs that would be created by this new development; the second (and in its way almost as important as the job-creation aspect), proving the actual need for such a development. Growing population . . . industrial expansion . . . Medley Green bursting at the seams . . . influx of car-owning commuters . . . overcrowded roads . . . inadequate car-parks . . . need for a large new shopping centre . . . the inalienable right of every human being to a decent home with a garage, and central heating, and double-glazing, and constant hot water . . .

The speech was recorded in the local paper, and Julian had kept the cutting. It was one of the first to be pasted in, and underneath he had written:

They've done it. It's happened. It's happened *now*, in May, just when the elder flowers are beginning, and I've seen the first hover-fly. The man says all that hedge at the foot of the hill is to come down, and of course the ragwort will go with it, and so there will be no cinnabar moths this summer. Nor next, nor for ever. The silver birches are going too, he says—in fact the whole of the copse, including the big oaks with the owls. The barn owls *and* the tawny owls.

I wish the nuclear war would start, then the human race would be gone too. At least the cockroaches would be left, for they are more resistant to radioactivity than any other creature.

May 17th. The same man was there, he's working one of the diggers. He agreed with me, yes, it's a bit of a shame to be cutting down the hawthorns just when they're in bloom—a grand sight, he says, looks like snow-drifts as you come over the hill; but it's the schedule, see, it can't be helped. If we don't keep to the schedule they'll be taking on another contractor, and then where'll we all be?

May 18th. I got up very early this morning, I was at Flittermouse
Hill before sunrise and had to wheel my bike over the ruts looking
for somewhere to lean it. The handlebars were all wet with dawn,
and the great oak I leaned it on was wet too, the bark was slippery
with wet, and I noticed they'd already marked it where the saw-
cuts are to go.

A bit further up, I stood very quietly and watched the rabbits
while it was still grey, the grass, and sort of misty before sunrise.
They are half-way up the hill now, I think the burrows further
down have mostly been destroyed, and they are scurrying around
making new ones higher up, all ready to be destroyed in a week's
time. Or maybe two weeks, depending on the schedule.

What can we do? There must be *something*. The demo was useless. Too feeble. Too few. There must be *something*, though; we
can't just let it happen; we *can't*.

On the way down, I met Mrs. Jakes, and told her about it—
about the rabbits making new burrows. She's one of the women
who were on the demo, and so I assumed she'd sympathise, and
help me try to think what we could do; but she just gave a little
laugh:

"I'm afraid I can't feel sorry for *rabbits!*" she said. "They're
nasty, destructive creatures, you know. They damage the
trees . . ."

Yes, that's what she said: "they damage the trees"; and actually
while she was saying it we could hear the chain-saws in the silver-
birch wood, slicing down trees at the rate of seven an hour. That's
what the foreman told me: seven an hour.

Something must be done; and whatever it is, it must be done by
me. I can see that now. I stood there, and I made a vow: I am
going to fight them. If necessary, to the death; and if necessary,
alone.

May 23rd. This morning, I stood all alone in front of one of the
bulldozers; but of course I was overpowered. No TV cameras this
time, they get bored if they have to spend more than half a morning on this sort of thing, and so there is no record of my solitary
humiliation. Two of the men were laughing as they swung me out
of the way. I raced them down the slope, and got in front again,
and we had a repeat performance.

The third time they'd got a little bunch of police waiting for me, and so that was that.

They didn't put me in a cell, by the way; they let me off with a warning.

A *warning!!!* I would like to have warned *them*, but I couldn't think how.

I shall, though, I shall.

June 2nd. The oaks are down now. I watched the last one as they tore it to pieces, the mighty branches groaning and resisting, but giving in, one by one, in spite of their enormous strength. Each one in turn cracks at last, and bends, and then with a last frightful tearing sound it hangs loose for one juddering moment, and then crashes to the ground, where it lies, waiting to be set upon after the tea-break. The young green leaves don't yet know that they are dead; they go on growing and unfurling themselves on the doomed twigs as if nothing had happened.

Of course, this is the end of the owls. In the early afternoon I saw a pair of tawnys flapping blindly in the sunlight, their nest of owlets somewhere down there among the shrieking saws.

June 3rd. It looks like a battle-field; and of course that's exactly what it is: part of the world-wide battle going on between human beings and every other living thing.

Last week it was the owls. This week it's the bats; the little mouse-eared bats that have hibernated in the chalk caves for thousands upon thousands of years, and who gave the hill its name. Now their caves are to be filled in to strengthen the foundations of the new buildings. There is a Bat Society of some sort, I rang them up, but they didn't think there is anything they could do, someone is on holiday, and anyway mouse-eared bats are not an endangered species. "They'll find somewhere else to settle," the girl consoled me; "Barns—derelict sheds—that sort of thing. They'll be all right."

And perhaps they would have been. At this point in the diary, personal narrative was replaced for several pages by newspaper cuttings.

"THE BATTY BATTLE-LINES ARE DRAWN" was the first and predictable headline, and throughout the article which followed Julian and his little band of supporters were referred to as the "Batty Battalion"—people, that is, campaigning to prevent the bats being poisoned as well as dispersed. The problem, as set out in subsequent articles and correspondence in the local paper, was roughly as follows:

The bats, displaced from their ancestral caves, had indeed sought other homes, many of the females with their babies clinging to them as they flew around scouring the neighbourhood for suitable dwellings—barns, derelict sheds and so on, just as the society had predicted.

But it was in one of these derelict sheds that the trouble had started—a garden shed, as it happened, belonging to an elderly widow. Going into it one evening for the first time in months, to look for a tin of paint she remembered storing there, she was greeted, as she opened the door into the dusty, dusky interior, by "a terrifying noise . . . like a great pair of scissors opening and shutting"—and while still in a state of shock from this fearful sound, "A dreadful creature flew right past my face, I thought it was attacking me, I thought my last hour had come . . . !" The unfortunate lady had had to go to hospital to be treated for shock; and no sooner had the outcry over this died down, than another woman, slightly younger but with bad nerves, had fallen down and broke her arm while fleeing in panic from what she thought was a vampire flying about in her disused garage.

"I thought it was going for my throat!" she explained to the reporter sent to interview her. "These horrible creatures—it shouldn't be allowed!" and went on to say that she was thinking of suing the council for damages. "They should do something!" she demanded, "These evil creatures should be got rid of! We can't go on like this!"

The council was worried; the argument swayed back and forth, and finally went against the bats. The general opinion was summed up by a letter in the local paper at the end of June:

"How anyone can plead for a creature that has already caused serious distress and injury to two helpless old women is beyond my understanding," fulminated the writer. "Does there have to be an actual death before the authorities recognise their duty to get rid of these loathsome and dangerous creatures? How much longer will our old folk have to walk in dread after dusk has fallen, terrified to set foot even in their own gardens . . . ?"

Powerful stuff: the pest-control officer got to work, and a week later Julian himself encountered one of these evil and dangerous creatures dragging itself along the roadside in the moonlight.

Was its wing broken? Or was it dying from the effects of the poison?

I couldn't tell, it was humping itself along in the moonlight, in this terrible tortured way, using its wing as a sort of crutch to drag itself along. So slow—only two or three yards a minute, moving in the direction of Flittermouse Hill: for all the world as if it was seeking its ancient haunts, struggling at this snail's pace to cover the hopeless miles that lay between it and its true home, the place where it would somehow be well again, able to fly again, to swoop, to shout, to feast across the moonlit sky.

I don't think this is all fantasy, I think, actually, it *was* trying to make for Flittermouse Hill, for bats do have a powerful homing instinct, and an unerring sense of direction. It would never get there, of course, long before it had covered the four or five miles it would be dead; but what purposeful effort it was putting into its utterly pointless progress . . . ! Such indomitable will to keep trying, to keep going, no matter how inevitable its doom.

I knew I should have killed it, put it out of its misery—but how? I dared not stamp on it, I was terrified that when I lifted my foot I would find it still alive.

Now, if I'd had a gun . . .

I'm going to get myself one. Must find out how.

And then, a few days later:

Got gun. Will shoot.

CHAPTER 23

But by now it was not just for an injured bat.

"I can't bear the fact that I'm a human being," he wrote.

I can't bear being a member of this monstrous species . . . A few nights ago we had some people in, and after dinner an argument arose about starlings: should they or shouldn't they be allowed to come and feed at the bird-table? "Starlings are vermin," someone said, "Of course you shouldn't feed them." "No they aren't," someone else argued, "Birds can't be vermin"—and so the argument went on—were they or weren't they vermin?

So later, when they'd gone, I looked up "vermin" in the dictionary.

"Old French, vermine. Lat., Vermis, a worm.

"Animals of a noxious or objectionable nature . . . who prey on, or are parasitic on, other species . . . wholesale destroyers of crops and other vegetation."

How perfect, how apt a description of the human race! Vermin! If you looked down from a high enough satellite, you would see them pullulating on every land-mass like maggots on a piece of meat, swarming like locusts through the forests and the grasslands, leaving dust-bowls and deserts in their wake, consuming and destroying and laying waste the food supplies of every other creature.

I've been collecting cuttings about the human vermin and their achievements, which I intend to paste in here some time, but in case I don't get around to it, let me summarise a few of them:

1) In a laboratory in the States they have succeeded in grafting a second head onto a dog. The two-headed creature lived for several days, and they have every hope that the next one will live even longer, though of course more money will be needed for the successful expansion of this line of research.

2) Somewhere in Japan they have a monkey's brain, still alive, as proved by the encephalographic apparatus monitoring it. What the apparatus doesn't monitor, because it can't, is what the brain is experiencing while it waits in vain to die.

3) A Science Correspondent in one of the Qualities writes:

"The good folk who bewail the disappearance of wild life have their heads—to put it kindly—in Cloud Cuckoo Land. The truth is that we live on a shrinking planet, with a human population of five billion—a figure likely to be doubled within less than forty years; there simply isn't room for creatures other than those needed for human food. By the end of the century, or soon after, all large mammals will have to go; and the smaller ones will follow, as well as most species of birds. To put it in practical terms: we just can't afford them; and anyone who thinks we can should be dragged forcibly out of his ivory tower and made to look squarely at the actual facts . . ."

4) [Another quote] "Fish-farms are no longer a novelty or a way-out experiment; they are fast becoming a necessity. Already large areas of the North Sea are so polluted that many of the fish are developing cancer. As the oceans of the world become more and more polluted and less and less able to support life, these farms will become a vital source of essential food . . ."

5) Meanwhile, while the oceans *do* still support quite a lot of fish, we have invented a wonderful new way of depleting them . . . Huge vacuum fishing-domes, the size of St. Paul's, sweeping over the water like a giant Hoover, sucking out of it every living thing, some to be brought ashore and sold, most to be discarded as useless, and left to die. In this new technology for destroying marine life, we in Britain are falling behind, it seems. More money is needed if we are to catch up with our rivals in Europe and elsewhere who are seriously out-distancing us in the destruction of life in the oceans of the world.

Well, that's just a few examples. I began collecting them quite a while back, for a Sixth Form debate on Conservation, but the habit grows on me—the few dozen cuttings I began with have become a few hundred. It's become an obsession, you could say.

I have heard people express the fear that the human race will destroy itself. I am more afraid that it won't.

I have also heard people agonising about how it is that a merciful God can allow earthquakes, floods, shipwrecks, aeroplane crashes etc. . . . . Me, I can't see the problem. A truly merciful God, looking down on the world as it is today, would surely order a cull of human beings, far more extensive than that entailed by the odd earthquake etc.

Well, I'm not God. *I* can't order this cull of human beings, I haven't the power. All the same, I do have the power to get rid of one of them. This very night. They will find me in the morning among the ruins of Flittermouse Hill, with a bullet through my brain. In case they don't know why, I will tell them. It is in order to end my membership of this awful species, and to save those bits of the planet that would have been destroyed to keep me going for the next sixty years or so. Four hundred acres of the earth's surface, they say, has to be covered with concrete to keep one Western citizen at the standard he has come to demand.

This is my last message to the world.

But it wasn't. On Tuesday, July 4th, there was a failed suicide attempt to record. As well as the first murder.

Much of the record was in note form, understandably hasty and incomplete, but not hard to piece together into an approximate account of what had happened.

It was not quite midnight, and the turf still warm from the long, scorching day, when Julian settled himself among the gorse bushes that still stood in untidy, battered clumps alongside the earthworks that were to become one of the new roads. The moon, a little past the first quarter, was just setting beyond the curve of the hill—Julian had planned the timing like this so that he would have some light with which to locate a suitable hide-out, followed by darkness in which to commit the deed.

Everything was ready—the loaded gun, the farewell note that was to be found in his pocket; and the thing that delayed him was something quite unexpected. It was that he couldn't get comfortable. Either he leaned against the gorse, and had to endure the prickles, or else he had to sit up straight, unsupported and ramrod stiff.

Fancy wanting to be *comfortable* when you are just about to die. I
wonder if other suicides have felt this? It's something the same as
taking your last look at things—you want your last sight of the
world to be of something grand and lovely, and in the same way
you want your body's last sensations to be of comfort and peace.
So anyway, I fidgeted about, changing my position—this way, that
way—till at last I got it right. Then I looked up.

Cassiopeia. Perseus. The Great Bear. In five minutes they just
wouldn't be there. Nothing would. At this thought I experienced
such a moment of panic as I don't know how to describe. I had to
wait for it to pass.

The gun felt heavier than I'd remembered, and terribly cold.
They say you should put it in your mouth, but I didn't have the
courage. I don't know why it should need more courage, but it
does, so instead I pointed it to the side of my head, and sat there
nerving myself . . . nerving myself. Other people have done it
. . . *I* can do it . . . just one tiny tug on the trigger . . .

"What the *hell* are you up to . . . ?"

The voice . . . the dark circle of the head sliced into the stars,
and straight away I pulled the trigger.

He died instantly. It seemed the purest chance that it was him
and not me. If he hadn't chanced to be walking on the grass
instead of along the lorry track . . . If *I* hadn't chanced to be
behind this particular clump of gorse rather than another . . . If
I hadn't chanced to take so long arranging myself in a comfortable
position . . . such trivial and arbitrary differences of time and
place, and then it would have been me, not him. So little difference—one man or the other. All random chance . . .

I remember slipping away through the dark bushes, not feeling
anything in particular. Only gradually it came to me what I'd
done. I'm a murderer now, I thought. It was the strangest thing,
though, I felt no guilt, nor even any fear of being caught, which of
course looked like being a near certainty; my footprints must have
been everywhere, and I hadn't the ghost of an alibi. No, what I felt
was an extraordinary exhilaration, such as I've never known before: a sense of enormous worth, of achievement. "I've killed a
man, I've killed a man!" I found I was saying to myself as I walked
down the street next day, as I queued for stamps at the Post
Office. "I've killed a man: *you* haven't, you poor drip; and nor

have you . . . nor you. *I* have—I've killed a man"; and I felt about ten feet tall.

Another thing: it seems to have wiped out completely the shame of being a failed suicide. It has given me such strength; *next* time I shall not dither and hesitate and fail, because now I am a person who *can* inflict death. I wasn't before, but now I am.

July 5th. The hunt is on: TV, newspapers, the lot, but somehow I don't feel it's anything much to do with me.

I'm an outlaw, I've put myself outside the law, and so its workings don't really concern me. I have crossed a frontier, and there is no going back. I find myself in a place of amazing freedom. I can do *anything.*

Sunday July 10th. Blazing hot day. Lying in the gorse, only slightly shaded from the sun, and watching the human vermin pullulating below. They are all over the building sites, screeching, picnicking, dropping trails of litter. When I half-close my eyes, and see through my eyelashes, they look like one of those hospital films of abdominal operations—a huge, shuddering mass of flesh, mindlessly pulsating and executing bizarre and monotonous convolutions. If I took a pot-shot into the middle of the mass, what would be the difference?

Ah, but I need my bullet for myself.

Or is it that I don't dare?

I wish I had more courage. Or more bullets. Or something. It's a cop-out, just shooting myself only, I ought to take a few others with me out of this over-populated world.

And that very night, he did. And the following night too. Though the entries at this point were only barely legible, they left no doubt as to the fearful facts.

Tuesday July 13th.

"THE MONSTER STRIKES AGAIN"

This is today's headline. Well, of course it is. But I ask myself, what are the criteria of monster-hood? In almost any other period throughout the history of mankind, what I've done would pass as perfectly normal. The young human male who aspired to any sort of important status in his tribe would have killed quite a few men by the time he was my age, certainly more than I have. The reason I'm a Monster is not that I've killed three men, but that I've killed them now, in the 20th century.

Who will be the next victim, everyone is asking, and so am I. How do I know until I see him? I knew this last time because he looked so miserable, this one, as he stumped along, glaring at the ground, his face all twisted up with years and years of grievance and bad-temper. I'd noticed him earlier, in the afternoon, jabbing with his thumb at a folded paper and snarling something about the front elevation. Having destroyed Flittermouse Hill and every creature in it, they aren't even going to be happy with their victory. They are planning already to be miserable and discontented.

I sat near his body for a long time, waiting for it to be found, and as the beginnings of dawn shimmered over his dead face, I saw with my own eyes the vastness of the peace I had created, the sudden gentleness. The grievances, the anxiety, the ill-temper, all were gone, and as the sun rose he lay with his blood soaking into the short grass, a sacrifice to the Powers of Earth, which of course are the worms and the soil-bacteria on whom the rest of life depends, and to whom these trickles of blood are a rare and wondrous feast. This is the first good, creative thing that this fat and pallid body has ever done: sacrificed at sunrise as so many of our ancestors—his and mine—must have been sacrificed likewise, on this very hill.

There followed a quotation from some author; Alice promised to try and track him—or her—down:

"Killing is an act of creation . . . Why is it a crime to kill? . . . It is, on the contrary, a law of nature . . . killing is a law thrust by nature into the very profoundest impulse of our being . . ."

The diarist adds a rider:

I don't know if this author *had* actually killed anyone, but he's certainly got it right. It's nothing to do with any "Lust to kill," it's the exercise of an ancient and deeply-implanted skill; one that has lain dormant all one's life, but is suddenly in perfect working order the moment occasion for its use arises. I would imagine that this is how a woman must feel having her first baby—the hitherto unused muscles of her womb suddenly springing into powerful and totally efficient action, with no practice, no previous training.

That's the way it feels. It's *easy*. That's the amazing thing.

But a few days later, a different note was struck:

July 17th. I feel shaken this morning, in fact a bit shattered, for last night it all went wrong. I fired from too far away, I think, and instead of being killed at once, he was injured. I hadn't meant that at all. I ran up to him. "I'm sorry . . . I'm sorry!" I told him, "I didn't mean to hurt you, I only meant to kill you!" I tried to help him, for lying there he looked like any other living creature in distress. But I couldn't do anything. I just got myself covered in blood, and so I ran away and phoned a hospital. Anonymously, of course, I don't want to put myself into their hands, just like that. Not yet, anyway.

It's amazing, really, that they haven't caught me by now, and I can't help feeling that my indifference to whether I get caught or not must have something to do with it. For a murderer, my behaviour must be very un-typical, and this may be putting them off their stroke.

One or two more, and then it'll be my turn. I'm glad I decided on that second gun when I had the chance; now, if something goes wrong, I'll still be able to finish myself off. I have the courage for it now, I know I have. In fact, it will hardly need courage, for I have become familiar with death, he has become an old friend.

Just before they come for me, I will do it. The rush of adrenaline will help me, as I see them closing in.

It didn't, though. They closed in too suddenly, perhaps; or the rush of adrenaline came too late. Or something.

Anyway, they got him. They took him alive, which he had sworn they should never do.

CHAPTER 24

Alice's words hung in the quiet room unanswered. "Do you want to throw it away?" she'd asked.

It was after midnight. She was exhausted—and so must Mary be after their day-long journey into tragedy. Had she made a mistake in more or less forcing Mary to sit down and read the diary with her? It was bound to upset her—to re-awaken all the dreadful memories—but was it not better, in the long run, to face everything that had to be faced, and then begin putting it behind you, rather than have it for ever hanging over you?

"Or shall we keep it?" she continued.

Mary still did not speak, but sat, head in hands; her mouth pulled into a thin, down-turned line, like an old woman by the pressure of her tense palms. Alice felt obliged to go on talking, to hold at bay, somehow, the terrible silence which threatened to become irreversible.

"The way it seems to me," she hazarded, not even knowing yet how she was going to finish the sentence; "The way one *could* look at it, I mean—well, in *some* ways hasn't reading it made you feel a bit better? I mean, obviously these were dreadful crimes, no one is going to argue with that—but at least he imagined he had a *purpose* . . . in his own eyes, he was doing it *for* something . . . fighting single-handed for a *cause* . . ."

At this last word, Mary's head jerked up, her eyes sharp with the feverish glitter of exhaustion as well as panic.

"*A cause* . . . ! But that's the worst thing of all, the lawyers said! All the time, preparing for the trial—they were insistent that the whole question of Julian working for a cause must be kept strictly out of it.

Juries have no sympathy for causes, they told us. They are likely to view a crime committed for a cause in a much worse light than the same crime committed for money, or revenge, or some other sort of personal gain. And anyway, they told us, the judge would disallow it. He would instruct the jury that the rights or wrongs of any cause whatsoever were outside their terms of reference; it was their duty to decide only two things: first, were they satisfied that the alleged crimes had been committed; and second, were they satisfied beyond reasonable doubt that it was the defendant who'd committed them. And of course it *was* beyond reasonable doubt. Julian never made the slightest effort to deny any of it."

"No, well, he wouldn't, would he?" Alice pointed out. "It's obvious from the diary that he *wanted* the world to know what he'd done and why he'd done it. He felt that he was striking a blow—making a huge, unforgettable gesture on behalf of—well, of life on earth. That's what he felt he was doing, and he wanted the world to know it. He didn't know, I imagine, all this about judges disallowing discussion of principles, of ethical fors and againsts, in court. Besides, he never expected to *be* in court, did he? He planned to finish himself off before it came to that. He says so—over and over again—and my reading of it is that he truly and honestly meant it. Not all suicides do; but I'm sure he did."

"Oh, yes. I'm sure too. He even talked of it to me—long before all this. When we first heard that they were going to build on Flittermouse Hill—that's when it was. He felt *awful* about it—I knew he did, though I suppose I didn't quite realise *how* awful. Well, I felt awful too, but of course it wasn't quite the same for me. I'd already left home, you see, I was at college by then, my life had already moved on to somewhere else, if you know what I mean, while his hadn't. He was still there, still at school, still living at home, right in the thick of it. I didn't realise— well, I did, but I didn't see what I could do about it; except go with him on those demos and things, whenever I was home; and a bloody lot of use *that* was!"

She paused, reached out absently for one of the biscuits which had been virtually their sole sustenance during the day.

"And another thing, Alice, which would have gone against him— the fact that it was not only a cause, but a cause that concerned animals. *You* know—the idea of valuing animal life above human life. It gives people the shudders."

"Oh—I don't know," Alice was beginning, thinking about this being a nation of animal-lovers; but Mary interrupted.

"It *is* so, Alice," she insisted. "It really is. You know how horrified everyone is if a motorist swerves to avoid a dog and hits a pedestrian? There's a national outcry. Whereas if he's swerved to avoid a sack of potatoes and had exactly the same accident, no one would have said a word; it would just have been an unlucky accident. And that time two or three years ago—do you remember?—when a man drowned trying to rescue his dog from a rough sea, and a policeman got drowned too trying to save him? It was a scandal for days—endangering human life for the sake of a *dog*. Whereas if exactly the same tragedy had occurred as a result of him swimming out after a lilo, there'd have been no fuss at all. It would have been just one more unfortunate bathing fatality. It was because it was a *dog*—an *animal*—that's what caused the moral outrage.

"It's true, Alice. People *do* feel this horror. And on top of all this his cause, as you call it—Nature, and animals and things—it could only have been harmed. A woman I know from the Animal Guardian Group said it would set the cause back a hundred years if it ever became known *why* Julian had run amok like that. I assure you, Alice— I've lived with all this awfulness for long enough to know this for certain—I can assure you, it's better to kill for sheer wickedness than for the sake of an animal. People feel like that. They just do."

"And do *you* feel like that?" Alice had hesitated for several seconds before putting the question; and straight away it was clear that she had said the wrong thing.

"It's not *fair!* It's not *fair!*" Mary cried. "Why should you expect me to feel differently from the way other people feel? I don't *want* to feel differently! I want to be *ordinary!* I want to feel the way other people feel, I want to think the way other people think. I want to think ordinary thoughts; and so would you if you'd been through what I've been through!

"Oh, Alice, it's not my *thing!* I've been dragged into it, it's like being hi-jacked in mistake for someone else . . . it's not *fair!*

"Sometimes, Alice, I envy him, I really do. I envy all these dreadful criminals because they actually did commit their crimes, themselves; it's in their nature to do whatever they did, they're kind of all of a piece with it. And I'm *not*. How can I be? It's not in my nature to be the sister of a murderer, I wasn't born for it, it's something I don't know how to be, something I *can't* be, it's impossible . . ."

By this time her voice was almost lost in gusts of exhausted weeping, and the single desperate plea was all that Alice could distinguish amid the uncontrollable sobs:

"I want to be *ordinary!* All I want is to be *ordinary!* Surely that's not much to ask . . ."

Actually, it is a lot to ask. Too weary to follow up this thought, Alice summoned up all her remaining energies for the task of persuading Mary to go to bed. Tomorrow—today, rather, for it was long after midnight—would be Saturday, the first day of the new job in the supermarket . . . and as this fact crossed her mind Alice knew, with absolute certainty, that Mary must be made to go to it, no matter what she was feeling like. It was a watershed, on the other side of which might surely lie the new life she had been so hopelessly seeking all this time. No way must she be allowed to oversleep, to lie in bed till it was too late to go, sobbing I can't, I won't and what's the point, my life is in ruins . . .

And so, heartless though it seemed at such a juncture, Alice reached out both hands and yanked Mary to her feet, tears and all.

"Come along. Pull yourself together"—the one phrase you must *never* use, all the books say so, as Mary would well know; which would make the shock of hearing it all the more salutary— "Come on, it's nearly two and you've got to be out of the house by eight—and properly dressed, too, looking your best, and how do you think you're going to do that if you go on crying all night? Let alone getting the money right in the till. Never mind that discrepancy of ten pounds, you'll be getting a discrepancy of hundreds if you don't get any sleep.

"Listen. You said just now you wanted to be ordinary. So, OK, *be* ordinary; an ordinary working girl off to an ordinary job at which she's ordinarily efficient and picks up an ordinary pay-packet at the end of the day. A girl who *looks* ordinary, too, not one with red eyes and a swollen face and can't stop sniffing . . . Now, get *on!* Out of that door, down those stairs, and into bed. I'll bring you a hot drink in ten minutes, and then that's got to be the last we hear of you until the alarm goes in the morning. Here you are—I've set it for seven, and if I don't hear you moving around by seven-fifteen, I'll come and drag you out of bed. Right?

"*Out*, then. Don't just sit there. Make yourself scarce. Which is Oldspeak for 'sod off,' in case you haven't come across it before!"

CHAPTER 25

The effect seemed to be little short of miraculous. Well before eight, Mary must have been up and away, or so Alice concluded, glancing into the room on her way downstairs. She had made the bed, too, and flung the window open at the bottom before leaving. Both good signs, though the latter was admitting so icy a blast of damp January air that Alice could not refrain from closing it. A pity: Mary's flinging of it open onto the wild, windy outdoors, after all these weeks of cowering away from everything, seemed to indicate a wonderful lifting of the spirit, a revival of confidence and hope.

Of course, this had been almost bound to happen, sooner or later. The living mind, just like the living body, is resilient beyond the wit of man to comprehend. Just as an injured body will instantly set about mobilising all the appropriate mechanisms of repair and healing, so also will the mind. Nor do these processes of repair demand any particular co-operation on the part of the sufferer. Without encouragement of any sort, a burned area of skin will form for itself a blister, beneath the shelter of which new skin can regenerate. It will do this whether the victim wants it to or not; whether he is conscious, unconscious, happy, unhappy, crossed in love, on top of the world, sunk in apathy, intending to die—his body will go on quietly doing its job regardless. So, likewise, will the mind. However great the trauma, however terrible the shock, or however hopeless the situation, the mind will very soon set in motion the forces of recovery. Even during the period of apparently total despair, the process will already have begun, far below the level of awareness, and the final breakthrough may take the sufferer himself quite by surprise.

Was this what was happening to Mary? Had she now reached the point when the forces of mental health were taking over, willy-nilly, regardless of the intractable nature of the dreadful facts? More hopeful about the girl than she had been for some time, Alice continued on her way down to the kitchen to make herself some toast and a cup of coffee.

Miss Dorinda was there already, just finishing her bowl of reinforced low-fat peanut crunchies, and full of complaints which (though she didn't say so) filled Alice with optimism. *That girl*, declared Miss Dorinda, had not only been washing her hair before seven in the morning —all that noise from the pipes, bath-mat soaked, and you should just *see* the basin!—but had been down here in the kitchen frying sausages. Sausages, if you please, the smell all over the house, at twenty-five past seven.

"Twenty-five past seven!" she repeated, thinking Alice couldn't have heard her, so casual was her response. For "Oh," was all she'd said, and had proceeded to switch on the toaster just as if nothing had happened.

"Twenty-five past seven! That's not her time, that's my time! My time is quarter past seven till quarter to eight, it's been my time for years, it was agreed right from the start! And if that girl thinks she can get away with defying the house rules . . ."

"I don't think she's defying anything," suggested Alice placatingly. "I don't think she knows anything about the breakfast times here. Until now, she's never been down at this sort of hour, has she, she doesn't come out of her room till . . ."

"You're telling me! I don't know what the young are coming to, I really don't. And that Brian, too, he's never up until goodness knows what hour either. What they'll do when us old ones are all gone, and no longer working ourselves into the ground to pay for their free this and thats, their social security, and their unemployment hand-outs . . . They'll soon find—"

"Well, at least she's got herself a job *now,"* Alice interposed hastily; "Mary, I mean; she's starting today—don't you remember? On the till at Brandgoods. She'll just about be there by now. And as to Brian— he's a musician, you know. A lot of the time he has to be working at home . . . practising . . . going through things for his pupils . . ."

"Well, and isn't that just what I'm saying?" snapped Miss Dorinda. "A musician . . . !" and it was clear from her tone that in her scheme of things being a musician was just one more way of being unemployed, and a singularly tiresome one at that, insofar as it involved keeping other people awake after 10:00 P.M.

" 'Early to bed and early to rise'—that was my mother's motto," Miss Dorinda finished complacently, laying down her spoon and dabbing at her lips with a tissue; and Alice forbore to point out that Mary's one and only attempt to live by this worthy maxim seemed to have caused nothing but trouble.

On and off during the day, Alice's thoughts turned anxiously to Mary, struggling with all that money and the intricacies of the unfamiliar till. How was she getting on? Were they telling her off a lot? Or upsetting her in some other, perfectly innocent, way, by asking friendly questions about her home and family? Once again, Alice found herself querying the wisdom of Mary's policy of impenetrable secrecy as a technique for minimising her troubles. For a technique it was, one of the many techniques the mind employs for self-healing; a method of protecting the injury from further assault while it slowly mends. Looked at this way, all this secrecy was Mary's life-support system, the healing method of choice for her traumatised spirit, as necessary as a bandage on an open wound, or plaster round a broken bone.

Still, life-support systems shouldn't be kept switched on for ever; sooner or later, the patient must start breathing on his own. Hadn't this time arrived for Mary? Shouldn't she start being Imogen again—or Midge—and let the truth be known? Brazen it out—let the whole thing be a nine days' wonder, after which it would gradually subside as everyone got tired of it, as they surely would?

It crossed Alice's mind to take a trip down to Brandgoods, at the far end of the high street, and have a peep at Mary while she worked; but she decided against it. With Mary's rooted terror of being spied on, checked up on, such a visit might reactivate all sorts of irrational suspicions. Also, on a more practical level, it might simply distract her from her task—get her pressing the wrong knobs, ringing up too many noughts and find herself charging £2,800 for a £2.80 pair of gloves. Or whatever it was that one was liable to do wrong on those machines— Alice was rather vague about it. For all she knew, some small slip not much different from a typing error might cost the firm hundreds of thousands of pounds.

In any case, it being Saturday, she herself was more than usually busy —Cyril in the morning, and no doubt he would stay for lunch, and the postman, Mr. Bates, in the afternoon, with his carefully prepared homework. Alice had given up for the time being the attempt to teach

him any grammar; she contented herself with preparing lists of all the
nouns, adjectives and verbs he would encounter in a given portion of
text, encouraging him to learn them, and sharing his delight when he
recognised them as they turned up. His other delight lay in criticising
Euripides for his handling of the plot. On this particular afternoon,
they were tackling Admetus's long speech about the difficulty he'd
encountered in trying to persuade other people to go down to Hades in
his stead; the dubious ethics therein displayed really got Mr. Bates on
the raw. For a wife to volunteer to die for the sake of a husband, that
was all fine and dandy, but it was a bit off for the husband to *expect* her
to do so, didn't Alice agree. And then dragging the poor old father
into it, too, expecting *him* to trot off down to Hades at the drop of a
hat! Mr. Bates was tickled pink when they came to the bit where the
old boy put his foot down good and proper, and quite right too! Put
Admetus in his place, after all that back-answering; "I'd like to've seen
what *my* Dad would've said if I'd even . . ."

And at that point, the telephone rang.

Now, it so happened that it was the custom at Number 17 Beckford
Road—indeed it had acquired almost the status of an unwritten law—
that everyone should wait for someone else to be the one to run up (or
down) the long flights of stairs to answer the phone; to be the one to
scrabble in the semi-darkness for a pencil with a point, with which
laboriously to transcribe the message for somebody else, with its characteristic content of unspellable names and long, out-of-town numbers.

The ringing went on and on. It was a question of who cracked first;
and on this occasion (as commonly happened) it was Alice. On the
eighth ring, with a hasty apology to her pupil, she hurried down into
the hall.

It was a male voice, and one strange to her.

"Good evening; could I speak to Imogen, please?" it enquired with
easy confidence; and for a moment Alice was completely thrown. Imogen—the name that Mary was keeping a total secret. The name by
which she was never to be known again. I'm sorry, you've got a wrong
number, Alice should have said, and should have said it instantly. By
the time she had collected her wits enough actually to say it, an awkward little pause had intervened, indicating a measure of uncertainty;
enough, anyway, for the caller to feel it worth while to argue the toss:

"Imogen," he repeated. "Imogen Gray. I understand she is residing
at that address—17 Beckford . . ."

"No . . . No . . . !" cried Alice—and was she, this time, rushing in *too* fast, suspiciously over-emphatic?—"No . . . No one of that name . . . No, not living here . . . No, we've never heard of her"— and she slammed the receiver down before she could be embroiled in further bouts of incompetent and ill-rehearsed lying.

Sitting down once more alongside her expectantly waiting pupil, she was dismayed to find herself trembling from head to foot. It was impossible to concentrate. Admetus's moral dilemma concerning life or death for himself and/or his wife seemed both feeble and contrived when compared with Alice's own moral dilemma—to tell Mary, or not to tell her, about this disconcerting phone call? To tell her would inevitably fling her right back into the state of obsessional distrust and terror out of which—or so it had seemed to Alice this morning—she was just beginning to emerge; *not* to tell her, on the other hand, would be outright deception, almost amounting to betrayal. Supposing something awful happened as a result of her failure to warn the girl of . . .

Well, of what? Of the possibility that someone from her past had tracked her down, was on her trail, was bent on exposing her? Inevitably Mary herself would see it in these terms—but did Alice have to? *She* wasn't the one in the grip of an obsession; she was able to look at the thing from outside, rationally, and from this vantage point she could already see the whole episode as probably quite trivial and entailing no dire consequences of any kind. After all, she had told the caller, quite decisively, that this Imogen Gray did not live here—why should he disbelieve her? The fact that someone from her former life was trying to get in touch with her was neither surprising nor sinister, and on being told that he'd got the wrong address, he would surely try elsewhere, or else give up altogether? Anyone would.

But, on the other hand, there was just the possibility that . . .

"Oy, listen to this!" Mr. Bates was saying, and he proceeded to read from the translation of Alcestis's dying words, as Death comes to fetch her away.

" 'His hand in mine, he leads me down to the House of the Dead . . . He has wings . . . his eyes are dark under his frowning brows . . .' "

He read the passage with great feeling, before subjecting it to comparison with his dad's last words, which, it so happened, concerned the lid of a biscuit-tin that someone hadn't replaced properly. "Air-tight! . . . Gotta be air-tight," he'd said, quite loudly, before closing his eyes for ever, and like Alcestis, seeing no more the sun nor the light of the day.

CHAPTER 26

The moral dilemma was solved, after a fashion, by Mary herself. In such good spirits did she arrive home after her first day's work that one would have to have been an outright sadist to confront her with a piece of news that could not fail to wreck her evening. Alice had never before seen her so full of fun and chatter; she had only to report that telephone call and she never would again.

They were in the kitchen, just the two of them, Hetty having gone to the pictures, and Miss Dorinda having gone to bed early with one of her headaches—a mild one so far, but poised to get worse should Brian start playing the piano; which he didn't, as it happened, but all the same, he might have, and that is quite distressing enough, as anyone nursing a headache will tell you.

And so by nine o'clock Alice and Mary were sitting companionably, one on each side of the big scrubbed table, finishing off the free hamburgers which (Mary had been assured) were legitimate perks for the Saturday staff, together with two tomatoes out of the fridge which didn't seem to belong to anybody.

"You know something, Alice?" Mary was saying. "It's like you told me; I'm beginning to see it now, and I really am getting—you know—not so neurotic about everything. Trying, anyway. You know what I do? Every time something starts to upset me—you know, someone looking at me, or something—I take a big breath, and I ask myself: 'What would Alice say?'"

"And what would I?" Alice asked, amused, and not sure whether to be flattered by this implication that her opinions were as predictable as all this.

"*Oh*—you would say that wonderful thing about other people not being interested in me—not *at all*. After feeling all this time that everyone's watching me, and perhaps recognising me— Oh, it was like a blood-transfusion to hear you saying that they weren't even interested! I couldn't quite believe it, but all the same it was wonderful just to *hear* it, to feel like a nobody at last! You've no idea what a help that is. I keep saying it to myself, whenever something happens that spooks me . . ."

Alice laughed.

"And what *are* the things that 'spook' you?" she asked. "Remember, I'm one of the oldies, and a schoolteacher at that, so my vocabulary only stretches *that* far"—she held up thumb and forefinger a fraction of an inch apart—"so I don't know what the verb 'to spook' really means. Give me some examples."

"Oh. Well . . ." Mary's face became grave, and she slowly wiped a piece of bread round and round her plate to catch the last scraps of meaty flavour before popping it into her mouth. "Well, the kind of thing I mean . . . well, like Hilda, she's the girl on the till just across from me; she's nice, she helped me when my drawer got wedged, I'd shut it too hard, or something. Well, anyway, while we were queuing up for our tea-break, she asked me quite casually, 'Have you any brothers or sisters?'—and Alice, honestly, I thought I was going to faint! Everything went black, I had to clutch onto the rail: and then out of the blackness I seemed to hear your voice inside my head: 'Don't be silly, Midge,'—wasn't that funny, you were calling me 'Midge,' not Mary— 'Don't be silly,' you said, 'she's not the least bit interested really, she's just making conversation, just being friendly.' And of course she was. The blackness cleared away, and I found that I could answer her in an ordinary casual way. Wasn't that good?"

"Yes, very good." Alice paused. "And what did you answer?"

Mary gave her a quick, sidelong look. "Oh, I said no, I hadn't, I was an only child . . ."

"I see." Alice began collecting up the plates, experiencing a sharp little pang of disappointment. Couldn't Mary have admitted at least to *having* a brother—surely an innocuous admission by any standards?

Still, it was a start. At least she hadn't told her companion to mind her own business.

"And then after lunch," Mary was continuing, "I got another scare —a worse one really, but just listen how sensible I was about it! There was this man, you see, who kept eyeing me. I'd noticed him before lunch too—he was standing just inside the door, and every time I looked up from what I was doing, there he was, looking right at me. A middle-aged sort of man, rather tall—that's why I noticed him, I think, he stood out among the rest of them, and he had one of those lined faces that looked more lined than they ought to be, if you know what I mean. Anyway, when I saw him again in the afternoon, that was really scary. We were fairly quiet just then, and I could see him edging nearer —I tried not to look, of course, but my hands were shaking, I was dropping the money, the customers were having to help me—they do, you know, they're awfully nice, some of them. I was terrified, you see, that he was going to *say* something when he got close up—and, oh, Alice, he did! He said, 'Well, well, my dear, I do believe I've seen that pretty face before, haven't I?' You can imagine how I felt! You ask me what 'spooked' means—well *that's* what it means, the way I felt that minute! I felt like screaming, and dropping everything and rushing out of the shop, leaving the till open with hundreds of pounds up for grabs! But I didn't. I *made* myself stand still and look unconcerned, and I *made* myself think the ordinary sensible thoughts that an ordinary sensible girl *would* think. Calm down, I said to myself, he's only making a pass, he probably tries it on with all the girls, what's so special about you? And it worked—I really did feel that I wasn't special, it was a real good feeling. I couldn't think what to say, though, so I just giggled a bit and looked away: Hilda says you should never do that—not unless you really do fancy them, of course—you should look them in the eye, she says, and slap them down good and proper when they start getting fresh. Else, she says, you'll find them waiting outside when you finish, and then it's a job to get rid of them, they can turn really nasty, she says . . ."

And actually, Mary continued, he *was* waiting outside at the end of the afternoon. She saw him standing at the extreme edge of the pavement, a cigarette burning down to nearly nothing between his fingers; but he didn't turn nasty. Didn't even look at her as she came out, let alone speak to her, and so she concluded he'd picked up another girl on one of the other tills, and was anticipating better luck with her . . .

"And you know, Alice, I think I'm pretty good at the job," she boasted; "I did pretty well with the money—I *think* I did. We don't count it ourselves at the end of the day, I thought we would, but Mr. Wayland comes round and takes it all, he tips it into a large bag, and they work it out at the back somehow. But anyway, I think it must have been all right, because they want me to come in again on Monday, because someone's off sick. And probably Tuesday and Wednesday as well. They wouldn't have done that, would they, if my money hadn't been *fairly* all right?"

Indeed they wouldn't, Alice agreed; though privately she did wonder whether they could actually have checked the money as quickly as all that. Was the day of reckoning still to come? She hoped not. To have succeeded at *anything,* even at a relatively unskilled job like this, would do wonders for Mary's morale.

"Good night, Midge," she found herself saying when they parted on the landing later on that evening; and Mary, though startled by the name, was unmistakably pleased.

"But don't do it when anyone else is around, will you!" she urged, glancing nervously up and down the stairs. "Not anyone! Ever!"

And Alice promised. Well, it seemed easy, as promises go.

It must have been nearly an hour later—well after eleven o'clock— when the phone sounded up and down the echoing stairs and landings, and this time Alice overrode the usual custom and went racing down the three flights to the ground floor, fearful lest Mary should get there first. This time, she knew what she was going to say to this tiresome and nerve-racking intruder. *This* time, *she* was going to ask the questions. Would you kindly tell me who is speaking, please? Do you realise what the time is? Will you explain why you are continuing to harass us when you have already been clearly told that we have no one of that name here?

She had embarked on more than one of these prerehearsed put-downs before she realised that the male voice she had at first not recognised was in fact Rodney's; so startled had he been by the freezing reception of his call that his usually precise and confident voice had collapsed into bewilderment and hesitancy.

"For goodness' sake . . . What on earth . . . ?" he protested; and it was not until he reached the word "earth" that she gathered who it was that was speaking.

"Oh . . . Oh, I'm sorry . . . !" she apologised, and could have kicked herself for putting him so effortlessly in the right before the argument, whatever it might be, had even begun. "I'm sorry," she repeated lamely. "I thought you were someone else."

"The lucky fellow!" he commented dryly—she seemed to be handing him on a plate all the best lines. "The lucky fellow, give him my best condolences, won't you, if he ever speaks to you again! Now, listen. What I was *going* to say—and if you're planning to bite my head off, at least wait until I've said it—I—we, that is—we'd be awfully pleased if you'd come round for a meal one evening? Long-time-no-see, and all that?"

Why did he have to change it to "we," spoiling everything? Why couldn't he have left it *"I* would be awfully pleased . . ."? What harm would it have done him?

And anyway, what was it all in aid of? Long-time-no-see was in no way a sufficient explanation. No, it was something Ivy wanted . . . or didn't want? . . . Let's guess . . .

"You want to talk about the house," she hazarded. "You and Ivy are moving."

From his sharp intake of breath, she knew she had hit the bull's-eye.

"How . . . how did you know?" he asked, baffled, as men so often are by a woman's capacity to reach a correct conclusion without reference to the relevant data. "Who told you?"

No one had; she'd guessed; but it would be more fun to let him—or, rather, to let Ivy—imagine that she, Alice, had access to some sort of information unknown to them. It would make Ivy feel nervous about all their mutual acquaintances, wondering which one it was. She would feel under scrutiny. Rodney wouldn't, of course; he wasn't a man to bother about being under scrutiny—well, the Rodney she knew wasn't. Had he changed?

"And so you see," Rodney went on, bypassing the mystery—and Alice could exactly picture the slight humping of his left shoulder with which he was accustomed to brush aside the incomprehensible—"You see, it's your *things,* Alice. I know you said you didn't want them, but the thing is, *we* don't want them either . . . Ivy doesn't. We're trying to get sorted out for the move, and she doesn't know what to do with them. She can't exactly throw them away, you see, and so . . ."

How do you *exactly* throw things away? Is it the opposite of throwing them away *inexactly?* Not aiming quite straight when you toss them towards the dustbin or the paper-salvage or whatever? For a moment, she indulged in a vision of Ivy doing just this—anxiously aiming object after object towards some receptacle, and failing miserably every time.

"So we wondered—Ivy wondered—if you could come round and go through them a bit? Your papers, you know, and all those wads of typed stuff, and all those half-finished bits of knitting? We don't mind storing *some* of it for you, if it could all be packed up somehow, but at the moment . . ."

This was just the sort of opportunity she'd had in mind, only a few days back; but Rodney was still speaking:

"And your *books*, Alice, surely you want your books?"

He had something there. She *did* want her books, even though she had, more or less, nowhere to keep them. In particular, she wanted the further volumes of Herodotus, so inflexible was Cyril's determination to plough through the lot of them; it would be a shame to discourage him, especially in view of his remarkable ability and propensity for hard work. She would be wanting the plays, too, and a number of Latin texts—Caesar, Cicero, Virgil. For some more coaching was coming her way—two sixth-form girls from the local comprehensive who wanted to take A-level Latin despite the current lack of a Latin teacher at the school; also an aspiring physics student who had decided (probably mistakenly, but who was she to argue?) that it would be easier to learn Greek and be done with it rather than learn by heart, separately, the ever-multiplying scientific terms of Greek derivation. On top of which, the prospect of some supply teaching was on the cards; the spring term, the term of colds and flu epidemics was just starting, and so supply teachers of every kind were likely to be in great demand—especially in this area, where the full-time teachers were currently digging their toes in about filling-in for absent colleagues.

So, "All right," she said, cautiously. "When?" After a brief bit of to-ing and fro-ing about dates, an evening was fixed on. Next Wednesday. For dinner, at seven o'clock.

By now, Alice found herself quite looking forward to the occasion, because, really, it couldn't go wrong. It was a heads-I-win, tails-you-lose situation. If the meal was nice—well, that would be nice in itself; but if it was awful, that would be nice too, as showing up what a rotten cook Ivy was.

If she was. Oh, well . . .

It occurred to Alice that there are compensations in being the discarded wife: the onus of being perfect now falls on the Other Woman.

CHAPTER 27

She arrived on the doorstep of her old home at six minutes past seven —exactly right according to Alice's grandmother, who had been an absolute mine of this sort of information. For a dinner invitation, the guest should arrive between four and seven minutes later than the appointed time; for afternoon tea, between five and twelve minutes; whereas for lunch you should be exactly on time, to the minute. Why this should be, Alice could not clearly remember. The late arrival for dinner was explicable in terms of allowing your hostess a little margin of time to be absolutely ready for you; but why was this not necessary at lunch-time, likewise? Her grandmother had explained it to her at the time—something to do with the servants, and the replacement of butler by parlour-maid for morning occasions . . . well, something like that, but the inner logic of it had escaped Alice's memory, presumably through long disuse, butlers and parlour-maids being thin on the ground these days.

Still, her grandmother would have been proud of her tonight. During the longish pause between her ringing of the bell and the sound of scurrying footsteps (evidently, Ivy was a hostess who needed the full seven minutes), Alice had time to look at her watch and congratulate herself. At least she'd got the timing right, and with a complacent smile she waited for Ivy—for she was sure it *was* Ivy, scuttling nervously like an overweight rabbit down the stairs—to open the door.

It was more of a shock than she'd expected, to be welcomed as a guest into her own home: to be shown where to hang her coat, on the very same pegs she had always hung it as far back as she could remember.

The sitting-room was a shock, too, though in a different way. The big serviceable work-surfaces on which the books and papers of one or both of them had invariably been spread out throughout the best part of twenty years—they were gone. There was no longer any proper solid table at all—just flimsy little coffee-tables with splayed-out gilt legs, scattered here and there about the room, each with an ornament on it, or a photograph of some bulbous baby or grinning relative; something, anyway, to prevent it being any use for putting anything down on.

And somewhere to put things down was exactly what Ivy was urgently needing, at this very moment. Moving agitatedly back and forth from glasses to drinks cupboard, she had managed to assemble on a tray three large wine-glasses, three sherry glasses and a brand-new packet of peanuts needing to be gouged open by some sort of sharp implement not yet to hand. With one hand she clutched this tray against her person, while with the other she was trying to pluck from the drinks cupboard, like a bunch of oversized flowers, a bottle of gin, a sweet sherry, a dry sherry and an unopened bottle of white wine. Her glance darted hither and thither along the well-stocked shelves; she was desperate, Alice could see, to remember where the corkscrew was, and also to locate some kind of dish into which she could decant the peanuts, when and if she could succeed in wrenching them open.

Her predicament was so familiar that Alice could have laughed out loud. Helpful though Rodney could often be with day-to-day household chores, whenever there were visitors he always behaved like this: disappearing without trace the moment the doorbell rang, and only reappearing when the difficult part was over—when the guests had been successfully divested of their coats; had been asked how they were, and been informed in tones of extravagant rapture of how wonderful it was to see them; had been seated in appropriate chairs, and supplied with appropriate drinks . . . Then, and only then, would Rodney re-emerge and take over his duties as eager and welcoming host.

This, Alice calculated, he would be doing in about five minutes' time; meanwhile, she took pity on the flustered Ivy; cleared one of the tottery little tables so that she could at least put *something* down, and offered to go and find the corkscrew.

"It'll be in the knife drawer, right at the back," she predicted confidently, and set off for the kitchen—wondering, as she did so, whether it was quite her place to be knowing more about where things were kept than Ivy did.

Rodney, as expected, had found himself something urgent to do to fill in the time until the guest could be assumed to be settled; with a felt pen, he was blacking in the pattern on the label round the coffee-jar. He jumped guiltily when Alice came into the kitchen, though not, in her opinion, guiltily enough in the circumstances.

"Corkscrew," she said, falling effortlessly into the old shorthand which had once existed between them, and proceeded to scrabble in the knife drawer, pushing her hand back and back among all the old familiar prongs and edges and spare bits of the mincing machine.

"That drawer could do with a good clear-out, you know, Allie," he was beginning, in tones of mild reproach; and then suddenly, like a man woken from sleep, he recalled who she was—or, rather, who she wasn't.

Her fingers encountered the corkscrew, and she pulled it out triumphantly. "Here!" she exclaimed, thrusting it into his hand. "Come on, we mustn't leave . . ." Now it was *she* who had to recollect who she was, and who she wasn't.

The situation was impossible. Their eyes met in a kind of visual shrug; each gave a little laugh and hurried to take refuge in the sitting-room, where the resumption of dinner-party formalities would help to prevent old and familiar habits from raising their unruly heads.

The meal was a disappointment. That is to say, it was neither good enough to be a gastronomic treat, nor bad enough to show up Ivy as a rotten housekeeper. Ivy's legs were a disappointment, too. As she stumped in and out of the room carrying dishes, Alice couldn't help noticing that they weren't, after all, as thick as tree-trunks, as she had been picturing them all this time. They were just rather fat, that's all, nothing spectacular. The rest had been just wishful thinking.

After dinner, and after coffee (quite good, though served in horrid little vulgar mugs with slogans on them: "ME First!" "Oops—Sorry!" and "Come Again!"—that sort of thing), the real business of the evening had to be broached. In a little procession headed by Ivy, they made their way upstairs into the spare bedroom where all Alice's belongings—or alleged belongings; much of it she intended to disown on sight—had been piled, higgledy-piggledy, to await . . . well, whatever was going to happen to them in the end.

"You see," Ivy was pointing out as politely as she could—because who wants to reveal herself as a fishwife in front of a newly-captured partner?—"I don't like having to rush you like this, but we do have to get this room clear, ready for the decorators. Before we can put the

house on the market the whole place has to be decorated from top to
bottom; the men are starting on Monday, and so you see . . ."

"Yes, that's right, no rush at all," put in Rodney warmly, just as if by
saying the exact opposite he was backing his wife up—this, too, was an
annoying way of his that Alice remembered well. "All we really want
you to do tonight, Alice, is to pick out the things you actually want,
here and now, and I'll give you a lift back with them."

"Just books it'll be," Alice was beginning firmly to stipulate, when
Rodney interrupted, his voice sharp with dismay:

"The *cuckoo clock!*" he exclaimed, rummaging behind piles of old
journals and pulling it into view. "Surely you want the cuckoo clock,
Allie? Don't you remember? I brought it back from the Black Forest
after that convention, and you were so pleased? You *must* want it!"

His dismay seemed quite out of proportion. After all, if he valued
the clock all that much, how had it ever got shoved away out of sight
like this?

"Of course I remember," she said. "But it's yours really, Rodney, you
bought it. Why don't you still have it in the bedroom, where it always
was?"

She had said the wrong thing. Had she meant to? Had some devil
inside her been prompting every word? After a moment, Rodney answered in a tight voice. "We can't have it there anymore. It keeps Ivy
awake."

It wasn't Rodney's words so much as Ivy's face that revealed to Alice
a hitherto unsuspected truth: the truth that, if she really wanted him,
she could have Rodney back. If she really set herself to do so, giving
time and trouble to it, using all her intelligence, pulling out all the
stops . . .

For the bond was still there. Neither of them could have failed to be
aware of it during those moments in the kitchen. A bond tough as old
boots, resistant alike to both neglect and rough-handling, sending out
shoots, like bindweed, in every direction, coiling around everything,
popping up everywhere, out of control, ineradicable.

Or almost. Of course, it *could* be eradicated, just as bindweed can. It
would die in the end, it was bound to, if it got no nourishment at all of
any kind. It was in Alice's power to nourish it, to feed it with new life,
starting this very evening. Or not to. She looked at Ivy's round, unhappy face, with a smudge of dust across the cheek, and she knew that
Ivy knew. And then she looked at Rodney, his bent head turned away

from her as he fiddled with the cuckoo clock. *Setting* it, for goodness sake! Setting it to the right time, seven hours out of phase as it was.

"Cuckoo . . . cuckoo . . ." the soft musical notes floated lightly in the still air up in this little room; and then, almost immediately, "Cuckoo"—a single note as he took the hand past the half hour. "Cuckoo . . . cuckoo . . . cuckoo"—three o'clock—half past—four o'clock . . . The sweet notes were like an accompaniment to Alice's unfinished thoughts . . . to Ivy's . . . to Rodney's . . . and at last it reached its conclusion; caught up with real time, with now-time; the nine sweet cuckoos marked the end of something.

"Time for the news," exclaimed Rodney, setting down the clock as the ninth cuckoo died away; and then, turning to Alice, "We have the telly in the bedroom now, Alice; so come on."

The danger was over; they were safe. For the time being, anyway. The sense of relief in the three of them was almost palpable. They were like three climbers, roped together, who had just achieved a miraculous escape from some fearful hazard of the mountains. Here they were, safe and sound, back on solid earth again, warm and comfortable in front of a TV set, two in chairs and one on the bed.

All the same, Alice found it hard to concentrate on the news; she'd heard it earlier, anyway, before she'd started out, and there wasn't much change. An insurrection somewhere; a twenty-four-hour strike of civil servants in some department or other; a widow of eighty-nine who had hit an intruder over the head with the family Bible and sent him flying. "The Lord helps those who help themselves!" she'd declared, cackling with triumph in front of the cameras, her face rosy and wrinkled like an old apple, and her top teeth slipping.

And then—just after what should have been the final item—a late news report:

"The news has just reached us that mass-murderer Julian Gray escaped this afternoon from Brimthorpe top-security jail. Police have set a cordon round the area, and there is hope that the man may shortly be re-captured . . . He is five-foot-eleven in height, light brown hair, and as far as is known will be wearing the prison clothes. Meantime, the public is warned that if they see a man answering to this description, they should on no account approach him . . . Highly dangerous criminal . . . it is believed that he may be carrying a gun . . . The governor of Brimthorpe Jail has told reporters . . ."

Ivy leaned forward and turned the knob. "It's nearly twenty past," she pointed out. "I want to watch that ballet thing"; and at once the room was filled with orchestral music. But Alice, already on her feet, did not hear a single note of it.

CHAPTER 28

Cyril yawned, and pushed his Goodwin's *Greek Grammar* to one side of Alice's makeshift table. It had been a rotten day, one way and another. First, the Bike Run had ended in disappointment. Instead of beating his own record by at least a step or two, as he'd confidently expected after all that practice, he had done worse then he'd done for weeks; falling off almost at once three times in succession, while they all laughed, and called him cissy. Not unkindly, exactly, it was only a joke; but all the same, they *did* call him cissy. Then, afterwards, coming here for his Greek lesson, what should he find but that Alice was in a hurry because of some rotten dinner-party she had to go out to, and so could only give him his exact hour, with no time for interesting conversations either before or after. Normally, they had all sorts of discussions triggered off by something in Herodotus; whether Cyrus, stirring up disaffection, was really just like Mr. Scargill, only lucky? Did the oracles actually influence events, as well as predicting them, rather like the opinion polls? Could there really have been giant ants in the Arabian desert that could run as fast as camels? That sort of thing.

But this evening, there'd been no time for anything of the sort, and of course he hadn't been invited to stay for supper either. True, Alice had told him, before she left, that he was welcome to go down to the kitchen and help himself to anything in the fridge that was labelled "A," but this was a pretty gloomy prospect, all on his own. "A-level" food—but what was the point of making a silly pun inside your own head when there was no one there to laugh at it?

Oh, well. He might as well stay for a bit, and get on with some homework. There was no point in going home; his parents were out playing bridge again, so there wouldn't be a proper meal there either, merely another bleak instruction—just like Alice's—about the contents of the fridge. Also, the baby-sitter would be there, the new one with the round stupid face and a ridiculous froth of yellow hair that seemed to need fiddling with all the time. Cyril found her terribly boring. She wouldn't even watch television, this one; she preferred to sit fiddling with her hair and making him feel that he ought to be talking to her.

Languidly, he reached down for his school bag, and pulled out his geometry book. Might as well get that over with; but while he was scrabbling in the further depths for his protractor, which seemed to have detached itself from the main box of instruments, he became aware of voices on the stairs. Hetty's voice, eager as always, bubbling over with sympathetic concern for someone else's business, and also another voice, a man's voice new to Cyril. He might be anyone.

On the landing just below, the footsteps came to a halt, and the voices too. There was a sharp "Rat-tat" on a door—the door of that sad girl, Mary something, it must be. A short silence followed, then the resumption of voices. By now, Cyril could hear what they were saying.

"I'm afraid she doesn't seem to be in," Hetty was apologising. "She works now, you know, a nice little job, but I don't know when she finishes. But I'll tell you what, I think I know where she keeps it—up in the other lady's room. She's out too, but I'm sure she won't mind . . ." and now the footsteps started up again, really loud this time, on the uncarpeted stairs leading up to the attics.

Neither flight nor fight being a viable option, Cyril froze into immobility. He didn't feel like socialising, certainly not with whoever this was, and so he kept his head down and his shoulders hunched against whatever was going to happen.

Nothing much did; or nothing that concerned him, anyway. They seemed slightly surprised to find him there—well, naturally; since they'd walked in without knocking they'd had no warning of his presence, but that was their look-out. At least they didn't try to engage him in conversation, beyond a "Well, my goodness!" from Hetty and a perfunctory and dismissive "Good evening," from the visitor—a large, ugly man with bent shoulders, roughly the age that adults usually were, and intent to the point of rudeness on his immediate purpose.

"It's under here," Hetty was saying, bending over the box-built sofa. "I saw they'd got it out of here when they were sorting it all out, and I know she wants you to have it, because she told me she was doing it for a friend who was in a hurry for it, his thesis or something . . . She told me you'd be calling . . . Ah, here we are"—and in triumph she dragged out the cardboard box that supported one end of the couch. "Here, you take it—it's a bit heavy for me . . ."

The man barely thanked her. Greedily, he stooped for the box, and grabbing it in both arms made for the door. Here, remembering his manners as one might remember to step over an annoying obstacle, he did throw a hasty word of thanks to Hetty over his shoulder. He then set off down the stairs with clumsy haste, easily outdistancing Hetty who stumbled in his wake, clutching the banisters and trying hospitably to delay his departure by such inducements as she could think up on the spur of the moment—from a nice cup of tea to the possibility that Mary (" 'Imogen,' as you call her, I'll never remember to call her that myself, I'm sure") might well be back any minute, and would be awfully disappointed to have missed him . . .

But he only hurried on the faster. Cyril heard Hetty's hospitable voice fade into an uneven wailing towards the lower regions of the house; and then the front door slammed and that seemed to be that.

Cyril was growing hungry. He waited for a few minutes to make sure that the commotion, whatever it was, had completely died down, and then set off for the kitchen to see what he could find. Rather to his annoyance, he found Miss Dorinda still at the cooker, stirring this and that in little pans, although it was already twenty to eight. Wasn't she supposed to be finished by half past seven? Evidently, the same thought must have crossed her mind, too, for she had whipped round in righteous indignation as he came through the door, had opened her mouth on a reprimand, and had then caught sight of the time. By a bare ten minutes, the bottom had fallen out of her grievance. It was maddening. Surely there was *something* she could tell him not to do . . . ?

But no; for by now Hetty had arrived too, and Hetty hardly ever allowed anyone to be told not to do things—certainly not Cyril, who by now was rather a pet of hers. Seeing him now, rummaging in the fridge for such oddments of cheese, bacon scraps and margarine that might turn out to be Alice's, she immediately put her foot down and urged him, if he didn't mind the bones, to share with her the remains of a delicious Irish stew.

Delicious it was; and of course Cyril didn't mind the bones. Actually, there were some rather interesting ones, the upper neck vertebrae, which looked exactly like faces when you'd picked them clean of meat and stood them up on end; but when he held one up for admiration, pointing out the eyes, the mouth, even the little projections that looked like ears, Miss Dorinda made a face of such disgust and aversion as quite took him aback. And not only this, but at almost exactly the same moment Hetty, too—most uncharacteristically—gave a little cry of dismay.

"Your *hand*, Cyril! Whatever have you done to your hand?"

He'd grazed it, that was all. Nothing to make a fuss about. Falling off a bike, he explained nonchalantly, and anyway it had stopped hurting.

All the same, a fuss was made. Hetty insisted on iodine—or, rather, tried to insist on it, the force of her insistence being sadly weakened by the fact that she couldn't find any, search as she would: weed-killer, worm pills, mango chutney, nasal spray—you name it, she had it, every damn thing except iodine.

In counterpoint to all this, Miss Dorinda was setting herself to improve the occasion.

"You see, Cyril?" she admonished, "You see what happens? Didn't I tell you you'd get hurt one of these days, going around with those awful boys? I know those flats—you'll get blood-poisoning, I wouldn't be surprised, cutting yourself on those filthy stairs . . . You ought to see a doctor, get one of those injections, tetanus and that . . ."

And then, as the search for the iodine continued, and Cyril resumed picking at his delectable bones as if nothing had happened, she felt provoked to continue with her theme:

"It's bad company you're getting into, Cyril, one of these days you'll be sorry. It's got a bad name, that Estate, that's where the muggings go on, and the robbings and the stabbings. Myself, I wouldn't go there, not even by daylight—not if they paid me!"

They wouldn't pay her of course, it was just a silly turn of speech. What they paid *her* for was to go back and forth, back and forth, day after day, month after month, year after year, along the same safe streets at the same safe hours to the same safe job; never any change, never anything different, all the time getting older and older and greyer and greyer and more and more disapproving. This, then, was the ultimate reward for not getting into bad company . . .

The front door slammed, and a few seconds later Mary was in the room, brandishing a frozen quiche which had come her way in the course of her duties, and asking who would like to share it? It was too large, she said, just for her.

Cyril, despite the Irish stew, was by no means unwilling to help her out; and while it heated up in the oven, Mary regaled them all with an account of her day; about the customers who never had their money ready, the even worse ones who wanted to pay by credit-card for one tin of cat-food and a tube of toothpaste; and the puzzling fact that so very few of them ever counted their change, or gave even a glance at the detailed and accurate receipts spewed out so patiently by the machine . . .

The quiche was OK; not as good as the Irish stew, though of course he wouldn't say so . . . and by the time they'd finished, it was nearly time for the nine o'clock news. Hetty particularly wanted to watch it, she said, because of that actress, what was her name, getting some sort of an award for whatever her part was in that film, what was it called, that there'd been some kind of a fuss about.

The TV set, being rather a nuisance in the kitchen, had found its way into the absent Mr. Singh's room on the ground floor, and thither Hetty made her way, followed, for lack of anything better to do, by the rest of the party. Mary had hesitated a moment—she had some washing to do, she said; but urged by Hetty, she came along with the others; as did Cyril, not because he cared about the news particularly, but because it was a way of putting off the time when he would have to return home to the boring baby-sitter. Miss Dorinda came because she always enjoyed a nice sit-down after her long day on her feet, and also because, in the case of TV, there was always a chance of being shocked by something.

It was a cosy little gathering. The splendid two-bar electric fire that actually worked was fetched from Brian's room—he was out playing at a concert, or something, and so couldn't possibly mind—and the four of them had just managed to settle themselves in a comfortable circle round the set by the time the main news was to begin.

CHAPTER 29

"Alice! Thank goodness you're back! Oh, thank *goodness!* They've gone *mad*, Alice, every last one of them, they've gone absolutely raving bananas . . . That poor girl sobbing her heart out, and the boy pounding up and down the house, calling out to her, and the telephone never stops going, and everyone on about a package gone missing . . . and now she's gone off in a mini-cab in floods of tears, and no money on her I wouldn't be surprised . . . *I* don't know, nobody tells me anything. And now there's that boy's mother ringing up asking where is he, why isn't he home yet, and *I* don't know, how should I? I don't even know why he's here, do I, let alone why he isn't! And on top of all this, as if all this wasn't enough, someone's been helping themselves to Miss Dorinda's yoghurt and left her a strawberry-flavour one instead, and if there's one thing Miss Dorinda can't stand it's flavoured yoghurt . . . Oh, Alice, what a mercy you're home at last, now we'll get a bit of sense hammered into it!"

It seemed an optimistic prediction. Rushing home through the rainy night, just failing to flag down taxis, just missing departing buses, Alice had been preparing herself either to break the frightening news to Mary, or, if she had already heard it, to offer what consolation and support it was in her power to give.

Well, Mary *had* heard the news, that was beyond doubt. But what then? Where had she gone? And why? What did she think she could do in the face of this alarming new development? What could she even *want* to do, so repeatedly had she asserted that her brother was out of her life for ever, that the whole tragedy was something she intended to turn her back on and try to escape?

What had changed her mind—if changed it was? Assuredly, to-night's news was startling and disturbing in the extreme—but surely a lesser tragedy, by any standards, than the original crimes them-selves . . .

"A cup of tea," Hetty was saying now, in something more like her normal voice; and Alice, aware suddenly of how cold and wet she was —her hair, her scarf, her shoes all soaked—roused herself to follow Hetty down to the warm kitchen. Not that she wanted a cup of tea—she was wondering already how she would manage to get it down—but there was something obligatory about it, which she and Hetty both recognised. It was bigger than both of them, this ritual cup of tea—this seal set on disaster, recognised by all, from broken-hearted widows to earthquake victims dragged out of ruins.

Under the harsh kitchen light, Alice could see that Hetty had been crying. Her plump, kindly face, usually so contented and full of all-purpose benevolence, was strained and streaky with uneven pallor; her hair, never very tidy, was standing up all ways as if she really *had* been "tearing her hair." Usually looking young for whatever her age was, tonight she looked old—for whatever it was.

"If only she'd *said* something!" Hetty wailed, slamming the kettle down noisily onto the gas-ring. "There we were, all sitting cosily round the telly, as snug as can be—and all of a sudden she leaps up as if she'd been shot, and rushes upstairs . . . and then Cyril, he rushes up after her . . . I heard their voices . . . something or other . . . I don't know—he was telling her something . . . or she was telling him . . . anyway, down she came, in floods of tears, and grabbing the telephone . . . I wish now I'd . . . but how could I, not knowing anything? It's set her right back, you know, whatever it is, that's the shame of it. Just when she was getting so much better—haven't you noticed?—a differ-ent girl these last few days. Only this evening I was noticing it, it did my heart good, it really did, watching her enjoy that bit of pastry stuff this evening. And a bit of colour in her face too, and having a laugh about that job of hers . . . and now *this* has to happen! I could've cried when I saw her face as she went out the door, all white and pinched again, like it was right at the beginning . . .

"I couldn't get a word out of her—not a word. If only she'd *said* something, Alice . . . if only she'd *told* me. But such a state she was in, I can't help wondering if she knew herself what she was doing . . . where she meant to go . . ."

CHAPTER 30

Mary knew where she meant to go all right. The problem was, how to get there before Julian. For she knew already where he would be going, and why he would be going there. How he had succeeded in escaping from his top-security prison she could not imagine, except that prisoners *do* escape sometimes, somehow or other. It must need a range of skills quite beyond her imagination, including a dauntingly-high intelligence, applied intensively to the assessing of weak spots in the security system and the moments of relaxed vigilance during the day's routine. It must need also unshakeable nerve, iron will-power, and a reckless disregard of consequences, all of which he had—my God how he had them . . . !

Speed . . . Speed . . . ! She had a sort of start on him, that was one thing, setting off as she did from London instead of from the bleak northern county where he was serving his sentence. What time would he have set off? "This evening," they'd said on the news, but of course evening starts early in institutions, the last meal of the day taking place much earlier than in most households. About six, perhaps? That was probably when they'd missed him—but how much earlier might he have actually got away? How many hours along his dark and rainy route had he come by now—hitching lifts, perhaps? Slinking along black verges as the water splashed waist-high from the wheels of passing cars? Seeking short-cuts sometimes across sodden fields of dead winter grass and black ploughlands?

"C'mon, Midge—race you!" The young voice, breathless with ambition to win, came to her across the years; but this time the race was for real, and no way could he be allowed to win it. *She* had got to win this time. Somehow, some way, she had *got* to get there first.

It wasn't difficult to find out the times of the late-night trains from Victoria; for a wonder, the Enquiries people had answered almost at once when she'd phoned. Nor was it difficult to order a mini-cab, though unfortunately they couldn't come at once—twenty minutes it would be, the girl reckoned. Thus there was nothing for Mary to do but to wait, biting her nails or not, as her self-control waxed or waned. There was no packing to do; she would not be taking an overnight case. Whatever was going to happen to her this night, going to bed would assuredly form no part of it.

Hetty was fluttering like a mother hen, getting in her way, bombarding her with endless futile questions: it was unbearable. The only way not to be downright rude to her—and even in her distraught state, Mary was dimly aware of the kindness and concern implicit in these flutterings—the only way was to get out of the house; to wait for the mini-cab outside, and never mind the rain.

The street was empty, and very silent. It was that hour of the evening when comings and goings have almost ceased; too late for anyone to be still setting off to anywhere, too early for them to be returning.

So Mary had the rainy darkness all to herself. To save time, she walked a little way along the street, in the direction from which the mini-cab would be coming; also, she wanted to get well away from the windows of Number 17, lest Hetty, peering worriedly out from one of them, would realise that she had not yet gone.

Twenty minutes. Twenty minutes isn't forever, but it can seem very like it in these sort of circumstances, so Mary braced herself for a long and nerve-racking wait; and her relief was enormous when, long before the twenty minutes were up—it couldn't have been much more than ten—she saw the black car nosing along the street towards her. It seemed to be having some difficulty in locating the right house, most of the numbers being so badly marked, and the street lighting so poor. Thankfully, Mary waved, ran towards it, and as the driver swung the rear door open for her, she leaped inside.

"Victoria Station, please," she panted, flopping down gratefully on the back seat.

The driver turned his head slightly, as if checking that he'd heard her directions rightly.

"No, dear, not Victoria. I'm taking you the whole way, right down to Medley Green," and now, as he turned further round towards her, she recognised the face—the bland, heavy face, scored by lines of aging adolescence—of the man at the supermarket. The man who had been watching her . . . had spoken to her at the check-out, and had been waiting outside on the pavement when she finished work. So proud of herself had she been for not suspecting him of any evil intent; for having mastered her paranoia at last!

"No—no!" she cried, struggling with the locked door; but he wagged his finger at her with menacing playfulness.

"Hush, dear, hush! You want the whole street to hear you? To hear that you're the notorious Imogen Gray, Sister of the Monster? Because if you create a scene, getting them running out and rescuing you, that's what I shall tell them. Try not to make me do that, dear, because it would be a shame, wouldn't it, a pretty little girl like you to turn out to be Sister to the Monster? They won't feel so good about you, will they, these cosy new friends of yours, once they know who you really are? That nice young man won't, for a start. I doubt if any young man will, once he knows. Imogen Gray . . . Imogen Gray . . . it's become kind of a nasty name, hasn't it, just lately? Not at all a nice name for a pretty little girl like you, I'd hate people to know about it, I really would.

"So come along, there's a good girl, I'll drive you down to Medley Green, and after that you can direct me. You know bloody well where your brother's hiding, you must do, that's what this jaunt of yours is all in aid of; aren't I right? And let me warn you, darling, not to start telling me lies and giving me the runaround. I don't like little girls who behave like that to me, I really don't, and I know just how to make them very, very sorry. So just remember . . .

"How do I know it's you? Listen, dear, your picture was in all the papers, remember? And on TV too, scuttling in and out of doorways, trying to hide your face. But it didn't work, did it, it never does, one can always get the glimpse, and for a pretty little glimpse like that, one's going to be extra attentive, naturally. I've been keeping the old eye out for you ever since, and so have one or two other chaps in the trade . . . Well, they would, wouldn't they? Did you really think you'd get away with it, holing up and giving yourself a false name? Listen, darling, you're worth the best part of half a million to the gutter press, there was never a hope in hell we wouldn't track you down in the end; and right now, with your brother scarpering like this, the price is going to hit the roof. And you know, if you'd been a good little girl right from the start, co-operative, you know, something might have come *your* way. But you were naughty, dear, really naughty, refusing to speak to the boys . . . dodging the cameras; stand-offish—toffee-nosed; that's not the way to win friends in this game, it really isn't. And then all those lies you told about the diary? *We* knew you'd bloody got it, stashed away somewhere—and by the way, *I've* got it now, thanks to your dear kind landlady; she knew just where you'd hidden it—wasn't that lucky? I could hand it to the police any minute I choose, and explain how you've kept it from them all this time. I won't, though, if you're a good girl. I might even let you have it back, if we could come to some arrangement . . .

"No, darling, don't be a silly girl, don't keep fighting with that door, it won't be the slightest use, d'you think I'm stupid? You'll only damage your nails; even your fingers, they might get damaged if you provoke me too far, and I'd simply hate that to happen . . .

"What paper do I write for? Darling girl, *I* don't write for any paper, that's a job for the other boys. I'm just the little rat who digs up the big stories; I rake among the kind of muck the gentlemen of the press won't soil their hands with—but they're not too proud that they can't recognise a good thing when I show it to them. And this is going to be the scoop of the year. It's got everything: a bloodthirsty criminal; a top-security break-out; a pretty girl with a secret . . . Wow!

"But listen; time's going on, you know. I've enjoyed our little chat, but we have to be on our way . . ." Glancing out of both windows to make sure the street was still empty, of pedestrians as well as cars, he started the engine.

Well, empty to all intents and purposes; just a young kid idling along, bouncing a tennis-ball or some such as he went. But, annoyingly, just as the car began to move, the wretched child muffed a catch, and the ball dribbled gently out into the centre of the road, right in front of the car —and with the child, of course, darting right out after it, the way kids do, never a thought for looking where they're going.

He gave two irritable little hoots on the horn; but instead of leaping out of the way as might be expected, the boy merely glanced up for a moment and stayed where he was, examining his ball meticulously, and brushing little bits of mud off it as if to test its quality.

Another, sharper hoot—the driver dared not make too much noise and so rouse the curiosity of the neighbours. Still no reaction. The boy was now dreamily bouncing the ball, up and down, up and down, on the road right bang in front of the car.

Violently, the window was wound down.

"Get out of my way!" yelled the occupant; but without result. The boy went on playing his game, apparently oblivious: tossing the ball in the air now, first with one hand and then the other.

The kid must be deaf, or daft, or something. Angrily reversing a few yards, the driver edged the car forward to the other side of the road, thus bypassing the idiot child.

But no sooner was he on course than—would you credit it?—the boy had moved across to that side of the road, and was once more slap in front of the car, playing his same futile game, this time with a little smile on his face.

Twice more the manoeuvre was repeated, with the same result; and now, maddened almost beyond endurance, the driver decided to turn around and make his exit in the opposite direction.

The boy had stopped playing with his ball for the moment, and was watching with interest while the car executed its U-turn; but no sooner had this been achieved than there he was again, right in front, bouncing his ball as nonchalantly as ever. The car drove savagely toward him . . . stopped with a jerk barely a foot away . . . but he stood his ground. His demeanour, though, was beginning to change; he was no longer cool and casual, you could see now his delight in exercising such effortless power over the clumsy great vehicle—all its speed, all its enormous horsepower locked up and useless in competition with his own slight, childish limbs. The thing had gone to his head: higher and higher he tossed the ball, smiling at each perfect catch . . . and now he was almost dancing, skipping and leaping as he reached and tossed; mocking, challenging, making an utter fool of the furious man behind the wheel.

Of course, by now Mary could see exactly what Cyril was trying to do; he had seen she was in trouble, was being taken somewhere against her will, and he was engineering her escape. Sooner or later the maddened driver would fling himself from the car and go for his tormentor; and in that moment Mary would be able to escape. She saw just how it was meant to go, and she was grateful—admiring, too, of his audacity —but she was also frightened. A man as angry as this one was becoming might do *anything*. She clutched her handbag to her breast, tightened every muscle, ready for the moment of escape . . . and waited.

But for how long? Cyril could go on like this for ever, he was loving it; but what about her? How long could *she* stand it, sitting here every nerve poised for instant action, and feeling, like a tangible thing, the towering masculine fury building up to explosion point only inches away from her? How long would *he* put up with it? How long would *any* motorist put up with it?

With a roar of ungovernable rage he wrenched open the door and flung himself into the road. Her moment had come: she was out and away, streaking down the dark street while her captor was charging at the boy, fists raised, breath rasping with primitive, uncontrollable fury.

And this was the moment when Cyril overreached himself. Glorying in the feel of his light, agile limbs, and supremely confident in his ability to out-dodge and out-distance this heavy, aging, out-of-condition assailant, he indulged for just one half-second too long in a final, mocking little skip, and his enemy was upon him: a huge arm, thick as a ham, powerful as a piston, swept across his vision, and he was flying through the air. The crack of his head against the kerbstone sounded like a pistol-shot in the empty street, and then there was silence.

CHAPTER 31

The last train from Victoria reached Medley Green just after midnight, and, as often happened, there was no ticket-collector on duty, no staff of any kind. Mary was the only passenger to alight, and the sound of her boots was loud on the empty platform. She walked through the silent, brilliantly lit-up booking office, leaving her ticket for someone to find in the morning. Or not. Or whatever the system was for these late hours of the night.

There were no taxis anymore, but Mary didn't mind. It was less than two miles, and every inch of the way was so familiar to her that she could hardly believe that when she arrived she wouldn't find everyone still there, just as they used to be: her mother in the big chair under the lamp, sewing; her father, not yet ill, poring over the accounts of whatever firm he was working for just then, and Julian, a young schoolboy still, sprawling on the carpet with his homework, idly massaging the dog's contented ears while he studied . . .

Once away from the dazzle and glare of the deserted station, Mary found that the darkness lightened, brightened, filled itself with shapes and shadows by which to steer her swift familiar course.

Swift it had to be, though already she felt a curious and not quite rational certainty that she would be there before him.

"C'mon, Midge, race you!" Again she seemed to hear the long-ago voice, filling with its faint echoes this stretch of road by which they had walked to school through all the years of their childhood.

The moon was rising now, but only just; a dizzy, lopsided creature it looked tonight, sprawled on its back just above the dark line of the trees at an awkward, uncomfortable-looking angle, and giving less light, almost, than the unimaginably distant stars.

What had she expected? She had known, vaguely, that the house was up for sale. When she and her mother had both fled, beaten down by shame and horror, an agent had taken over, and it looked, now, as if he had done absolutely nothing; broken windows, sagging porch, and the garden a dark tangle of overgrown vegetation. Perhaps it had proved impossible to find a buyer for so haunted a dwelling, pictured on television night after night, with little crosses helpfully marked on it to show viewers where this or that awful thing had happened, or been suspected, or marked off by the police with lengths of tape. A house that no one would want to live in, ever again, one-time residence of a family that no one now would ever want to know.

She pushed open the garden gate, now lurching drunkenly on its hinges, and made her way slowly up the path to the front door, the huge dank weeds, heavy with wetness, brushing against her at every step. Now that she was here, within yards of the thing she'd rushed so frantically to reach, all the hurry seemed to have drained out of her; she wanted to be slow . . . slower . . . to know nothing . . . to find nothing . . . to go away leaving everything unresolved.

"Pull yourself together," Alice had said: a very wrong thing to say (as any psychologist will tell you), but all the same it had been useful, somehow, at that one particular moment.

"Pull yourself together!" she now repeated to herself, experimentally; for one of her training it had all the force of blasphemy, and the adrenaline leaped accordingly, enabling her to face the next move.

She looked up at the broken windows, all out of reach. She would have to break yet another, one on the ground floor.

The crash and the glitter of the flying splinters took her breath away for a moment, like a plunge into ice-cold water; and while she stood recovering, it occurred to her that this was actually a good sign: if Julian had got here before her, surely she would have found a ground-floor window already broken?

Or maybe not. You couldn't tell. Someone who could do the things Julian had done, and break out of a top-security prison into the bargain, wasn't going to be daunted by a climb through the broken glass of an upstairs window . . .

In she crawled, over the now rotting window-sill, and lowered herself into what had once been the sitting-room. It still was; nothing had been changed. In the oppressive darkness, she could make out the looming shapes of all the old familiar furniture, each item exactly where it had always been. No one had done *anything*. Even the books were still there, sinking into dust and decay, each one still in its proper place, no doubt, exactly as her father had arranged them while he was still able to arrange things.

The lights wouldn't go on. She tried each of the familiar switches in turn; but it didn't matter, she didn't really need them, so familiar was every step of the way across the room, through the hall, and up the stairs.

Julian's room, of course, was greatly changed; the to-ing and fro-ing of the police, and their intermittent searches, had made that inevitable. There was very little left that she recognised.

But the alcove was still there; the alcove at the back of the room, facing the windows. And not only was it there, but by some small, happy chance the moon had moved around to shine right into it at this very moment—the poor lopsided thing was now well up above the trees, and the light, to her dark-adapted eyes, was almost bright.

Down on her knees, gently lifting the lino, pliable from long use, she felt eight years old again—no, six. This had been hers and Julian's secret, sacred place. It was their magic chest, their witches' strong-room, their deepest dungeon below the castle moat; and though of course it was much too small to get into themselves, their toys had all managed to get into it—soldiers, teddies, sugar-mice, turn and turn about, playing out their variegated roles in many a long-forgotten drama. And as they grew a little older, it had become a storehouse of secrets, of all precious things unfit for adult eyes—code messages, magic spells—bits of rock that might have been brought on a flying saucer from Mars.

Gently, with infinite care, Mary eased up the board from under the lino, and pulled it free. Awash in the pool of moonlight, she bent down and peered deep, deep, into the dusty darkness that wasn't quite darkness.

The gun wasn't there.

The shock was so great that Mary thought for a moment that she was going to faint: so sure had she been, so absolutely certain that this was where he would have hidden it.

So he had arrived before her! This, at first, was the only thing she could think of. He had got here first, had gone straight to the secret place—and now he was off and away, once more at large with a loaded gun. New horror—new tragedy—and she was powerless to prevent it.

Too late! Too late! Maybe only minutes too late!

Slowly, common sense began to seep back. Perhaps it wasn't like that at all. Perhaps the second gun had been found long ago. Even with the actual murder weapon safely in their hands, their investigations had continued for many dreadful days.

Or had the gun never been here in the first place? What was it that had made her so certain—so suddenly, overwhelmingly certain—that it would be? Until she'd read the diary, she hadn't even known that there *was* a second gun.

She must have been crazy. And yet, crazy or not, this irrational sense of certainty was still with her: it would not go away.

She peered again into the dusty hollow under the floor; she tried, as well as she could, to examine the loose board, the curl of the lino, to see if they showed signs of recent disturbance; but of course it was impossible to tell. If only she had a light!

Well, that mightn't be impossible. It could be that the electricity had been turned off at the main. Or—just as likely—that the current was on all right, but most of the bulbs broken. In that case, there might easily be one or two still working in one or other of the rooms; she could bring one up, fix it in the socket here, and really see what she was doing . . .

It was even easier than that. The very first light she tried, the kitchen one, went on immediately and dazzlingly; and there on the floor, deeply etched in the thick dust, were footprints, a man's footprints, and almost certainly fresh ones. She traced them out through the kitchen door, along the passage, and even up the stairs so far as she could see before the darkness of the upper regions took over.

The only thing was, all these prints were going in the same direction, up the stairs. None were returning.

CHAPTER 32

Footsteps leading away into the darkness, and none returning—this is one of the archetypal terrors of mankind, and it was several minutes before Mary could summon up the courage to search the house.

It didn't take long. Several of the light sockets, as it turned out, had live bulbs in, and it was soon evident that there was no one there. Mary—Imogen—was on her own in the deserted house.

And the footprints? Well, no mystery really, now that her first moment of panic had subsided. As a result of some small alarm he could have made his exit by one of the back windows upstairs; or—for some similar reason—he could have taken his shoes off for extra quietness, his stockinged feet making no discernible mark on the dusty surfaces. Anything.

The essential fact was that he was no longer here. And so he must be somewhere else. Once again, Mary had that strange sense of absolute certainty. She knew, already, just where he would be.

She had already traversed three or four miles, some of it at a run, but somehow she wasn't in the least bit tired. All the way, she had been peering tensely ahead, straining her eyes into the uncertain light, imagining, every now and then, that she could indeed glimpse a slender, swinging figure, now here, now gone, in the feeble half-light of the waning moon.

That young, swinging, questing stride that she remembered—would it still be his after all that had happened, all that he had become . . . ?

There! What was that . . . ?

The shadow ahead shivered . . . melted sideways as she came

nearer . . . loomed again across her vision—and it was only the lean-ing hump of an old, old tree, balancing between life and death in the damp, almost windless air.

She was beginning now to feel the slope of the hill pressing against the soles of her feet; her steps shortened in response to the steepening gradient. All round her now rose the raw mounds of construction work, great gashes of blackness criss-crossing the centuries-old turf, throwing up huge hillocks of tortured earth as far as the eye could see. The irresistible power of destruction was everywhere; the glimmer of huge plastic covers glimmered over mysterious piles of things; cranes, diggers, and things like interlocking tanks stood silent under the stars, ready for the onslaughts of tomorrow.

And yet, the scene seemed different under this elvish light; gentle, somehow, and impermanent. Less like a brash new building-site than like the ruins of some ancient city: which of course it one day would be. One day, the bats would be here again, darting in miraculous zig-zag flight in and out among the crumbling walls of supermarkets, establish-ing their homes and breeding-grounds in the caved-in ceilings of bet-ting-shops and pin-table saloons. One day, the grass and the brambles would grow over the washing-machines rusting back into the ground in the roofless laundrettes . . .

She recognised these thoughts as Julian's thoughts. This was the way he must have seen it as he passed this way ahead of her so short a time ago; this was his vision, these were his very thoughts, that she was picking up as she toiled upwards, on and on, towards the place where she knew he was going to be.

The raw, half-built road came to an end at this point. From here on, a rough, slippery track led towards the wooded ridge that the bulldoz-ers had not yet climbed. Here, for a little longer, the turf was still springy beneath one's feet; here, wet swathes of winter bracken caught in the darkness at one's ankles; and as she drew nearer and nearer to this last surviving patch of ancient woodland, the gibbous moon seemed to dip and leap drunkenly among the leafless twigs with every step she took.

She came upon him almost at once, and at first she thought he was asleep, so peacefully did he seem to be reclining among the brambles and the coarse tufts of winter grass; half-sitting, propped against a dark mass of tangled winter vegetation. The sound of her soft footfalls on the dead leaves did not seem to rouse him—but she could see, now, that he was not asleep. In the glimmer of moonshine that made its way through the restless tracery of twigs overhead, she could see that his eyes were open and very bright, staring straight ahead with an intensity rendering him oblivious to small distractions.

Her next thought was that he was dead. But no, for even while she watched, his right hand moved a little, stirring ever so slightly the wet, dead leaves as he lifted it.

There was no mistaking now what it was that glittered in his grasp, nor the quiet purpose with which he held it against his head.

She lunged forward through the undergrowth, and immediately there was a mighty noise, a blow on the shoulder that sent her spinning with a sharp cry; and above and through it all, she heard her brother's voice, for the last time:

"Oh *no!* Oh, *Midge! No . . .*"

And then came the second shot, she heard it echoing from tree to tree, from bush to bush, and shuddering at last into silence.

Not quite silence, of course. There was still the faint stirring of the night air; the whisper of one more leaf circling down from some twig or other; all the ordinary little sounds of a winter woodland, continuing as if nothing had happened.

And of course nothing had: just one more death among the billions and billions of deaths which had gone into the making of this rich earth; to the making, over countless millennia, of Flittermouse Hill and all that grew upon it.

CHAPTER 33

The two invalids were both in hospital, and both recovering fast—
Cyril from a broken collar-bone and concussion, Mary from the gunshot wound in her upper arm. It was Cyril, conveniently in a London
hospital, who was perhaps getting the most visitors. His family came
first, including Sophy (even though she was manifestly under fourteen,
they'd still let her in), who explained to him, wide-eyed, that Tracty
also had broken his collar-bone and banged his head ever so hard, and
was all bandaged up— *Look . . . !*

Then came Alice who, on his urgent request, agreed to bring Herodotus later on; not yet, because he wasn't supposed to read until the
doctor had seen him again and tested his reflexes and so on to see how
his concussion was getting on. All nonsense, in Cyril's opinion, because his head had almost stopped aching, and he could read perfectly
now, the print no longer jumping about, not even the small print in
newspapers. This latter he'd been able to put to the test—despite the
ban—earlier in the afternoon, when, to his immense delight and surprise, Winston had come to visit him, proudly clutching a much-folded
page from the local paper, in the left-hand column of which Cyril's
adventure had been briefly recorded, albeit not very accurately, giving
his name as Cecil, his age as eleven, and his exploit as the foiling of a
hold-up by an armed robber attempting to make his getaway. Well, of
course, the chap *was* a robber in a way, even though (as Cyril had
learned since) the box pinched from Alice's room had only had junk
paper in it; the diary (about which the whole fuss seemed to be cen-
tred) having been extracted by Alice herself that very evening, and
stored away safely in her old home.

Anyway, the story the way the paper told it was still pretty good. It made him out quite a hero, and featured a rather smudgy picture of him grinning into the camera on some holiday or other; not bad; and, as Winston pointed out, anyone could see it was him and not this pocky Cecil person, and so not to worry.

What Cyril was actually worrying about, though, was the Bike Run. So badly had he done last time; and now, with his collar-bone, he'd be out of it for weeks, getting quite hopelessly behind.

But here, too, Winston repeated his injunction "not to worry."

"We're off it," he explained. "Right off it, somehow. We aren't having no more bike meetings for a bit. It's not much fun now, not without you, nigger"—and for a moment Cyril could hardly breathe, so overwhelmed was he by the honour just conferred by this long-coveted, scarcely hoped-for name.

So happy was he, so proud, that when later on Miss Dorinda, of all people, came to visit him, it hardly got him down at all. It was nice of her to bother to come, of course it was, and she'd brought a huge bunch of black expensive grapes, which was nice too. Besides, by now he was quite used to the way she talked. Having asked him how he was, and having told him details of the various cases of head-injury, some fatal, some not, among her ever-widening circle of people who knew people who knew people—after this, she found herself, irresistibly, drawing the moral of it all:

"Well, I'm very thankful to find you no worse, Cyril, but I do trust it'll be a lesson to you. I've told you before, haven't I, that running around with all that riff-raff the way you do, and getting into these dare-devil scrapes—I've told you, one day you'd be sorry! And now it's happened! I only hope you've learned your lesson!"

He had, too. He had learned that the pain of a broken collar-bone, of a concussed head, were as nothing compared with the joy and triumph of partaking in such an adventure; of defying an opponent much bigger than yourself; of getting your picture in the papers, and finally, in recognition of all this, being called "nigger" by the leader of your gang.

So, "Yes," he said meekly, in answer to Miss Dorinda's question.

Meanwhile, in another hospital, a good many miles to the south, Mary's visitors sat in Reception, waiting obediently for it to be two o'clock. Alice and Hetty had come together, by train, after quite a struggle to dissuade Brian from coming too.

"No, Brian, we *must* see how Mary feels first," Alice had insisted.

"She's had this tremendous shock, you know; and now to give her the additional shock of learning that you know all about it—who she is, and everything—when you are the very person she was above all trying to hide it from . . ."

This was the tail-end, really, of the discussion that she and Brian had been engaged in, on and off, ever since the news broke.

"Why didn't she *tell* me?" he'd kept reiterating. "It wouldn't have made the slightest difference to how I feel about her—why should it? It was only her *brother*, for God's sake. How can anyone be held responsible for what their *brother* does? I'm a brother myself—I should know!"

And then Alice had tried to get across to him the real core and essence of Mary's terror and withdrawal; her sense of being contaminated, of being irrevocably touched by evil; of being for ever unmarriageable, unfit even for a love-affair, because of the "bad blood," the faulty genes, that she must be sharing with her brother.

He had pooh-poohed the entire thing.

"Faulty genes, my foot! As if there could be special sets of genes that inexorably turn a man into a criminal, or a bus-driver, or an in-tourist guide! It *can't* be as specific as that! Of course, I grant you that to be a way-out fanatical criminal like this Julian, you'd need *some* inherited qualities. Like courage, for instance; and dogged determination. Like the ability to care desperately about something, and the strength to defy the whole world in support of your conviction. Just the qualities a chap would have needed in Nazi Germany if he was to defy the regime . . ."

All very well, Alice had protested; but you've left out the *negative* qualities. Ruthlessness. Greed. The actual ability to kill a human being at all, in any circumstances whatever . . .

Well, greed didn't come into it, did it, in this Julian's case? "And as to the ability to kill a human being, everyone has *that*—every male, anyway: *Homo sapiens* would never have survived without it. It's inhibited, of course, in our sort of society, but once something happens to make the inhibitions crack . . . Honestly, Alice, the actual inherited qualities you need to become a spectacular criminal are exactly the same as you need to become a spectacular anything. *I* probably need them to get to the top in my profession, and God knows whether I've got them! Though actually, Alice, I forget to tell you, it *does* look as if a bit of luck may be coming my way at last! You remember that chap I was sending some of my compositions to—that evening you were on about the Blu-Tack—remember? Well, I've had a cable from New York, and he wants me to . . . Oh, Alice, I'm so longing to tell Mary about it! I'm sure, once I saw her, I could . . ."

But Alice was adamant. It all sounded much too exciting, too sudden, too overwhelming for an invalid still in a state of shock. All she would promise was that she would ring him from the hospital and tell him as much as she could about how Mary was feeling.

Mary, too, had been trying to get a clear idea of how she was feeling. Yesterday, coming to from the anaesthetic, and before she had begun to recall anything at all of what had happened, she had been conscious of an enormous sense of happiness and release, unfocussed and apparently without cause. Only as consciousness slowly returned, and clear memory, did she realise that this huge happiness lay at the very heart of a huge grief.

Julian was dead. The brother she had loved was back; the dark, bitter last months of his short life were now over. He was safe in the past.

Safe in the past. All the while he lived, while he still existed in the world, the dreadful and continuing present was blotting out completely the whole of the happy past, as if it had never been.

The present has this awful, tyrannical power. It arrogates to itself a total and absolute importance over and above all other moments in all of time. It is a spurious power, though. You have only to wait, and it, too, will become the past, its awful domination at an end . . .

Would Mary's mother, already on her way from Spain, be thinking these same thoughts? Mary hoped so. Now, at last, they would be able to mourn for Julian properly, together.

She must rouse herself now—Visiting Time was at hand. Already, at the far end of the ward, she could see Alice and Hetty making their uncertain way among the beds, glancing questioningly this way and that. Their pace quickened, smiles brightened on their faces, as Mary waved to them.

As promised, Alice went straight to the telephone when her visit was over, leaving Hetty to finish off the snippets of news from Number 17 with which she'd been regaling the invalid. Such as that—would you believe it!—*Horsa* was back! After seventeen weeks, and so fat and glossy too, whatever had he been up to? The only thing was, he kept eating out of Hengist's dish, no way of keeping him out of it, and oh, the kerfuffle! Oh, and another thing, another truant returned—Mr.

Singh! He seemed to be in fine fettle, too, his troubles (presumably) all sorted out, which was a grand thing, Hetty was delighted. Here, the only thing was that he didn't want the TV set in his room. Where in the world it was to go Hetty couldn't imagine, such argy-bargy it caused in the kitchen, as well as blocking the way to the broom cupboard . . .

That sort of thing . . . Alice smiled as she picked up the receiver. Already she was visualising Brian hovering in the dark, cluttered hall, on tenterhooks; and when, sure enough, the receiver at the other end was snatched up almost before the end of the first ring, she rejoiced that the message she had for him was so exactly the one he was hoping for.

ABOUT THE AUTHOR

Celia Fremlin's first novel won an Edgar Award from the Mystery Writers of America. This is her sixteenth novel, and her sixth for the Crime Club. Her previous books include *A Lovely Day to Die* and *The Parasite Person*. She lives in London.